An Innkeeper's Diary

An Innkeeper's Diary

JOHN FOTHERGILL

Introduction by Craig Brown
Illustrations by Peter Bailey

The Folio Society
London   2000

An Innkeeper's Diary was first published by
Chatto and Windus in 1931. With a few minor
exceptions, the idiosyncrasies of spelling and
capitalisation of the original text have been
retained in this edition.

This edition published by arrangement with
John Fothergill and Jane Fothergill.

Set in Walbaum at The Folio Society.
Printed in Great Britain by St Edmundsbury
Press, Bury St Edmunds, on Balmoral Wove
paper. Bound by Cambridge University Press,
in quarter cloth, with paper sides printed
with a design by the artist.

Contents

Introduction

John Fothergill once wrote of innkeeping that it was 'the only occupation wherein one can be brought to know and embrace all humanity'. Yet the embrace to which he subjected most of humanity was more often a half-nelson than a hug.

The portrait he paints of himself in *An Innkeeper's Diary* is of a put-upon host in a permanent state of war with his ghastly guests. In this way, he is the forerunner of Basil Fawlty of Fawlty Towers. The two share that explosive but not uncommon mix of a deep belief in etiquette coupled with furious rudeness. They are both idealists, dreaming of creating a paradise on earth, if only they can first get rid of the riff-raff. Both are more concerned with throwing guests out than attracting them in. Fothergill relates a set-to with 'a scrubby undergrad': 'The fellow said, "I'll never come here again," to which I replied, "Yes, but will you give me another undertaking: to tell all your friends not to come?" '

An Innkeeper's Diary reads like a despatch from the front line of the losing side in a long drawn-out battle. Yet in all respects other than the purely financial, Fothergill made the Spreadeagle at Thame a notable success, 'the first Good Hotel', in the words of Hilary Rubinstein, founding editor of *The Good Hotel Guide*. When Evelyn Waugh published his first novel, *Decline and Fall*, in 1928, he gave a copy to Fothergill, inscribing it to 'John Fothergill, Oxford's only civilising influence'. Later, in *Brideshead Revisited*, Anthony Blanche takes Charles Ryder to dinner. ' "We are going to

Thame," he said. "There is a delightful hotel there".'

Fawlty is far from being John Fothergill's only heir. The angry restaurateur should be as rare as the blind dentist or the flamboyant Cistercian, but England is full of them. Two of the most famous in recent years were Peter Langan and Kim Tickell. 'Patrons of Langan's haunts were only safe when he lay like a white whale in his crumpled suit, snoring sonorously on the floor in the gentlemen's lavatory at his Brasserie' ran the *Daily Telegraph* obituary of Peter Langan. Once, when a distraught lady approached him bearing a cockroach she had found in the ladies' room, he took it from her and studied it closely. 'Madam,' he exclaimed, 'this cockroach is *dead*. All ours are alive.' He then swallowed it, washing it down with a glass of vintage Krug.

Kim Tickell was perhaps closer in character to John Fothergill, in that his abuse sprang from snobbery rather than alcohol. It seems likely that this snobbery (both came from what used to be described as 'old families') led them into a certain amount of self-hatred, looking down on themselves for being, as it were, counter-jumpers in reverse.

Tickell − or Joseph Hollick de la Taste Tickell, to give him his full name − ran the Tickell Arms, outside Cambridge, up until his death in 1990. Like Fothergill, he wore eccentric dress (in his case eighteenth-century breeches and silver-buckled shoes). A notice outside his pub listing the categories of people who were banned − left-wingers, long-hairs, CND-ers, jean-wearers etc., etc. − grew longer with every passing year. If ever a borderline customer asked for the loo, Tickell was in the habit of saying, 'Along

the corridor, turn left, you'll see a sign saying "Gentlemen". *Ignore it and walk straight ahead!'*

But Fothergill was the pioneer. In a way, he gave
proprietorial abuse a good name, for, again like Fawlty,
however awful he is, he somehow never loses our sympathy. But there is, of course, an essential difference
between Fothergill and Fawlty: Fothergill is real.

Or is he? 'I'm better than this Diary, the product of
the fag ends of my daily supply of energy,' he writes at
the end of this volume. 'Let people reading it think,
perhaps, less of me than I really am.' Like Evelyn
Waugh, Fothergill wrote up his diary in a state of
exhaustion at the end of the day, and this tended to
emphasise his crabby side. Waugh's letters, written
in the morning, reveal a far more sympathetic and
rounded character, and I suspect that if Fothergill
had written his diary when the day was still fresh
and before his dreams had been put through their
daily mangle, he would now be remembered quite
differently.

Or perhaps he would not be remembered at all. It
was Fothergill's Licence to Abuse that made *An Innkeeper's Diary* such a popular success when it was first
published in 1931, running to four impressions within
the first year. There is still something very funny and
even strangely endearing about this potty hotelier
daily breaking loose from the straitjacket of flummery
to hurl insults at every ragtag and bobtail who has
had the impertinence to venture through his portals.
Fothergill's vocabulary of abuse is matched only by
the range of its targets. He disapproves of shop girls,
undesirables, bounders, haughty females, uppity sales-
men, the ill-shaped and the ill-bred, the second-rate

and the proud, people who want to see the bedrooms first, people who only want to use the loos, people who ask if the beds are well aired, people who only want to look at the garden, people who request mint sauce with their lamb, people who only drop in to shelter from the rain . . .

Reading *An Innkeeper's Diary* is rather like sitting in the upper circle at a Dame Edna Everage show, confident that, whoever he turns on next, it can't be you. Yet if the book were purely a compendium of snobbery and vitriol, it would never have attracted such affection. Not very far beneath the surface, the book reveals something by turns fragile and heroic about the complicated personality of John Fothergill. It is this, I believe, that gives the book its unexpected humanity.

The inter-war years were a bleak time for British catering. Fothergill was a crusader for 'Real Food', and rather than get all his produce from one central hotel supplier, he ferreted about with a single-mindedness blind to profit, paying regular bills, as he points out, to Athens, France, Norway, Jaffa and Italy. Small wonder, then, that the Spreadeagle was frequented by such grandees as J. M. Barrie, G. K. Chesterton, Mrs Patrick Campbell, Jerome K. Jerome, John Gielgud, John Betjeman, Elizabeth Bowen and George Bernard Shaw. Fothergill mentions these guests (who wouldn't?) but only in passing: he seems more comfortable stamping his foot than blowing his trumpet.

His tetchy, snobbish persona was a Gothic mask. The mask is undeniably entertaining and provides the book's mad energy ('Are these biscuits a home-made effort?' asks one poor guest, to which Fothergill answers back that they are 'not an effort but an achievement') but it is the occasional glimpses of the face beneath that make it poignant. If he writes of his life as though it were a battle, much of that battle was, I suspect, with himself; a battle between the person he once was, and the person he had somehow become.

Who was John Fothergill? More particularly, who was he before, at the surprisingly late age of forty-six, he decided to reinvent himself as an innkeeper, checking in as the permanent guest of his own caricature? The answer – never more than hinted at in *An Innkeeper's Diary* – is bizarre and unexpected. Fothergill was – or, at least, had been – an aesthete and dilettante, art student at the Slade, aspirant architect, gallery owner, friend of Robbie Ross and Reggie Turner, disciple of Oscar Wilde. After Wilde wrote *The Ballad of Reading Gaol*, he distributed fourteen copies to close friends. One of these copies was for John Fothergill. 'To Rowland Fothergill,' read the inscription, 'Architect of the Moon'.

John Rowland Fothergill was born at Grasmere in 1876, the descendant of George Fothergill, a Norman baron who had been granted land at Ravenstonedale by William the Conqueror. His mother died of scarlet fever when he was just two days old; his father was a somewhat stern, distant figure. It may have been his childhood neighbour, John Ruskin, who first gave the young Fothergill a taste for art: talking to Harold Acton and his friends in the 1920s, he would describe Ruskin's 'very little bedroom in his beautiful house in Coniston, a little bed, a few sticks of furniture but about a dozen sumptuous Turner water-colours'.

Aged twelve, John was sent to Bath College, where his only distinction lay in drawing elaborate maps of Greek battles and designing programmes for school concerts. At Bath, he fell in love, he wrote in his unpublished and unfinished memoirs, with a boy called 'B. McC.', 'the only real and able love of my life'. He was determined to keep the relationship platonic, and 'with heroic effort' he managed, only to find that an older boy had taken 'B. McC.' away 'and seduced him properly'.

By the time he arrived at St John's College, Oxford, in 1895, he was already a dandy, wandering into lectures in a grey hop-sack tailcoat with extravagantly long tails, a gold hunting-horn in the buttonhole. However, he failed his first exam and was forced to leave after only one term. He then seems to have killed time in a dissolute manner, living off a meagre allowance in a bedsit off Marble Arch, waiting for the inheritance that would be his on his twenty-first birthday. Around this time, he met Oscar Wilde. Though poverty made him no stranger to the pawn-broker, it never crossed his mind to get a job. 'My father and his ancestors had never had one', he recalled, 'and I hadn't any qualifications for a profession'. By this time, his father had been informed by Fothergill's brother-in-law that his son was 'a homo-sexualist'.

Fothergill celebrated his twenty-first birthday on 27 February 1897. Three months later, on 18 May 1897, Oscar Wilde was released from Reading Gaol, catching the night boat to Dieppe the next evening. Fothergill spent six days, 'a sextette of suns' in Wilde's phrase, with him that September. Wilde attempted to entertain Fothergill with his old brilliance, but, wrote Fothergill, 'he was too broken and friendless to do it well'. Wilde, still pining for Bosie, did not conceal his fondness for the good-looking young Fothergill, who possessed, according to one writer, 'clear eyes, smiling mouth, and an air of cynical sophistication'. 'Two loves have I: the one of comfort; the other of despair,' said Wilde to Fothergill, 'the one has black; the other golden hair.'

Back in England, Fothergill received 'some charming letters' from Wilde, but, believing any future friendship too dangerous, took the cold decision to drop him. 'I actually wrote that it was not "politic" to go on with it. What an awful expression!' he later recalled. Wilde answered that he did not know what Fothergill meant by 'politic', but he received no reply.

A year later, Fothergill took a snap decision that was to haunt him for the rest of his life. He had been walking down the Via del Corso in Rome when he saw Wilde sitting alone at a table at Aragno's Café. 'He sat so still, looking at nothing, and had that same, sad friendless face . . . I passed on, and never saw him again, but my tragic picture of it all sickens me still.' It was to be the last time he ever set eyes on Oscar Wilde.

Also in Rome, at the Caffè Greco in the Via Condotti, he encountered the beautiful American artist Romaine Brooks, two years his senior. Together 'there was not a single ruin, gallery or monument we did not visit'. It was a romance of sorts, though more passionate on Brooks's side than on Fothergill's: Sir Harold Acton believed Fothergill to be the only man Romaine Brooks ever loved. When she died in 1975, aged ninety-six, his was the only photograph in her apartment.

But after three months, Fothergill pursued his original intention of leaving for Greece. Six years later, the two met up again on Fothergill's initiative, but, Romaine Brooks was later to note in her memoirs, a spark had gone out of him: 'The brilliant boy . . . had become dreary and faded.' She painted a picture of him which her biographer, Meryle Secrest, said, 'caught, in the way the expression of the eyes contradicted the set of the mouth, a certain ambivalence, as if she sensed the inner bewilderment masked by the show of determination'.

In 1905, Fothergill enrolled at the Slade School. There he met Doris Herring, who was to become, very briefly, his first wife. He never mentions her name in his diaries or letters. She refused to consummate the marriage, and they split up. Fothergill had some sort of nervous breakdown, and went to recover at a home in Church Stretton where, he later recalled, 'they took mainly ex-idiots'.

Through his twenties and his thirties, Fothergill continued his life as an aesthete. With a friend, he brought the young Jacob Epstein over from America, helping to pay his keep. He also translated E. Löwy's *The Rendering of Nature in Early Greek Art*, contributed the essay on drawing to the eleventh edition of the *Encyclopaedia Britannica* and dabbled in an art gallery in Oxford. It was not until 1920, when he was forty-four, that he married for a second time. Kate Headly Kirby, practical and businesslike, 'masculine-looking with a leonine jaw' in the blunt words of Humphrey Carpenter, was to be his anchor in the years ahead. Aged forty-six, finding that 'I must do something for a living', the two of them bought the Spreadeagle at Thame, and he took on the profession, the role and the character for which he was to be remembered. Five years later, he was to write, 'Fifteen years ago, I was the best-looking and worst-mannered gentleman in London, and now I am the worst-looking and best-mannered thing in Thame.' The transformation of John Rowland Fothergill was complete.

An Innkeeper's Diary was the first, the jauntiest and by far the most popular of the three volumes of diaries John Fothergill was to publish. Though it contains occasional bouts of self-pity of the 'I don't know why I bother' variety, it is also the least reflective. But as he grew older, and a poor head for business forced him to move from the Spreadeagle first to The Royal Hotel, Ascot, and then to The Three Swans, Market Harborough, his tone turned from comical anger to lyrical melancholy, and he ruminated more on his past. 'In my bad moments I get again that heart-shaking remorse, regret and repentance for all the ignorance, violence, standing alone and lack of love towards everyone in my horrid past, and some are dead and will never know my remorse and some I shall never see again,' he writes in *My Three Inns*, adding, 'I have lived all my life with a broken heart.' From The Royal Hotel, he goes on a religious retreat, and says to his confessor, 'I cannot pray – I can only repeat – the silly – little wish – I made when – stirring last Christmas pudding – that Kate – and the children – should be happy.' 'And there he left me in tears', Fothergill concludes, 'and I never saw him again.'

Even in these days of serial newspaper confessionals, this makes uneasy reading. That it should have been written in the 1940s by a man more inclined to hide behind a mask is testament to a kind of heroism. Fothergill was a man whose dreams had been let down by his life. In the end, it was appropriate that he should find consolation in remembering something that had been told him by the man who had previously filled him only with remorse. All those years ago in Berneval, he wrote, 'Oscar Wilde once told me that when he went to heaven, Peter would meet him at the gate with a pile of richly bound books saying, "These, Mr Wilde, are your unwritten works." '

If Peter had ever been brave enough to have approached John Fothergill, I doubt the two would have got on. His beard and open-toed sandals would have marked him down for immediate derision. But who needs the unwritten works of John Fothergill? The written works are, to my mind, quite good enough. *An Innkeeper's Diary* is the perfect English bedside book: sometimes snobbish, sometimes batty, often touching and always very, very funny, it is worthy of the embrace of all humanity.

CRAIG BROWN

TO

KATE

too good for words

TO OUR

GENEROUS STAFF

and to the

KIND VICTIMS

of our

INNKEEPING

Author's Introduction

This Diary or 'Tired Notes', as I entitled each volume of them, was started to remind us in our old age of the Spreadeagle Inn, before and after we changed it to what it is now, and with the same pious purpose it has been continued. Lately, however, it struck me that it might interest others. I can justify my immodesty only on the ground that though public and professional men have written copiously of their shop lives the tradesman, businessman and so on have been too secretive. Very interesting would be a collection of journals, technical as well as intimate, of grocers, farmers, nurses, commercial travellers and so on. Such experiences and confessions, moreover, might vindicate them: the grocer, for instance, before Mr G. K. Chesterton for not 'splitting a bottle of fish sauce' with his customer, or commercial travellers for hanging their hats over pictures, or farmers for doing what they've always done, or nurses for behaving like tyrants, or it might not. And it might modify our feelings and behaviour towards these people and so bring into their lives some of that uncommon and peculiar happiness that we have had here from the great majority of our victims. This simple Diary, then, is my contribution to such a hypothetical collection – *an Innkeeper's, and nothing but an Innkeeper's.*

The first pages of the Diary were written up *en bloc* from memory and from some contemporary notes in order to bring me roughly up to the date when I started it regularly five years ago. The present publication is the result of selection and a certain amount of collating of entries on the same subject; the dating of the Chapters, therefore, is correct only generally. Where the subject is of a private sort, I have suppressed names and sometimes altered immaterial details so as to prevent, I would hope, the identification of the persons concerned, because, though I owe no malice, of course, to tell only of the delights of this life and suppress what is trying or ludicrous would be to fail in my purpose in publishing; and for the same reason — to complete the picture — I have allowed myself to publish personal feelings which were often momentarily prejudiced by circumstances and domestic matters that are ordinary.

I would fain excuse what is dull or unappetising or arrogant because of the narrowing effect upon the mind of a too absorbing and exhausting occupation and of the difficulty of editing one's own Diary, especially when it is not written for publication.

Spreadeagle, Thame, 1931   JOHN FOTHERGILL

An Innkeeper's Diary

1922—3

The Old Regime

I imagine that everyone who has had a career of any
character has his amicological tree to the root of which
he can trace his chief relationships and interests, his
good or ill, in life. My tree grew out of Robert Ross,
amicus amicorum, and its two main branches were my
friendships with E. P. Warren and twelve years' Greek
archaeological study and surroundings, and with Will
Rothenstein, his family and friends, Tonks and Steer
and so forth, Will, whom I have watched inventing
innumerable geniuses, helping and fighting for them
and with them, and getting, in return, different treatment at different times. This, then, with Westmorland
blood, the most precious in England, has been the
main source of what I have to give as Innkeeper, and
even that is far from enough. But it was more than
enough to disqualify me for any of the usual jobs when
in 1922 I found that I must do something for a living,
so I was compelled to take an Inn. Here at least I
thought I might still be myself and give to others
something of what I had acquired before making this
clean-cut departure from the past.

There are always plenty of Inns to be had, as many
as houses, and as inaccurately described by the agents. I
looked at a great number, but all of them had clienteles
and traditions, or definite trades or attractions, which
were not my traditions, attractions, etc. At last, seeing
this place advertised, I got my dear friends Montie and
Lady Pollock to go and vet it. Lady Pollock wrote 'very
shabby but very possible' . . . I took it and thought I
saw my chance of running a most splendid farmers'

pandemonium in this almost unknown patch of rural England . . . The ceremony of 'Change-over' was a lurid proceeding. After the signing of the deeds and handing over of the money in cash, I and the two – in this case – preceding proprietors (the last one had held this 'little goldmine' for only a year), our respective brokers, solicitors, and valuers ate a coarse silent lunch together, after which each of them put a pound note into a plate 'for the new proprietor's wife', which time-honoured act of generosity was followed later by the vendor's valuer telling me that he had omitted in his valuation the price of a cocoanut mat in the hall, 'about which nothing need be said now'. The Valuation (*sic*) of the furniture (*sic*) agreed by our two valuers (*sic*) was £1,400. Some weeks afterwards I sold it all, save the knives and forks and the very common crockery, for £85 at public auction, and brought in my own on the following day.

Besides the almost total loss on the furniture, the selling of it lands me in a predicament because, when I should want to retire, I must either sell or try to sell my own furniture at its proper value, which no Inn-keeper would give me, or sell it empty, which would be as difficult, or refurnish at great expense. No wonder under these conditions the poor Innkeeper has to stick to his beastly sticks, and the hard beds that pitch as well as toss and roll.

On the first day I gave it out, as I had been advised, that there would be free drinks in the evening, and we were filled to the doors and emptied, like my dead friend John Marshall's sister Pro who, he said, had 'such a big voice that she could fill St George's Hall and empty it'.

The House Public

No owner of a licensed house could ever feel, of course, that his house was his own, but I think this particular public house must have been exceptionally public. Not only indoors but in the yard and garden people wandered at will, each for his own little secret business, or with his own particular time-honoured privilege or abuse. One old farmer had to have his Market Day dinner for 1s. 6d. at the end of the kitchen table as he was often sick on the floor. In the Billiard Room they played little but many didn't pay. The billiard table was a curious one. Some thirty years before, the then proprietor watched in silence some yokels play 100 up in about 1½ hours for one shilling when he burst into a pleasant stream of frightful oaths and said he'd have in future an Innkeeper's billiard table which soon arrived, hollowed out towards the pockets. Thenceforward the locals played quicker and better, and all were pleased.

Proceeding slowly up the yard I'd watched every Tuesday evening for almost two years what looked like a man carrying his own cross before him and then returning with another (for a friend perhaps?) and disappearing into the coach-house. Later he would go up again with a barrowful of timber, till I was brave enough to ask what all this gear was. 'Oh, my fish stall; I store it here during the week, you see.'

When we'd been here a day or two Kate (wife) wandered into the garden with Michael, aged 3, to explore it. At the end, under the trees – one of them a huge walnut for which the High Wycombe seekers of Queen Anne furniture used to offer me rich sums up to £6 – they found an old shed with a green thatch in holes, they pushed the door open, and peeped inside, and in the dark corner near the door they saw crouching a man with an evil, black and white face and a sack standing in front of him. Kate withdrew the child, talking cheer-

fully, and came to me. I collected the degenerate gardener, who was for once luckily on the premises, and to
my surprise the horrible-looking fellow was still there.
I pulled him out and found that he'd merely been steal-
ing a sackful of our walnuts. I rained all the worst curses
I could invent upon him, under which he began to grow
restless. He put his hand to his hip-pocket – 'Look out,
sir,' said the gardener, half aloud, 'he carries a pistol', at
which I quickly dried up and told him to get back over
the wall. I discovered later that he was a harmless pil-
ferer, and, of course, never carried a pistol.

At that time the classical joke in this town was:

Schoolmaster. 'Where do knives come from?'

Scholar. 'Please, sir, the Spreadeagle.'

Hearing a crash in the kitchen I looked inside and
asked what was broken; a kitchen boy on his first day
with us from a pauper home replied wearily, 'Only a
jug, sir.'

We used to sell beer in casks to the farmers, but
they 'lost' so many of our casks that in the end we gave
it up, having to pay £40 to Messrs Ind Coope, which
but for the kind intervention of their Mr T. R. Tame
would have been £80.

The Inn was always empty save on Tuesdays, when
a hundred farmers and kindred trades overran the
place, literally from top to bottom – we were not *in* it
but the dirt and noise was. We were frightened to
death. After four or five weeks I noticed that the girl in
the bar was selling cigars (in wine glasses) pretty
freely, so I made up my mind timidly to ask her where
she got them from. 'Oh, in the cupboard by the nursery.' I went and looked for the cupboard, but couldn't
find it, so I asked and looked again, till the third time I

got brave and made her explain exactly where it was, when I found the door to a recessed hole in a dark passage wall covered like the rest with oak-grained wallpaper. I now braced myself to ask her for the key which she haughtily gave me and I found some 5,000 cheap cigars being dried to tinder, because the cupboard overhung the hot kitchen below.

I was told I mustn't decline drinks offered me but that I should keep the 'innkeeper's bottle' – containing a harmless coloured drink. I didn't do this, but one day the late 80-year-old Captain Howland (late QM Oxford Yeomanry), courteous and tactful old thing, asked me to have one. So along with his gin and water on a tray I brought myself a glass of cold water – they both looked so alike – for the drinking of which he gave me ninepence.

Here they used to keep an eagle (*aquila spuria*) in a sort of meat safe in the back yard, which apparently amused the sort of people who came here because we get enquiries for it even now. Fortunately it died just before we got here, teased to death by a charabanc crowd.

Thame People

G. N. Clark of Oriel told me that the (then) Provost's father, who had been a parson here, said that Thame was remarkable for its miserable human nature – 'even its vices and faults were miserable'. But I have found their only characteristic, whether fault or virtue, is peacefulness. When we first came here they often told me that the High Street, 190 feet across, is 'the second broadest street in England'. As it is usual for people to boast about rather than belittle their

...teased to death by a charabanc crowd.

town I was puzzled till I discovered that the Thamensians avoid all occasion for strife. Hence if they tell a foreigner (and you are a foreigner here for your first generation in the town) that the street is second broadest, the man from Marlborough or Oxford or elsewhere grants it you and there is no strife. A charming person, G. A. Cohen (ICS on leave), came to us and wanted to hunt with his nice family three or four days a week. I sent him to a job master who quoted so much per horse per day as would have amounted to £40 a week whilst telling him that he couldn't hunt three days in any case, so there was no strife and no Mr Cohen, who took his leave and his money to Bicester. For Johnny McNaught, whilst staying here in full training, I found a sparring partner to take him on, a fine enormous fellow, with a local reputation. But twice McNaught waited for him and in vain. Avoidance of strife again.

Once I ran out across the road to stop a man maltreating his little horse, and the brute (not the horse) ran across to meet me: 'Now then you bloody foreigner, get back to your house or I'll set about you.' As I didn't speak, he flicked at me three times and sent my spectacles broken onto the road. There was a crowd already drawn by the man's noise with the horse, but when I looked round for witnesses they were all rabbitting into their holes, avoiding litigation. Of the two I caught, one said he hadn't been looking my way and another that he had only just come out. As I came inside, St John Ervine, having watched the incident from upstairs, struggled past me and, partly out of kindness, partly to *seek* strife, caught up the man and gave him a perfect hell of oaths and names. He very kindly gave evidence for me at the Petty Sessions, but the case was adjourned because the defendant's witnesses 'were on holiday'! – They are always on holiday. At the next sitting these witnesses, now returned from their holiday, gave the credit to me for all the fine language that St John Ervine had used, with the result that the magistrates must have had before them a picture of a drunken brawl and fined the man 10*s*. and me nothing. In the report of the proceedings in our local paper I was spoken of as 'Fothergill'. The Editor was rather shocked that I, a newcomer in Thame town, had caused strife.

Freemasons

But certain sections and coteries are not so easygoing. When we first came here we did the Freemasons' feeds

and they always complained. Moreover, taking advantage of our doing little business, they beat us down in
price. In fact we started badly with a feast in the first
week of our taking over, when at the advice of our predecessor, a Mason, we fed them at almost cost price. I
ventured to ask him what was the good of that, 'Why,
for advertisement, of course.' But I soon found that it
was only an advertisement for the same thing again.
They were very hard masters, and Kate and I trembled
at the end of each meal to get their complaints. 'Mr X.
had to wait for his sweet, Mr Y.'s fish was cold.' After a
couple of years of this the secretary came to pay a bill
saying, 'Mr Fothergill, I want your opinion – the Tyler
didn't have fish for his dinner last night.' (The Tyler is
a sort of doorkeeper and, in this Lodge, has the full
meal kept hot for him to eat in the kitchen afterwards.) 'The Tyler didn't have fish. What do you think
about making a reduction from the bill?' – I wondered
whether I could afford yet to offend these people. 'My
opinion is, Mr W——, that it's the pettiest complaint
you have made to date, and as our temporary cook is
the Tyler's wife the fellow ought to have got a good
dinner here. Moreover, you ordered dinner for thirty-
six, and by over-catering I served forty-two and so
saved your face.' – 'Remember, Mr Fothergill, there
are many in the Lodge who are deeply dissatisfied
with their treatment here, and are agitating to go elsewhere.' Even at that I thought we couldn't yet afford
to let them go, so I became pleasant and finally the
secretary said, 'What if I sign the cheque in full and
you give the man a shilling?' I shouted with laughter,
opened the door to him and they never came again.
And now a confectioner, who had recently become a

Mason, does for them, and there is no more occasion for strife.

The Farmers

As for the farmers' meanness, selfishness and all that's irreconcilable, we had so much of it in the first years that even now, when we have been boycotted, to use their own term, for five years, the sight of Market Day opens wounds. 'The Old Spread has always been the farmers' home' was their cry when I told them that I would have to change their one-day-a-week market room into a dining-room for everyday use whilst giving them a much better room across the archway, and I showed them my books to prove that to do otherwise would be ruin. But they had no mercy; we argued for hours together about it. On Market Day as many as sixty farmers, dealers, and corn-merchants (there are six now) wolfed a 4s. 6d. dinner here for 2s. 6d. a time, and I had to put before them three different kinds of joints which they carved themselves. Meanwhile I looked on and thought and felt like Penelope and the Suitors. Once, before delivering a helping, I ran it out into the kitchen to weigh it – one slice weighing a pound and three ounces from the thick of a boiled leg of mutton. A Rent Audit dinner used to be held upstairs in what is now No. 12 bedroom. 'What's that room doing now?' asked a much-respected farmer soon after their clearing out. 'It's had people sleeping in it for six weeks.' – 'And next year it will be empty', was his gracious prophecy. Another farmer of first rank used to complain to the parlour-maid about not having enough fish, so happening once to see him as he sat down I quite kindly asked him to explain his difficulty, when, before half a dozen people in the room, he roared out, apropos of nothing, 'Well, you're the biggest liar on earth and a traitor to the country.' I persuaded him, perfectly sober, to leave the room, and five minutes afterwards I met him again in the butcher's shop. 'You're a dirty German and a damned man.' I now told him that if he spoke again I would . . . and he dried up, never to speak to me again. Poor good man, he was only letting out in his own way the concentrated feeling against me of the farmer clan. I tried my best to understand them, and some of them, perhaps, tried to understand me, but it didn't work. They are medieval and they treated me as an interloper from 300 years later. Those few that remain I like. Some of them like *me*, the rest disregard me.

The total of the Christmas collection for my two market-room waiters from ten regular customers amounted once to 3s. 9d. for serving 520 four-course dinners. When I couldn't help expostulating with the two of them who had given nothing, they were obdurate. There is no collection now. Mr X., a big farmer, came into my office with this: 'Mr Fothergill, that strong beer you sold me was bad, poor stuff, and I recommend you not to sell it to any of us farmers, and I am not going to pay you the whole £5 10s. for it.' I now decided to wrangle with or give way no more to farmers, so I pulled myself together and said, 'You *must* pay, and I'd remind you that it's just nine months since you had the beer and my profit is only a few shillings.' After a lot of argument he paid in full. I had to fill in his cheque for him to sign, which is the custom here. Doubtless this was necessary in earlier days either because they couldn't write, or often enough couldn't hold a pen, but now it is from laziness and the satisfying feeling of seeing the dealer doing some more work for his pay and at the same time you give him a drink. The next Market Day he came up to me with a pleasant, knowing smile, 'Mr Fothergill, that beer was like wine, I didn't know it could be made like that nowadays.' And all that manoeuvre just to beat me down a shilling or two! I believe these tactics are called 'leg-pulling', but, I think, only when it doesn't come off. He never asked for any more beer.

Thinking that I ought to try to persuade the farmers that I was not the sophisticated, ill-meaning person they thought me, I advertised in the Bar:

Wanted – Thirty good men to eat the following
dinner on Saturday, January 20th (1923)
Tomato soup
Fish – brown stew
Venison
Jugged Hare
Plum Pudding
Toasted Cheese
Filberts   4*s.* a head.

I prepared for the twenty-five who said they would come and only thirteen came. Two bottles of whiskey were bought, which gave me a profit of 3*s.*, whilst the meal just paid expenses. They were very pleasant, and perhaps were doing their best to forget that I was an interloper, and, for the moment at least, to realise old times. The venison was in an almost solvent state when it went into the oven, but solid was the stench all over the house when it was cooking. It was all eaten. Romilly John had just arrived here, and his pleasant smile, neat fringe, slouch and untidy belcher instead of collar were very popular even if I wasn't. It was his father's idea that I should teach him innkeeping; it was Romilly's idea to teach it to *me*. So after the venison feast he and I argued with all the passion of a theological discussion how best to carry an oblong tray, whether by its breadth or length, till 2.30 a.m. When I was quite broken down, we went to bed, only to argue again the next night about his fad of mead and exclusively home-grown products, and so on. Romilly must have thought me very loathsome, to take him so seriously.

Fat Stock Show Dinner

We used to do the annual Fat Stock Show dinner organised by the auctioneers. We gave frightfully good food and the plum puddings were made from E. P. Warren's extravagant American receipt, and a horde of elderly curious-looking waitresses came over in a one-horse van from Aylesbury in the charge of Mrs Balls. Finding, after accurate costing, that at 5s. a head we made only 10s. profit on the food, and for that they drank little and complained much, I told the auctioneers I would be quite glad if they would go elsewhere if they wanted to, and take with them the memory of some raw boiled mutton that unfortunately had been served the last time and had left its rawness upon some of them ever since. However, I wrote to the 'County' chairman of the proceedings saying I was sorry for his and a few others' sake that they should have to move into the Town Hall and fare less well in that gaunt place. He wrote me a charming letter in reply. In his speech at the dinner it was reported to me that he spoke differently, 'If John Fothergill doesn't want *us*, we damn well don't want *him* (applause),' – so I wrote and asked him if he had really said what I had been told, and I had no reply. Once when this masterpiece of feudal survival was being driven in a hired car an old woman got in the way and they had to slow up. Up he sprang to his feet, purple in the face with rage, and shouted, 'You d-d-damned old fool! You d-d-damned old fool! If I had my g-g-gun with me I'd shoot you!' And I'm sure that this was not like the rage of an upstart because his progress had been impeded but because he felt that the woman had acted stupidly in her own interest and deserved the extreme penalty for it.

But it is not difficult to sympathise with these difficult farmer people. The farmers didn't like to be
ousted from where they had been for generations
before the War and for which they had once paid properly. I came just after the War, and in their simple way
they thought it was I and not the circumstances that
was the cause of raising the prices and bringing in a
new clientele, though I didn't raise the 2s. 6d. dinner,
and I lowered the price of spirits. Neither they nor the
people nor the shopkeepers welcomed the sight of
people with energy to shame their slow ways. To tell
them that to support us here and to brighten up their
houses would be to make themselves and their heirs
richer was gratuitous, because they are happy as they
are and their heirs would be likewise. I don't regret
our first awful years of strife here, but I am grateful
now to be almost as peaceful as my fellow townsmen.

The Commercials

Commercial travellers have been spoilt by their having hotels kept on purpose for them. They have been
numerous enough to be worth spoiling for their custom and drinking, or at least, 'treating' capacity. Our
mineral waters traveller told me he still has to give
over 25s. a day in drinks. But now they stay no longer
in the little places but do their rounds in a car from
only the biggest towns. For those who asked for 'blan-
ket beds' we used to keep a pair apart, bringing them
out when wanted.

    Once a commercial came and of course asked for a
steak. I said, 'I've some very good saddle of mutton
and jugged hare. Wouldn't you have that for a
change?' – 'No, I want a steak.' – 'But I don't keep

steaks, and if I got you one I know it would be very tough.' — 'Look here, I've had a steak five days a week for thirty years, and I want a steak now, if you *please.*' — 'But I don't please; I guarantee that it will be utterly tough.' — 'Never mind, I'll have it.' I had tried to save him and the reputation of the place even amongst commercial travellers, so now I went into the butcher's and asked for the toughest piece of steak out of the freshest animal he had, and between us we got a beauty. It seemed almost illegal. I felt like Mr Tasker. I didn't see him again, but he told the parlour-maid that he had had to leave half of it. Once I sent a commercial up to a little timber room that we had just discovered and beautified. He looked at it and said, 'Well, I'm used to a certain modicum of comfort', then he poked the bed. Katie (Lomas) said, 'You needn't do that.' Then he asked if this was the only hotel in the town, and she said there was the —— and he'd better go to it, and he did. Soon after that I took up to the same room a funny-looking little businessman. 'Well, it's a curious room.' — 'What's the matter with it?' — 'Oh, it'll do for the night.' — 'Probably it is one of the prettiest rooms you will ever have slept in.' — 'Is Aylesbury far from here?' — 'No, quite near.' — 'Are there any hotels?' — 'Yes, lots, but they are normal while this is abnormal.' — 'I'll take off my boots', he said with a good smile. His bill was enormous and he insisted upon my sharing with him a bottle of fizz before he left at eleven o'clock next morning.

One of the old regime rolled up in a car and demanded a 'number'. When I told him the house was full, as indeed it was, he flew into a rage, and shouted that he'd been here for forty years and never known it so before. I accepted the compliment in proud humility.

But though we did the commercials well and charged low and gave them clean sheets and were polite, they never came twice. Hotels are their homes, so they are naturally particular about their atmosphere. Only two survive, nice people, and they come with appalling regularity. Mr Paul, of Spillers and Bakers, who reads good books, and Mr Rose, of Peter Rylands.

So, gone the furniture and Freemasons, gone the farmers, commercials and charabancs, and dead three customers at the Bar, who brought us in £800 between them; yes, and customers that we had taken over in the valuation, dead within three years! (If only I'd insured their thirst at Lloyds!) We had now lost almost all that we had paid extortionately for and now had to formulate a policy whereby we could be of service to some other section of the community.

1923–4

The New Style Begins

Wilson Steer came to stay for his summer's painting, and Montie Pollock sent George Behrend here for the same purpose. Without one another's company I don't know what they would have done because there are no subjects here, and the weather was worse. Anyhow, in five or six watercolours Steer created for the first time grandeur for this open town and market-place. One evening, to relieve the monotony, I told old Steer that we'd a baby just born. He looked very frightened at first, then asked, 'Is that true? I didn't know it could be done so quietly.' God knows what he expected. And it was done cheaply as well as quietly, for when Dr Summerhayes sent me his bill of £7, I told him that he had acted under false pretences, for if I'd known that it was to cost only that I'd have had twins. It was cold and Mr Janes-Hawkins opposite did a brisk trade with Steer in waistcoats. The following year when they were at Long Crendon nearby (it's good to think that it was here that Steer and George Behrend founded their summer friendship which has lasted to this day) I told Steer that he had shocked the proud artistic inhabitants by painting an ugly and the only new house in this Mrs Allington village, and he replied, 'But it's really the only thing in the village to paint!' Or was it that it happened to be the only thing to be seen from his front door? Behrend is incredibly industrious in spite of his doing such good work. Next year Steer wrote from Bridgnorth:

. . . Behrend has just received a letter from Balmoral couched in these terms:

DEAR MR BEHREND,

The King has heard with much pleasure and interest of your unique achievement in painting 12,700 water-colours, thus exceeding the number painted by the late A. W. Rich, and also attaining a further record of 1,400 water-colours in one season.

His Majesty warmly congratulates you upon these remarkable feats whereby you have established a new and greater record in the history of our national art.

Yours very truly,

STAMFORDBRIDGNORTH

N.B. Whilst Behrend was doing his last two water-colours at Bridgnorth he was in possession of a four-leaved clover sent him for luck.

The year after that Behrend wrote from Shoreham,

we have no news as we have barely recovered from grief at the failure of Steer's recent attempt to swim the Chan-nel. He started, full of buck, and was in the water exactly two seconds when, owing to the excessive chop-piness of the Channel, he regretfully returned to the beach where he partook of a hearty meal and redonned his waistcoats.

And yet it was Steer who got the OM later and not Behrend.

Henry Tonks came the next summer, and though beaten for subject like the others, stayed on out of his goodness and painted and presented me with a panel in the Dance Room experimenting with every known and unknown medium. When Tonks dies I shall really feel that the population of the world is one less.

*

To a farmer at the Market Day Ordinary, whilst watching him carving an entire calf's head, jaws, teeth and all, I remarked, 'Isn't it strange that with calf's head, which is such soft and easily masticated stuff, there should be provided a complete set of teeth to eat it with.' Farmer silent.

The Hypocrites' Club

Unfortunately I made no notes about this amazing party at the time, though I believe notes upon its doings were collated by one of the party. It was the last, the funeral bake meats, of the just-suppressed-by-the-Proctors club. Being ill-equipped at the time for so big a party as fifty, I was too busy and exhausted to remember much about it, and I knew very few of them personally. I have a clear image of David Plunket Greene, 6 ft 9 in. high, dressed in white flannel trousers and a thin white vest, and Lord Elmley had a purple dress suit, and as he was 'by way of coming of age' he supplied the sixty bottles of champagne which I set out, 9 inches apart, down the middle of their table, 40 feet long, that ran close against the wall of the dance room, the rest of which was clear for dancing; and Turville-Petre, who later went to the East to excavate anthropologically and discovered with his umbrella the oldest known skull within a day or two of his arrival. Rudolph Messel, even better looking than Turville-Petre, and quite the vainest, or rather the only vain one, of the lot. The Greenidge brothers, pleasantly quite mad. Robert Byron, shrouded in lace trimmings, slept blissfully on a sofa after dinner, pre-visioning Byzantine art, upon which two years afterwards he was considered an authority. Two of them squatted in the hearse outside

and smoked – the 'flesh-cart' the coachman used to call it when he and the gardener took it out for me at £3 3s. a time, until I sold it for £1. Harold Acton made the great speech with his Big Ben-like voice: 'Gentleman, deeeeear gentlemen, I wish to propose the toast of "the B—a—r—d—y" ', a speech full of incredible precocity and rare quotation that would have surprised Aubrey Beardsley. The dancing was terrific. I have an image as of wild goats and animals leaping in the air. It must have been a record party in Oxford's history. Feebly efforts were made to carry on the good work, but Harold, who was a real person, had gone down, and it finished *pro tem*. I was not sorry, because the subsequent 'aesthetes' were mainly silly and they came here.

I am grateful to the Hypocrites' set. Whatever their indiscretions and unpopularity in Oxford, they did like good furniture and a beautiful room, good food and wine and they practised conversation; in fact, they liked all that this place stands for and through their coming here frequently at our beginnings, they helped, unwittingly perhaps, to keep away the bounder and to give us a name to discriminating and saner people.

A neat little commercial man came into the hall followed by his wife followed by their boy. 'Can I book rooms here provisionally?' – 'Oh, yes.' – 'But', he would insist, 'provisionally?' – 'Ah, yes,' I said, 'you mean with provisions?'

This may seem invented in Aberdeen. Six days ago a Scotsman arrived and booked a room for a week. Before he had got through the second door into the hall he made excited enquiries about what whiskey I kept and ordered a bottle to be sent up at once. 'Now at least for some spirit trade', I thought, and ever since I have sold him nothing but syphons.

On a very cold day when no one had come to lunch I found a female sitting by a wonderful fire, spreading out carefully sandwiches, bread, butter, cake, wine and a glass on a table. I told her that a room cost something in upkeep which justified a charge or at least a request for the use of it, whereas if she went into a field the farmer wouldn't object because he doesn't light a fire in it nor sweep the grass nor polish the trees, so she said she'd go if I wished and I said I wouldn't mind if she did. A year before that, when still almost no one ever came to lunch, though we always had big joints

frizzling in the oven for the imaginary 'people', a girl
I'd once known quite well came in and asked if they
could lunch here, and I thought delightedly of the
joint of pork frizzling in the oven and of my usefulness
to the public. (Soon after I came here, being troubled
about occupations useful and parasitic, I asked H. C.
Fulford, a huge and kindly barrister, if I had done the
right thing in turning this into a decent place, so he
gave me his pronouncement: 'As you are not expensive
and do not cater for the extravagant, and as people
must have holidays and recreation, you are fully justified in doing what you are.') I told her I'd be delighted
for them to lunch. 'Where can we sit?' she asked. 'Anywhere you like', and she chose a table. 'Our luncheon
is in the car', she said, and going out she returned with
sandwiches, bread and butter, her husband, cake, a
literary friend, glasses and wine, and they sat down
together. Rather resenting this unexcused buffoonery,
I made nasty remarks *en passant*, e.g., 'Augustus John
and Dorelia were here last weekend, *they* brought
their *beds.*' No one smiled. And afterwards they asked
for a glass of sherry all round for the good of the house.
I did my best to dissuade them, but they won. It's
all right and that, but it was not business-like of them
or me.

A Dining Club

I had a letter from the Queen's College, asking for an
elaborate dinner, for two, each dish meticulously
described; for instance, pheasant (shooting had begun
only the day before) without 'bread poultice, gravel or
fried counters', and so on. But disliking to have undergrads spending extravagantly I got ready a very nice

meal, though I winkled their oysters, so to speak, all
the way through: chicken, for instance, instead of gun-
warm pheasant, and for aubergines stuffed cucumber.
They arrived and weren't undergrads after all, but, as
I learnt afterwards, T. W. Allen, Fellow of Queen's
College, and Dr Cowley, Curator of the Bodleian, the
two undisputed reigning epicures of Oxford. Allen
had, at least, his bottle of Château d'Yquem 1914, and
'Cowles' his Château Lafite 1907. After dinner, said
Allen heavily: '*We* are a dining club, we've dined
together for twenty-five years. Once we had a guest,
but never again. This is the first time we've dined out
of College, but we shall return.' They never did. I
couldn't tell them the reason why I had economised, I
was so sick about it all. Anyhow Dr Cowley, at least,
got knighted later.

A thin, wild-eyed young man came for the night. For
supper, I gave him a huge helping of jugged hare,
which he ravished in a few moments, so I gave him
another. Hearing next morning that he'd gone out
after breakfast 'to get a shave' and hadn't paid his bill,
I put the horse into the old omnibus and galloped to
the station. He wasn't there and I never saw him
again, but the fellow who drives beer about for me told
me that he met the man at a pub that morning, and
asked him to come and have a drink at the Spreadeagle. 'No, *thank* you,' was the reply, 'I don't like their
beer.'

Affectionate old Mr Asquith came again with his
pretty niece Cara Copland, and we did the crawl of the
house and garden, looking at his favourite things.
When seeing him off he said to me, 'You couldn't have

made us better gifts of hospitality – Greek honey, nec-
tarines and Travellers' Joy.' He always has sherry
instead of tea. I made another distinguished infringe-
ment of the law when C. S. and Mrs Orwin, hardy
periodicals, came with some others at tea-time to talk
about a party. People at the next table might have
been surprised to see what was a bottle of sherry like
rich brown tea being poured out of the pot, and each of
us loudly declining milk and sugar.

Frank and Mrs Mackinnon, KC, came for the night.
What touched me was that, starting on a six days' holiday, they had stopped here, only 25 miles away, for
their first night. So, too, Sir John and Lady Dashwood
of 15 miles away a few days later, but *they* went one
better. We were quite full and they pretended to be
delighted with two horrid little rooms in the yard
which an obnoxious young couple of cockneys had just
before turned up their noses at.

Face Money

Last Sunday we had thirty-nine folks to tea and I noticed that they were almost all ill-shaped, ugly or ill-dressed. I came into the office and complained at having to work for such people at 1s. 6d. a head. Charles Neilson said, 'That's easy — put up a notice, "Buy our masks at 1s. each, or pay 6d. extra".' So I went in and told Phyllis to charge 6d. face-money each for the worst cases. Thus for the first time in history seven people without knowing it have left an inn having paid 6d. each for not being beautiful. Surely this was a more praiseworthy action than the usual one of charging people extra because they *are* beautiful, well bred and dressed?

An old gentleman arrived for the night, aged 73, after a 90-mile ride on a push-bike from Southampton. Though otherwise perfectly sane and pleasant, he said he objected wherever he went to paying 6d. for a cold bath. So I had to extemporise a defence for the irritating charge. Each room has to pay its share of rent and roof and upkeep, besides the cost of the plant, water, towel and soap, and the keeping of others out, otherwise the room might be used as a bedroom for which presumably he didn't mind paying. Recently, however, we've raised the price of the room to make the bath free — on the Dutch principle of a sixpenny thing post-free for 8d.

1925

The First Four Days' Holiday

We are just finishing four days' holiday after three years' daily work from 7 a.m. to often any hour after midnight. Naturally, our only thought was food. Our first meal was luncheon at one of the big long-established hotels where we stayed the night. The people were inferior and the *hors d'œuvres* good, but the rest of the meal I couldn't eat for its falseness and tastelessness; price 6s. Next day we lunched very well at a little restaurant. But how he put it across us, that patron, who, when he comes here on Sundays, has always two vast helpings of our wonderful meat. Then miles away to an equally noted hotel in the country. Here I costed the 7s. 6d. dinner, scrap by scrap, and it totalled 1s. 4d. a head.

The Last of the Charabancs

The honorary secretary of a suburban motor club that was to have tea here, eighty of them, came in advance with a party to luncheon. After swinging the lead a bit he sent for me to tell me there were vegetables for not more than three out of the five of his party. I said, 'You've come very late and you've had a delicious salad and everything has been to my utmost satisfaction.' This scotched him *pro tem.*, but he rose again afterwards to demand a reduction for shortage of vegetables. With ill-breds like this about it was consoling to be told by the Fagans at the next table that 15 years ago they came together and are happier today than ever and are keeping their fête here for two days. At tea-time, to our surprise, only a handful of the eighty club-members turned up and I learnt that their revengeful secretary had warned them off, so they missed a very good tea and later the RAC ruled that the secretary should pay up for the full eighty. But this was a pleasant experience compared with sixty chara-banc men we had for 'dinner' from the East End. I saw their horrid charabancs coming along the clean and empty Sunday street, swoop down upon us and pull up. The sixty strong, great burly, black broad cloth-suited brutes with buttonholes all the same coloured target, leapt out and, already semi-tight, swung round to the back of the charabanc and began to pull cases of beer out of the boot. With quick courage I had the beer put back. They swarmed over the yard and into the big room where they ate, *inter alia*, 1¼ lb. of meat per head and got quite drunk. Later Kate came to tell me they were all out in the yard again, cursing and yelling out for me and at the same time a deputation of three came in to tell me that I had grossly underfed them and that they wouldn't undertake to get the men out of the place unless I knocked off 6*d*. a head. I gave way meekly and out they went. How much better to have called in the police and got their money. Our last charabanc party.

Since becoming butler, I think I've discovered why wine has to go round with the sun. In Italy, if you pour wine into the glass of the man on your right with the back of your hand downwards, it is an outrage, I suppose because it is casual, because to do it other-wise would be arduous. Well, if you make a universal rule that wine should go round towards the left or 'with the sun' (to avoid the word 'sinister'), no one can offend. The butler therefore needn't observe the rule, tho' he does.

I offered four shy undergrads at luncheon 'plum pudding or chapel harlot'. I told this my spoonerism to a lady who asked me if our 'Thame Tart' was a variant of the same delicacy.

Of two perfectly decent people but of the self-centred order I asked as they arrived for the night, 'And where are you going on to?' – 'To Shropshire; we only stopped the night here because we thought it was going to thunder.' What can you do with such tactlessness? And they made it worse later by saying that they'd been here before! So presumably only a thunderstorm would bring them in again. Next day the woman of another couple, less decent and very pretentious, standing before the beautiful Sheraton four-poster given me by Michel Salaman, said to Katie Lomas, 'What a funny old bed! Is it clean?' Katie, aghast, told her all the beds were clean. Then the woman proceeded to turn it back and over. Soon afterwards I caught them sitting in the garden. 'You have offended me and the whole staff by your examining that bed.' – 'But I *always* do it.' – 'Yes, but when I received you, you should have known at once that you were in a most distinguished Inn kept by a most distinguished gentleman. Have you ever eaten raw asparagus? Try it!' and I pushed some into her hand and went away feeling rather staggered by my awful self. Albeit I felt that if only for the sake of the decent people who ultimately are to be supreme here I must continue ever to battle with the second-rate and the proud. A lady wrote asking for rooms for a week for the Colonel and herself, her son and daughter, maid, chauffeur and car, ending with 'the beds must be comfortable and well-aired'. 'There you've dropped a brick', I thought, so I replied giving full details as to how I could accommodate her, but added merely as a P.S., 'We do not air the beds', and I never heard any more.

The reason why you get such a poor reception at the average English Inn is generally because the proprietor knows that he cannot or will not do you well and, being at bottom a Christian, he hates the sight of you as a living sacrifice. I myself find it difficult at all times to receive folks with perfect confidence and send them away with a clean heart.

Guy and Storm Chapman

For the whole winter, a very hard one, Guy Chapman and Storm (Jameson) have been with us swallowing their breakfast every morning in five minutes and smashing their horrid little car at 50 miles an hour to Prince's Risborough for the London train. A lovable couple and a good blend: where she is masculine he is feminine, and vice versa. Kate loved her from the start; I didn't. Bless her untidy head which in these six months has made a dear grease-mark on the wall by 'Chapman's table'. Guy gave me his pretty little cookery book, Ann Blencowe, 1694, which he published himself, and I managed to get out of it the following dinner for them.

> *Pease soup*
> *(but done in the superfluously elaborate way of*
> *all old recipes)*
> *fried oysters*
> *drobed beef*

allmand flumry
biskett (Mrs B.'s way)
Lady Gage's surfett water
('so strong as to fill a common chamber potte in
12 hours')

They pronounced it excellent and used it in their
Times advertisement of the book. Later . . . Poor Guy
and Storm have to live at Tonbridge for their boy Bill.
We got a letter from a landlady in Kent, they having
given us as references. We thought it was generally
rather an insolent one; anyhow 'his wife' instead of
Mrs Chapman wasn't proper; so Kate wrote what was
also a fitting epitaph to their many months of sojourn
here: 'Mr and Mrs Chapman are charming and honourable people. You are fortunate to be in a position
to do them service', which is characteristic of Kate's
directness when she has a conviction.

Some Scotsmen

'Financier, complete with wife', said Charles Neilson,
as an immense Scotsman, holding her violet pressed-
leather jewel-case, helped out of the car his tiny little
wife draped tight in black satin – and then dined. He
told me his family had been on their estate since the
eleventh century. After dinner he stood up and said,
'I'd like to reward the waitress,' who was not forth-
coming, so he put down on the table a pile of three or
four coppers. 'Blast his Scotch carefulness,' I thought,
but somehow I couldn't dislike their great kindness in
other ways, so I took them out, and having shown
them how to get to the garden I ran back and, being
ashamed before Phyllis, took half a crown out of my

pocket to exchange with the pile of coppers, but when lifting them up I found two half-crowns below. 'Eleventh-century unostentation,' I thought, but afterwards I wondered why he'd done it so. Was he afraid of the little wife's seeing his generosity to the girl or did he think I'd snap it up myself if it looked worth while? But I decided in terms of the eleventh century.

Three polite actions, all Scotch.

(i) Father Traill, sitting talking with me in the office, had put his burnt-out match and all his cigarette ashes on his hat before I noticed his difficulty;

(ii) E. M. Wrong, of Magdalen, started putting his ashes into the turn-up of his trousers.

(iii) Lord Skerrington, who before going away said, 'Mr Fothergill, could you spare me a couple of dozen of your excellent East India sherry?' – 'Yes, of course.' – 'But', he said, 'at a reasonable price, I do not consider 105s. reasonable; will you allow me to give you 125s.?' and many another lovely courtesy. Unhappily the two last are dead now. Lord Skerrington, after three weeks here, told me how much they had liked it and how they would never stay here again. His only passion was to be on Roman roads and a new bit every year. But Lady Skerrington, who used to arrange their annual trips with devastating circumstance and detail, wrote to me two months later that they would look in on us on August 6, ten months hence, at 4.30, and they did!

The Rats

Rats overrun the house. Having consulted the relevant department of the Ministry of Agriculture, and spent £14 on its recommendations, I fell back on our local surveyor, who kindly promised to send a man to catch

them, and a few days afterwards there came to the
kitchen door a ragged bundle of a man looking himself
more like a fat and dusty rat, with bright little eyes, a
pointed nose, and a crafty smile. They told me in the
kitchen who this specimen was, generally in trouble,
and from whom the children always ran screaming.
They said that he catches rats in his mouth and throws
them dead over his shoulder. I took him down to the
cellar and watched him anxiously for an hour or more.
Once he got a rat into his pocket somehow, but it got
away, and I was glad to get this odious character away
also. Yesterday a girl came screaming down the stairs
from the lavatory calling out, 'There's a rat – there's a
rat!' and fell into the arms of her young man waiting
below in the hall, who tenderly folded her to himself –
for the first time, as it looked to me – she had indeed
done well to sustain the rat emotion so long and use it
so opportunely. This morning I told H. G. Wells that
I'd been trying to stop rats' holes for two hours before
breakfast. 'Oh, you should get that stuff that makes
them so voracious that they eat one another up till the
last surviving rat goes conscientiously into every hole
and corner and finding none to eat goes out into the
yard and dies – conscientious.' Wells can turn everything to fun. When he'd been here three days I told
him that up till now I used to say 'All's well that ends
Wells', but that now I recanted wholesale.

*

Professor Gordon, leaving Poetry, urbanity and other LCs at Oxford, comes here annually for three days and lives quite another life with war cronies, Peter Gregory and Behrens from Bradford who treat him without respect. Gordon has the most taking and intelligent smile I know, whilst I tell Jock Lynam that when he comes into the room with *his* smile we might as well switch off the lights and economise.

When I get an order in the kitchen for four helpings of beef, as raw as possible, I know it's for Curtis Bennett and his friends, and 'Is this bloody enough?' I ask when I give it them.

Proper Innkeeping

It is easy for a grocer to decide what quality of goods he will sell to his best advantage, but he needn't trouble about the quality of the people he sells them to. Nor does any hotel-keeper; he leaves it to luck, and so to ill-luck. I've never heard it said of any hotel that they have any particular class of people as clientele, unless it be some residential place where they can easily pick and choose. Here I've determined not only to have proper and properly cooked food but to have only either intelligent, beautiful or well-bred people to eat it. Although barely paying our way, we've declined dozens of applications for rooms simply because we don't know the people, or the writing or the address don't please. To several of the commoner undergraduates I have said that I don't want them here with indiscriminate girls, and yet some people will argue with me that I am compelled by law to take them in or feed them! My answer is, 'Either I give them bread and cheese in a back room or fill the place rapidly with

men and prostitutes or the undesirable kind of undergraduate and let go the polite atmosphere that pervades the place and our polite staff too.' Few realise
what I go through to get and keep for it the atmosphere this place now has. After all, Innkeeping is
the only profession where one's business is also one's
home. If it be thought eccentric or arrogant to encour-
age only certain kinds of people to share your roof and
floor, is this not, in fact, always done? The beery Innkeeper has beery friends and discourages the others
and so on, and the man who has no particular character or leanings but thinks of his hotel first and his
home last merely makes a characterless business of it.

Three years have gone and still no one comes here
to stay in the winter save a few flukes, accidents or
thunderstorms. But I stick to my opinion that there are
enough decent people to people this Inn and until we
are known to all these we can remain empty. During a
recent Bank Holiday none of the five delightful, but
quite incompatible, parties knew that they were being
manoeuvred daily and nightly to sit in different rooms
and places in the house with fires so as to keep them
separate, whilst the big drawing-room with a blazing
fire at each end was left in possession of a party of four
who got there first and who read aloud to one another
all evening.

On the whole I've decided that it's not good to scrap
with your clients, even if only because it takes too
much out of you to win should the client really want
to finish it out, but certain people have to be tamed.
When there are plenty of decent folk about, quite
happy and content, it seems unjust that someone
should be trying on airs as he well might amongst a lot

of foreign waiters in one of a 'Chain' of hotels owned by a man in London. Today a red-haired man with a pretty woman chose to be nasty instead of mildly amused at the menu. 'What does the "Big Three" mean?' which I'd written for short instead of Beef, Pork, and Mutton, and then he said 'Μαυροδάφνη trifle' meant nothing to him! 'Anyhow, the food will', I pleasantly replied, and told him that if he had used his intelligence he could understand the 'Big Three' — to which he replied (quite properly, I suppose), that he didn't *want* to use his intelligence. When I was out cutting his food Kate told me he had made a very unpleasant entrance so I took the meat to him in order the more to tame him. He said he had come 80 miles here to lunch. I said, 'You mean, to pick a quarrel.' — 'How's that?' — 'Well, you arrived in a very disagreeable mood and I'm ever so pleased to see you so agreeable now' — and so we became friends. I think this must be the last scrap I shall induce. It is beastly enough to play the pig in a Hotel but it's still worse for the host to be a pig too, for he has such an advantage over his guest.

Mr ———, a German, whom X—— brought over with a party to spend the day with food and dancing, lives in great wealth at ———, just as he lived there all through the war. After lunch he bought and mislaid two pounds of our cheese and wandered round all afternoon crying, 'My sheece, my sheece, vere vos he?' Once, having had bad treatment in a Monte Carlo restaurant, he said to the waiter, 'Ziz vos not treatment for ze Englishman,' and to Lady W—— who told him that after all he was a German and that during the war his heart must have been in Germany he said, 'I do not know vere my heart vos – my stomáck voz in England and I stay mit my stomáck.'

If ever I had a private house again I should feel badly the want of a Sign outside. Even the open house that some people keep is generally arduous and expensive compared with what a Hotel can be with all its surprises if run strictly to a standard of breeding and intelligence. You are doing something, the door opens, you go to meet it. It is not a visitor whom you have invited weeks ago arriving now reluctantly only to find the feeling mutual since your moods have changed meantime. No one visits you out of duress or courtesy. So you know you are desired at the moment, and what is easier than to take up the feeling?

Comfortable Words

I asked Lord What's-his-name, a nice appreciative newcomer, what brought him to such a God-forsaken place as this. 'I used the RAC book, but what on earth brought *you*? A sense of humour?' Mrs Scrutton said this evening that she resented people coming here, as she felt it like a private house. Mrs Sefton-Cohen told me that Sefton-Cohen (a Government prosecutor) asked her to remind him to pay the bill 'as it was the last thing one would think about here'. Beautiful Henrietta Bingham came late to dinner with a friend at the fag end of the food. They had a shabby meal, and I told them why. 'We've enjoyed it immensely,' said H. B.; 'the ends of your dinners are better than the beginnings at other places,' which was as prettily said as it was untrue; but the motive was good. Such compliments are indeed nourishing. But there are people who tell me 'how jolly' it must be to keep a Hotel; these are the very people who would be generally incapable of doing the work or attending to the detail which alone makes an Inn fit for decent people and good for compliments.

We had today the most delicious pork ever eaten. To two hesitants with their 'no "*r*" in the month' I replied that there was an '*r*' in Fothergill, which was supposed to and did reassure them.

The parting words of St John Ervine after staying here and being ever so kind, with Mrs Ervine for three weeks just as he was getting into our old horse-bus for the station were, 'I don't like Thame, and I don't like the people'; so I replied, 'We must say with Milton, "The mind is its own place, can make a heaven of Thame or a Thame of Heaven." ' Perhaps he didn't like them because the people here avoid strife?

Where else would you get a sweet in a 4*s.* lunch that costs 4½*d.* a head? It doesn't seem much, but in other and expensive places it would cost 1¾*d.* or less.

There must be a specific Innkeeper's love for his charges. Or perhaps it's the same as the hospital nurse's. It's little that one can do for them, but I believe a constant watching tells its tale over against the inertia of the Innkeeper who wants not to keep the Inn but the Inn to keep *him*. I'm sorry I cannot allow myself to indulge in a saintly sadic love of the often disagreeable and conceited commercial traveller, lest he come again and disturb by his incongruity, his hat on the pictures, coat over the sitting-room chairs, and leather bags beside writing-tables, but one afternoon we melted towards a poor fellow travelling for something in which he had done no business and missed the 'bus. We had him to tea and he told us all about his children. At 7.30 I took him solemnly into the dining-room and asked him to sit down and gave him dinner and wine and waited on him in an amusing roomful and sent him away pathetic in his embarrassed grati-tude. I am so tired!

My affectation of styling myself 'publican' in official and other documents must stop — I had to explain on the telephone to an Insurance Office that I was not my own barman in order to save paying a much higher life premium.

A patronising or perhaps well-meaning woman said, 'You ought to do well here; I suppose it's the best hotel in the town.' I replied, 'Well, we don't fear com-petition in Thame, but there is, indeed, a hotel a few miles east of Baghdad which is giving us a little trouble at present.' Probably she is still going round saying that she'd been talking kindly to an Innkeeper about himself at Thame when he suddenly began talk-ing about Baghdad!

Miss ——, of whose hypochondriacy I had been forewarned, told me on the first morning that she hadn't slept at all. I said, 'What a privileged person! Because to most of us it is given to enjoy lying in a lovely bed for only a few minutes in the morning when we ought to be getting up. It is as if we are unconscious through the whole meal and only wake up in time for the savoury,' and I quoted a poem of mine which I once used to good purpose on myself when in like condition:

O would to God the giftie'd gie us
To flee ourselves as others flee us.

1926

The Signpost goes up

I told the auctioneer who, like the rest here, is sniffy and grudging of our new Signpost, that it alone would bring into the town £40,000 in the course of the next ten years, which is putting it low, and he sniggered. The original Sign when I came had merely the name of the Hotel with 'luncheons and teas'. In 1923 I sketched out the eagle on it and 'Carrington' Partridge painted it beautifully. Spenser Hoffman did the beautiful lettering. It used to hang out from the house 15 ft over the parapet on iron bars and tie rods upon which Timms, blacksmith of Long Crendon, when 22 years old, mounted his beautiful ironwork in 1834. After ninety-two years of swinging and vibrating, the part of the house where it was fixed was getting disintegrated. So in the summer of 1924 I wrote to the Council asking permission to put the sign up on a post on the pave-

ment, which they wouldn't have had power to do had I not told them that it would take the place of an ugly lamp-post which I would light at my own expense. The Council came in force to interview me on a summer evening at eight o'clock outside the house when dinner was in full swing, and I was in a white duck dress-suit, and it began to drizzle. I was given permission. I showed my ½-inch drawing to the late H. J. Birnstingl, who suggested two important refinements, e.g. the lead cap and the lanterns for which he gave me full-sized drawings. Later the Post was published in an architectural journal crediting Birnstingl with 'the general conception and details' and me with being a good innkeeper! Fortunately I had working for me Mr Cook, ex-shipwright lieutenant RN, who besides shaping and fluting the Post in the back yard, helped Eaton in the erection of it and was the real genius and *sine qua non* of the Post's existence. Ralph Timms of Thame adjusted and added to his grandfather's wrought-ironwork to fit the frame which also he made. My chief difficulty, in which I had really no help, was the strength and fixing of this huge iron frame, so I wrote an apologetic letter to Dorman Long, Battersea, and they replied that our local blacksmith should be well able to advise and that they themselves were unable! How kind we English are to one another! So I had to do my best. The sign, frame and ironwork measures 10 feet square, and the height from ground is 23 feet. It was Mr Cook's idea to slightly taper the 4 feet in the ground and drop it into a fitted cast-iron socket, so that it will, as it shrinks, always keep tight. In order to give another 15 inches depth, one Lanyon, engineer and rubber planter, who was staying here,

suggested dropping from the corners of the square
plate at the bottom of the tapered socket four 15-inch
rods with flat plates on the bottom of these, so the foot-
ing is now 5 feet, which Mr Howland surrounded with
3 tons of concrete. Afterwards I started making out the
cost and gave up when I reached £190. When he saw it
up, Mr Robinson, the surveyor, was very nervous as 'it
was a much bigger thing than the Council ever anticipated', which 'was more like this', he said, kicking a
scaffold pole. 'What', he asked, 'would they do if every
publican and eating-house in Thame asks to put up
a sign?' I told him that if they could find lamp-posts
to substitute signs for, it would be much to the good.
This evening, Spencer Jackson, good old man, iron and
brass founder and inventor, came in and said he had
proposed me and I had been elected with acclamation
a member of the Chamber of Commerce . . . And now
the Brewers of the 'Black Horse' next door have hung a
new Sign against their House, a black quadruped
printed (!) on beaverboard. But as the other side is only
a reproduction of this the animal is seen walking into
the house by the upper window, giving his hindquar-
ters to the street, ἵππος μελαμπύγος.

Sir X. Y.'s 'secretary for all his art affairs' came with
his sister and his son in a solid silver Rolls with gold
fittings to lunch. After lunch he asked that his sister,
who had come with oil-paints, could take a note of my
pink in the drawing-room upstairs, Norman Wilkin-
son had told him about it, to carry out in Sir X. Y.'s
new house. Now if Sir X. Y. had come himself I might
have been delighted, but as it is he is getting something for nothing which is not correct, and, worse still,

without knowing it. It would have been better had these people gone in and stolen their colour notes. My objection to this business is perhaps hypersensitive, but it smacked of a popular notion that a public-house is a public place for which the owner pays a heavy licence in order to have the privilege of being a philanthropist to all and sundry without acknowledgment. In other words they wouldn't have done this to a private house.

Mrs Greiffenhagen said that in fifteen years' time our sons would be able to take over the Hotel. This rather shocked me at first, but why should it? True, the publican has to deal with all sorts, but so does the doctor and businessman, and there never was a more interesting or stimulating trade − you get people at their best and out for the best; not like a doctor's or lawyer's or grocer's clients; for who would go to these willingly? But here is the only objection − it's a perpetual grindstone. There is no time for contemplation of your job and little enough time to enjoy your patients. Moreover, I think that a Hotel is a job to retire to, as ex-boxers do, or to take up at any rate after you have had a good time and learnt what is good in people, their houses and food. The born and bred hotel-keeper must necessarily be inexperienced.

Ernest

Ernest Thesiger turned up for the first time, and when I asked him why he'd come he said it was so long since he'd been in a lunatic asylum. He told Ian Strang, whom I had asked to do a series of etchings here, that he saw me run excitedly into the kitchen and say, 'Mr Thesiger is here to dinner, open quickly a box of sardines.'

Capitalism

I told T——, anticapitalist, that when I first started
business I thought the other wine merchants were
charging too much and now that I knew the risks and
costs of things I was getting less certain about it. For
instance, I found the other day 24 bottles of good wine
in a broken heap on a collapsed shelf, and 'the worst of
it was that the customer had to pay for those bottles!'
'Then', said T——, with his little eyes bright, 'I don't
think much of your "risks" if the customer has to pay
for them.' 'But', I explained, 'if he *didn't* pay for the
risks as well as the costs, and overhead charges, licence
and everything else, I couldn't afford to be a wine merchant, nor could anyone else. In short, I don't stock
wine for myself but for the public. As wine merchant I
am simply his servant, and the fact that the public has
to pay £1 for a thing everywhere else when *I* think I can
sell it for 15*s*. is beginning to make me feel that I may
be giving my capital and services too cheap.' 'Then, at
last, you have identified yourself with the trade,' he
said – implying, as I found out, that I was in a combination to fleece him. To which I replied that I was not *certain* of anything, but that business had at least taught
me caution before condemning coal owners and everyone else. I told him about staff – how lovable ours was
but how hard it had been to teach some of them and
keep them up to it so that they may profit themselves
and the town long before we were enriched. With no
business experience, this Utopian fellow yet persisted
in 'the real argument and reason at the back of the
General Strike'. H. G. Wells had been reading T——'s
latest book and I asked him if it was good. He said that

there was one joke in it which made it worth the 7s. 6d.
It was the counsel of a friend to a feeble man who
declined to allow his wife to go and get a child elsewhere – 'Better love hath no man than this, that he lay
down his wife for his friend.' It was my joke, which I
had told to T——— some years before.

An elderly gent was dining with a young man in the
little room where each table is inclined to overhear the
other. He graciously told me that I had a very good
wine list but questioned my Brandy's being '1865'. I
told him it was a mere silly name and that it didn't take
me in either. But he said he'd try it and that he knew all
about wine. When I asked him how he liked it he said,
'Frankly, I don't.' It happens to be good brandy and
everyone in the room heard this expert's opinion,
which was embarrassing. Then he went on to say that
he noticed that I had no 'Château Burgundy' so I had to
tell the expert that there was no such thing as 'Château
Burgundy'. 'But what about Château Yquem?' I replied, 'Yquem is not a Burgundy.' As I was leaving
the room he said in an undertone to his young friend,
'But there *are* Château Burgundies' – when I rudely
interrupted, 'I tell you definitely that there are NOT.'
The next evening in the same little dining-room a very
rich and good-hearted American had been brought to
dinner by two nice people. He sent for me and told me
my claret had 'neither bouquet, nor taste, nor colour' –
to which pronouncement five people in the room had
to listen. This wine being one of my lesser favourites I
was rather shocked, and his bottle was in perfect condition. I gave him a bottle of fat Burgundy instead. Later
I saw him spending a long time with Katie over the

bill – so I went up to see what was the matter. 'Mr
Fothergill, what is 10 per cent on £1 11s. 6d.?' Not bad
for a big businessman. Before going he insisted on a
liqueur all round and said he'd come again 7,000 miles
to dine here. After all, 7,000 miles is only like across the
road to this sort of American who is exactly like, in his
good heart, figure and rather brutal ways, the Lan-
cashireman, but with money added.

It's hard to be governess as well as cook, but it's
only by great vigilance that we've won a reputation
amongst the better-class undergrad, or, rather, lost it
with the worser. The fool or bounder seldom comes
now, or if he does he behaves as nowhere else. One has
to watch him from the moment he comes into a
charming dining-room with his hands in his pockets
and his cap on, if he only used one. It's no pleasure to
go and tell eight 'hearties' in the common-room that
people in the hotel might be bored with the sound of
their hunting horn, or that I don't like girls who are

not sisters or suitable companions, or not to swing on
one leg on an eighteenth-century chair. The other day
I told some lads who seemed to be blowing up for the
idiotic to go to those places in and around Oxford
where the furniture was made for breaking and the
food for vomiting. Once a party of two undergrads
with two delightful girls arrived and asked if they
could bring the gramophone in to dinner or 'was it
against the law of the house?' I told them it was
against not my but God's law to take about a musical
instrument in public places. Once four undergrads had
made a noisy start at dinner, so I asked them not to
behave like Reading students. 'I *am*', exclaimed the
most typical Etonian of the four, 'a Reading student!',
which repartee surprised them all into home behaviour again. (Reading wasn't then a University.) To
make this an Eton or Stowe of public-houses will be no
joke, but it's got to be done. In an altercation I had
with a scrubby undergrad, the fellow said, 'I'll never
come here again,' to which I replied, 'Yes, but will you
give me another undertaking: to tell all your friends
not to come?' – This enraged him into saying he'd
report me to the AA, of which he was a member, and I
told him he might as well tell me that he was a member of the A & NCS. Togo Maclaurin, who realises my
difficulty so near Oxford, said, 'Yes, if you gave me the
management of this place I could wreck it in a week.'
Yet to have to dinner the pick of charming or clever
youths is a vast privilege and a knowledge . . . Four
years later – partly, perhaps, owing to the above
scrubby undergrad's having carried out his undertaking so diligently, we almost never get an ass or a try-on
from Oxford and I no longer expect it.

Oriel College

The ancient 75-year-old Provost, Mr Phelps, without ever having been to this place and no one knows on what informations, ordained that the annual Fellows' dinner, never before held out of College, should take place here and should be considered *'an integral part of their sexcentenary celebrations'*. So after having lunched with 600 and tea'd with 1,500 they came over here. We had them in the little dining-room on the big round Regency table with a strip of rosewood and brass inlay near the edge, and in the centre Phyllis had put a low black bowl filled with concentric rings of orange geums and yellow-green feverfew. They had green-handled and silver pistol-handled knives and forks with prongs four, three and even two. Katie said they got hopelessly mixed with them. They ate on a Pinkston Bourbon sprig service with a few courses on Ming plates and Crown Derby. The Provost had coffee for himself and neighbours in a service of early Ginori on a superb boat-shaped brass bound gallery tray: the others had a Queen Anne coffee-pot and old Worcester. They ate up everything. There was a choice of three sweets. When I asked Katie how they were getting on with these she said, 'Oh, they can't make up their minds, so I'm making them into three separate courses,' which they solemnly ate through. They drank but little, and went into the garden afterwards. Kate saw one or two go back for their menu cards. 'How sweet!' G. N. Clark told me it had been 'the pleasantest event in their joint lives'. They were, as Clark promised, a remarkable collection of Don types, the Provost is wonderful to look at, a blend of

Zeus and Jesus, and Clark did most of the entertaining. I told the Provost that it was a most honourable
day for us and away they went.

Once Frank Wedgwood sent a telegram from 'Etruria'
to stay the night with Mrs Wedgwood, so I dined them
from beginning to end on old Wedgwood. They were
perfectly charming in every way but never said one
kind word about the crockery. Later I complained
about this to Sir Ralph Wedgwood, who replied con-
solingly, 'But you must realise he *makes* it and
naturally feels all old Wedgwood to be in competition!'
   I proposed to the Proctors that in my own interest
they might 'approve' us as they do the City restaurants, and though they said it was the first time they
had ever thought of outside places, it was done there
and then. Relations with the Proctors have always
been 'mutually respectful'. They've been here offi-
cially only once. In our very early days the Chief
Marshall (Bulldog) came in at about 10 p.m., and
asked if a certain charming and talked-about lady had
slept here after a big party given to her by Jimmy Bartram. This party had been forbidden by the Proctors at
the eleventh hour, so the whole thing, food, cooks,
guests and crackers, was transferred here. A proctor
told me afterwards that they knew they were coming
here, but could safely leave to me the conduct of this
party (which, being a strange selection of boxers,
peers, poets, hearties, aesthetes, and two pretty ladies,
was of itself a guarantee of dullness). Owing to the exi-
gencies of the case, they had to be seated at two big
round tables with a smaller round table sandwiched
between. Bartram covered and piled them high with

masses of white crackers and white flowers, making them look like the freshly filled graves of the charming lady, her husband and little son. I told the Chief Marshall that the lady had slept here alone with her lady friend. 'Have you any undergraduates on the premises now?' — 'No, none.' — 'Thank you.' But why there shouldn't have been I never asked. I told him that I'd like to talk to the Proctors one day about undergrads and Innkeeping. He said they were outside, so I asked him to bring them in. As he was the devil of a long time I went out also to see what was happening, and saw in the darkness three black figures coming up the street. At that moment two cars loaded with youths, making a loud and silly noise, dashed out of the archway and drove past the black figures, one of which jumped into the road to take the numbers. After a pleasant interview I added that I thought it might now be necessary to explain that those youths were not undergrads but Welsh Guards (Willie Makins, chief rouser) who had been dining here after the steeplechase. 'Of course, Mr Fothergill, it wasn't necessary, we would have believed you.' For all that, I don't know how otherwise they could reasonably have done so.

After many days of unsullied pleasantness we've had a day of loathsomeness, which began last night at 12.30 a.m. when an old woman, looking like a procuress, with a very pretty girl and an old car riding on its near hind rim, asked for rooms and food at one in the morning. I gave them delicious food and two wonderful beds, breakfast in the sunny little room and took them into a gorgeous garden. Then they complained to Katie about having to pay 1s. for garage because their

filthy little car had been left in the yard and not inside
the garage, so Katie took off the shilling. I caught the
pretty girl on the steps outside – 'I'm sorry about that
shilling for garage,' I said. 'Oh it's all right,' she replied
with a forgiving air. Then I gave her and the old
woman four minutes' talking-to by the Town Hall
clock. The Fagans left after a fortnight's stay, after
which I was pulled out of the garden to see an elderly
man in a Rolls with a pretty girl who wanted me to put
up a poster for a highbrow handicraft show in Oxford,
which I declined, and he went off – I had to talk to an
undergrad for sprawling about on his chair and
putting his feet on the mantelshelf. A woman and husband then came in a Chrysler to sell me Macquoid's
English Furniture, and when I said I had it already
they asked me where they should go next? I told them
that their method was a wrong one, and in the evening
I took up to No. 7, our best room, an awful couple of
people – having already three commercials in the
house – and he turned to his miserable wife and said,
'Will this do?' But happily we had seventeen very
decent folks to dinner, which rounded off the bad day,
and Hogarth (Ashmolean Museum) rang up to say
that they couldn't come to dine after all because their
car had broken down and would I send the bill?
Antique politeness.

'Questionings, misgivings'

As you get more and more tired out and in need of a
holiday you worry more and more about the food and
the people. Is the food good enough? And aren't the
people too kind? To the first question I have to bear in
mind always that the dinner is only 5s., the usual

price at places where the food is uneatable, in rooms
unbearable, on white cotton tablecloths, partaken
either solitary or with any old kind of lodger or
passer-by. I have to force myself to believe that about
two hours working at the food myself in the kitchen
before dinner and seeing to the helping on each plate
must tell the tale to the eater of it, unless I am imbe-
cile, and that a steady increase of people even in bad
times is a proof that our efforts are successful. But
meals fail at times from beginning to end and sometimes the super-smart come from London expecting
Boulestin. Bertie Meyer, for instance, with a party of
exquisites, asked for salad in midwinter with the Sunday lunch, and last night a splendid Hispano-Suiza
slid up the yard covered with escutcheons. 'Belgian
Embassy?' I asked the silver-grey chauffeur as I passed
him in the Bar, 'No, sir. Spanish Royal Family.' They
were a pretty girl and her husband, with three gentlemen who looked like butlers discharged for taking
liberties. The pretty girl said they'd heard the food
was so good. But as it was not *à la carte* she would eat
almost nothing and the meal was bad in any case, and
we had no time to make nice things, there being fifty
others dining at the time. I didn't mind the 'Royalty'
so much, but I feel it's so rude to disappoint, foreign-
ers especially. But when people come again and again
how can you reward them? You feel you must; yet if
you do, for instance, give them a bottle of wine, when
are you to repeat the dose? Or will they feel compelled
to drink wine on the next occasion when they might
not want it? Or mightn't some for that reason avoid
you altogether? How are you to face people who, after
coming regularly, have you to a splendid meal at their

own homes and then come and dine the following day and you let them have a bill! We ourselves can't have dinner-parties here, for we are busy just at that time and so I resort to little gifts of Greek honey or the banal giving of a glass of good brandy, and wonder how it's all going to pan out – this debit and credit account. Perhaps – most certainly, we shall never get out of debt with these nice folks who make our lives bearable or delightful, but we must include all in the common ledger to find that the nice folks merely pay for the few disgruntled ones who try to treat us like coolies but don't come again, or make a still more inclusive account to find that we are getting kindness and affection because so many other places are loathsome.

It was exciting to have here the Reverend laughing Hugh Embling before going to Corea to be Bishop, because Clarke Hall once told me the story about his asking for a lot of young criminals to be sent to a bit of a farm he had in Essex – 'Here you are,' he said to them, 'this is your farm and you are responsible for it – get on with it.' After a week all the tiles had been stripped from the roof and every implement made useless. Soon afterwards it became a going concern in their hands. Whatever the influence of this striking personality effected, Embling was modest and humorous enough to add to the story that he had a very useful and muscular sailor to look after the boys!

Peter and Kathleen Clegg, RN, came here for ten days' honeymoon – they were both so beautiful, but she especially lovely like the Helen on the Makron vase, and their ways were so charming that they ate into our minds. (They lunched again here on their anniversary.)

Romney Summers brought in a man to dinner. He told me he had overtaken him just outside Oxford, and that they had raced here, and then going level up the straight in the town he'd invited him to dine here. They had a magnum between them. Afterwards Romney backed his faithful Vauxhall through the archway out into the street. I said, 'I wish you wouldn't do that, coaches and fours didn't do it; besides, it looks as if we hadn't any room inside.' Then followed the other with his Bentley, backing also. I told him the same story, and when he knocked up against the side I added, 'In any case, you can't drive for little apples.' Each of them apologised quietly. Romney then told me that the other man was Clement and at the same moment, having now got his car into position for answering my charge of little apples, seemed to lift it bodily up and jumped into the darkness like a thunderbolt. Romney drove the other day from Glasgow here, 430 miles, is it? at an average of 36 mph, which is nothing compared with the beautiful Lady Marjorie Dalrymple-Hamilton, who told me she took her two children in a small car from London to Ayrshire, 450 miles in the day! 'Slow infanticide,' someone said when I told him of it.

Out of the affectations and tiresome struggles peculiar to the literary people and their children of the 'nineties emerges Olivia Sowerby (Meynell as I knew her last), a sweet and distinguished lady with delightful children and a practical husband.

Oliver Baldwin came to dinner early, and as he was hanging about when three respectable Hull solicitors arrived for the night with their luggage, Oliver, just like his kindness, offered to help me with them upstairs. Loaded with two big bags he stood patiently whilst they allotted their rooms. At dinner I asked them, 'How are you getting on?' and they replied, 'We are mightily pleased with our quarters,' to which I added, 'And what do you think of the porter of your luggage, the Prime Minister's son?', which made them sit up. Oliver wants to abolish the Public Schools and have all educated alike, as, indeed, most of us parents would, so that the Duchess and her daughters may be scullery maids if they shall have been beaten in the race by those who are scullery maids now. Anything, I suppose, to get us better scullery maids, for I'm sure that those we have now would make far better duchesses and far more daughters.

Agricultural Show Day

This is the fourth we've had and it gets easier, and in fourpences and shillings we turned over £75. The first Show that we had here the Inn was inundated with peasants and ham teas. There's fun in it, if it wears your feet out a bit. Two women brought in their car and backed it alongside of the little dining-room window and pulled out their sandwiches and bottles and lunched. I was waiting my time to tell them of it when right in front of them a man shouted out to me, 'Where's the Gent's urinal?' I pointed it out and turning to the women said, 'You've chosen a bad place for your lunch, with the Gent's urinal in front of you and our perfectly good dining-room alongside of you – better taste would have placed you higher up the yard.' So they said they had really intended to have it in my garden, and then at 8.30 they wanted to pay 1s. for garage for the whole day. After talking some time to an old woman at lunch she said to me, 'It's a very fine day, waiter, for the Show.' And into this crowd came Dunstan Skilbeck, bon vivant, jester and farmer, bringing Arnold Dolmetsch and Carr-Saunders to lunch and tea; and a young artist, a French viscount from Wendover, sat upstairs and painted the night Fair scene without; and an old man with a whore told Katie to tell me that 3s. 6d. for a four-course meal was a swindle, and when I went to him afterwards to invite a scrap he only smiled pleasantly; and John Nash and Daglish came, and after the beer-drinking masses had gone so had six of my good silver-plated tankards.

Walter Payne brought a lovely sight, Doris Lytton-Partington (now his wife) to dinner – after which he drew from his pocket a very long cigar for her and a very small but exquisite one for me. W. P. runs only forty theatres. I used to see him on Theatre Owner Committee Meetings. In perfect silence he used to let the thing get more and more boggled, then suddenly deboggle it by six or seven wise words.

About a year ago two Oxford aesthetes arrived in a car from Cambridge bringing a Cambridge aesthete of great elegance. The lad descended from the car with his arms outstretched, pushing the air, as it were, with the palms of his lovely hands in an undulating motion. Preceded by these hands he entered the house. At tea I said to them, 'I have a friend (Michel Salaman) who is thinking of not sending his sons to Oxford because he's been told that the moral tone there is not as good as at Cambridge.' – 'It's a lie,' screamed the exquisite,

throwing out his lovely hands with passion and indignation. 'Cambridge is *far* worse!'

'You've altered this room since I was here five years ago,' said a farmerish old man and his wife lunching in this distinguished, beautiful dining-room. 'Do you like it?' – 'Well, yes – it's clean and respectable now.' – Humiliating comment is salutary when you are beginning to get satisfied, still more salutary is a visit to a private house, Michel Salaman's, for instance.

A party of five people journeyed from —— to dine and they sat the meal through in almost perfect silence. Feeling that they might blame me or the place for a very dull evening I went up and tried some bright chatter on them, but they only stared at me till at last the parson, in as friendly a manner as he could muster, apropos of nothing, asked, 'Now, what is your population here?' I replied, 'It's not *my* population, thank God, but there are about 3,000 of them,' and we all relapsed into silence again. However, by way of excusing my inadequacy I might have told him of our grandfather Crawshay who is said to have had 300 children in South Wales, yes, and with a separate maintenance ledger for the twins!

Jermyn and Mrs Moorsom came here for the first night of their honeymoon. I gave them roses on their table, 'Red Letter Day' and 'Independence Day', and Mrs Moorsom had appendicitis within a fortnight. He wrote afterward from Hawick, 'Your Inn made all the others we went to seem very uncomfortable.' Jermyn is centred in his sheep, his soft-faced brother Raisley is centred in himself, and they've both got lovely wives.

... *after the beer-drinking masses had gone so had six of my good silver-plated tankards.*

1927

Past Generations

It is a privilege, though one works for it, to have here so many bits of past generations — people one has known by name for forty years and some never seen, and being perfectly delightful. Martin Conway, Harry Melville, Jerome K. Jerome, Professor Margoliouth, John Lane, Barrie, Madame Génée, Miss Horniman, O. Bradbury, Mrs Colin Hunter, Mrs Patrick Campbell, Ernest Rhys, Nigel Playfair (for wasn't he at Oxford with me?), De la Condamine the learned dandy. He takes me round my own garden and, with that scarlet intonation of the 'nineties, tells me or seems to tell me as much as might John Nash or F. A. Hampton, and they say that he performs the same feat with doctors and, I suppose, with everyone else's pet swindle in life and has never yet been found out. Then 'Vernon Lee', Mrs Jopling Rowe, Father Rivers and so on, why, the list makes my eyes water! And to think that these brave people, though having represented the worst decades of English life and art should be still at large! It is a privilege to be able to cater for them and their eminent successors of the present generation in return for their own clever tricks; a double privilege, because an artist cannot expect to return the hospitality of the musician by showing him his pictures, nor the musician the novelist, and so on, but an Innkeeper can and ought to be able to do for each of them with security of appreciation; a triple privilege, because an Innkeeper, being in no aesthetic or intellectual enclosure, can appreciate the tricks of everyone.

*

When I was measuring Count George Zichy on the wall, 6 ft 7½ in., I asked him if he was a descendant of the great Zichy. 'Yes, grandson, and allow me to present to you my friend, Prince Lázló Esterházy, grandson of my grandfather's colleague.'

This last summer I bought, bottled and had bottled for me 9,000 bottles of Bordeaux and Burgundy. The question whether it pays me to have so big a cellar I leave to answer itself – no accountant could answer it, because the circumstances here are peculiar.

A Joke

David Maxwell brought the young Duke of Norfolk with Kittner and Bob Wilberforce to dinner. Bob looks like a big fair American baseball hero, but is English.

The Duke is shy and solid and I said to him, 'We've read a good deal about you lately as being Chief Butler of England, and now' – pouring wine into their glasses – 'I find it pleasant to be doing you out of your job for once.'

Regrets

Empty house, and only a few passers-by to lunch – rain, the publican's ruin and no one to dinner. Nice people have been here in the past and may never have the chance to return. Nice people have come from inquisitiveness, perhaps, and will never come again, and certain nice people can't come, well, ever again at all. Everyone knows of us and there never was a greater *succès d'estime* save Will Rothenstein's un-dated pictures.

Guy Vaughan-Morgan brought one Massey, Canadian, and his pretty wife to lunch. Cohn, of Oriel, dined with Brooks and two others, all Dons. Cohn, though a clever and original little thing, wrote a book called *The Fool*. As I was turning it over at the bookstall on its day of publication I found him standing at my elbow, looking already tired, so I bought it. I wish more Dons would come here, but as they get free meals in College it's not to be expected. Without doubt our dinner and its sur-roundings are the best bargain in England. When Maisie Somerville, one of our foundation-stones, told some people that ours was the most celebrated hotel in this part of the world I objected to her limiting the area, but she had in her mind Clough Williams-Ellis's astonishing invention at Portmerion. I said that hotels like his, the Beetle and Wedge, Philip Sainsbury's, and perhaps others and mine had no competitors or comparisons, simply because they are expressions of different individualities and, as such, are not for universal appreciation. This Inn, 14 crooked miles from a town, has been created in four years out of none of those factors that are the making of hotels that otherwise could never have existed for a day, not golf nor shooting, hunting, riverside, seaside, climate, landscape, main road, nor jazz and cocktails – I have used only food, wine, furniture and people with which to express myself in the language of Innkeeping.

Innkeeping

Mary Dowdall won't grow old, she is a lovely person. Mr and Mrs Barrington-Ward (Christ Church) came to dinner – she, delightfully pretty and boy-like, with pale face, bright teeth and black silky Eton-crop. He, shy. Mr and Mrs Orwin and family came for their silver wedding – golden themselves. Patrick de Lázló and Derek Jackson, physicist, are of the most urbane, attractive and appreciative dining couples that we have here. Yes, it's courage chiefly that one wants here; you get seventy to lunch on Sunday, but this is reduced to a poor average when you get three the next day, and so on all the week perhaps.

The Twelve-Foot Patagonian

When we were at Weston-super-Mare we discovered for 2d. on the Old Pier a mummy of a Patagonian 12 ft high with two heads. I told Philip Gosse about it, the Author of the *Pirates' Who's Who*, etc., odd and disgruntled to look at but in reality a cheerful, whimsical and generous creature, and he told me it must be a

fake, a very jolly fake and much to be encouraged and
believed in. So I wrote to an important doctor at
Weston, to ask him kindly to examine it, giving my
undertaking to keep it secret should he have to
pronounce it a fake. I enclosed a letter from the distinguished bacteriologist, Dr John Freeman, assuring
him of my bona fides. The important doctor replied
that his time was not his own, that he had never heard
of a man of that height, therefore it must be an ingen-
ious fake. He would like one day to see it but he was,
he feared, a confirmed sceptic. It required some in-
genuity to thank this busy man for his trouble. So I
appointed a Commission of Enquiry, consisting of Guy
Brown, physicist, the radiologist at Weston-super-
Mare Hospital and a local doctor who kindly inspected
it thoroughly and found 'no perceptual evidence' of its
being a fake. Commander Gould in his fascinating
Oddities has exploded to his own satisfaction the
Patagonian giant 'myth', but he did not know of this
one. Trippers go and see it for 2*d*. They are sure they
are being taken in, and for 2*d*. they don't mind it but
they don't talk about it when they go home, hence the
poor thing's obscurity. I told young medical Rhinelander that this huge fellow might be after all no
corroboration of the giant 'myth', being probably only
a potential 6-foot twins like the Ward twins of 6 ft 4 in.
each, boiled into one, the heads only claiming separate
identity. But Rhinelander held that the man must
plainly have been from one egg, with an extra head,
just as some people are born with six fingers and lambs
with extra heads. At least two women have asked me if
he lived long! I hear it's now in the local Museum. I
told David Garnett about it and the elements of a

tragedy that Kate had invented. He said he would make a story of it. Today at lunch, months afterwards, he had done nothing about it so he started at once to dictate his story before the fire to his companion. Some time later I asked him to write for my *The Fothergill Omnibus* and had no answer. A year afterwards he crept in to lunch saying that he dared not say he would do it because he was so afraid that he wouldn't, and yet wouldn't say he couldn't because he would so much like to, so he couldn't reply, which ugly complex I imagine had also kept him away all this time. He's so lazy and lovable.

A curious solicitor, Cannan Brooks, brought a young Australian, Alfred O'Shea, to lunch who afterwards asked if we had a piano and if he might sing, so I sent them over to the Market Room where there is an old piano, which, for lack of space, we keep out of doors during the summer. Later I heard peals of mighty wonderful singing so I rushed round for an audience. I could find only two little scullery-maids and a dear temporary cook, weighing 19 stone, and in this shape we stood in a row behind him, much to his delight when he turned round afterwards. What will happen to this young man? Will he get eaten up by a rich woman, or continue to sing to any person and any piano?

Uniforms for Every Worker

Being the South Oxfordshire Hunt's steeplechases we had five or six horses for the night, including the Prince of Wales's, who didn't come here himself. A party of Welsh Guards – Willie Makins, Dowding,

Cyril Heber Percy, Higgon, Ackroyd and two beautiful
sisters Pritchard lunched and dined. It's rather a bor-
ing job getting people to clean their boots after shows
of this kind when coming into the house. In the hall
Cyril Heber Percy, malapert lad, came up to me and
asked in shrill voice, 'Are you the head waiter, or do
you merely provide the music?' A white jacket he
knew, but buckled shoes were confusing. I was too tick-
led to reply appropriately. As for my buckles and white
coat, every tradesman ought to wear a uniform, and
not only for giving at least an impression of cleanliness
but to inspire confidence, i.e. godliness. One wants to
feel that the man you are consulting is, *pro tem.*, like
God, wholly devoted to his job. How could a parson
massing in mufti impress, or a barrister or jockey or

Every tradesman ought to wear a uniform.

God or even a Hamlet? But there are many classes of tradesmen who fail us in this respect – the doctor could perfectly well wear a frock coat now that they are obsolete, just as the African medicine man wears a top hat, and the solicitor and hotel-keeper, especially the upper-class one. In these people, one doesn't want to see a perfect gent in plus fours but something super-human. One comes to them as helps and comforters, not as competitors or perhaps inferiors. I've always felt here that it's bad manners to appear in ordinary clothes, even to the plants in my garden, and, when not wearing a white coat, I have hoped at least my buckled shoes, which I've worn for thirty years, would carry me through.

At lunch there were two people, perhaps Colonial, a nice-looking woman and her husband, fat and bald save for some rust-coloured hair, rust freckles and a rust-coloured suit. He asked for Evian water, which I said I hadn't got, but I added, 'You ought to try our Thame water – it's supposed to be very good for – rusting tanks'; and seeing the quite accidental but apt application to the rusty fat gentleman I turned to the woman and said with a smile, 'Rather a rude thing to say, wasn't it?' However, they promised to stay here on the way back from Malvern.

Two Old Gentlemen and a Wine Cork

We had a good few to lunch, including a very courteous old gentleman, J. Roskill, KC, with a party of six. At the next table, two old boys, of the London Club variety, had Mouton de Rothschild '14, and they said how splendid it was. When they had finished lunch, for

something to say, I asked again, 'And did you like the
claret?' – 'Oh, it's . . . all . . . right . . .' with a drawl. I
was surprised by this complete change of attitude
towards the now emptied bottle, when one of the old
boys exclaimed, 'It's not Château bottled!' – 'Why, of
course it is and a very good bottle, because I tasted it.'
'Yes, you *say* "Château Bottled" on your list, but look
at the *cork*,' which he handed me. On it was branded
'John Fothergill, Thame'! So I explained the peculiar
circumstances by which I occasionally opened a wrong
bottle and immediately afterwards recorked it with a
new cork. But they were unconvinced. 'Have you a
bottle with the *original* cork in it?' I brought one up.
'Ah, that's the real thing,' said one, and the other
winked approval. 'Good God, do you still doubt me? I'll
open it and you shall taste it,' so bang went my money
on these old pretensions. But in vain: 'That's something *like*, Charles,' he cried, and this of a cellar-cold
wine when their own had been perfect – 'That's more
like it,' said Charles, then turning to me, 'you should
know that my brother is a great connoisseur of claret.'
The brother winked agreement. So I had to speak. 'I
deny that either of you know anything about claret at
all. In the first place you, the connoisseur, gave me a
shock when ordering the wine by asking me if Mouton
Rothschild, one of the five best clarets, was a red wine.'
At this the connoisseur George turned to his brother
and reproved him for giving him that reputation. 'I
never said I was a connoisseur, Charles,' and they had a
little recrimination for having landed themselves so
well. 'Secondly, besides not knowing claret, you don't
know ordinary human nature: it never struck you that
if I wanted to cheat you I wouldn't have left the "John

Fothergill" cork on the table in front of you.' So I left them, looking forward myself to a good bottle in the evening. I saw one of them in the hall later. He made no advance, so I said, 'I'm sorry about the claret business, but I really couldn't help it.' — 'How old are you?' snapped the old boy. — 'After thirty, age has nothing to do with the question. I hope the day may come when you may be able to like wine by the taste and not the cork — though it's improbable now.' And so they left for ever. But there's a pathetic sequel, for which I'm more sorry. Back to that Club they'll go, but never again to talk together about wine, since each knows now that the other knows nothing about it, and if one of them is dining with clubmates like himself he will have to look round before he joins in the usual wine talk to see that his brother is not within earshot. It really wasn't my fault. Mr Roskill, who had overheard the whole thing at the next table, told me afterwards that he wanted to give them a disinterested summing up which I wish he had done.

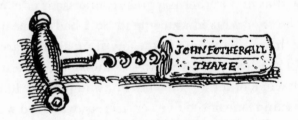

In the lavatory, having lost two good books, I put Baily's translation of Lucretius hoping that that would stay, but not even that — so now I've had for some months Theo Mathew's (barrister) *Forensic Fables* on which I've written 'IRREMOVABLE'. Mrs —— said to her husband, 'We've got a good story for Theo when we get back' — but Theo knows of its place already, for he wrote to E. S. P. Haynes that I was 'evidently a discriminating person'.

When E. W. Harding and I sat together in the summer afternoons at school writing 'lines' I little thought that thirty-two years thence I should be selling his handsome son a dinner! This evening he came himself. 'How pathetic', I said, 'that you are now a colonel and I a mere publican.' — 'Yes, but I am a bad colonel and you are a good publican.'

A lad called Duguid dines here often — a delicate, quiet, long-fingered lad of infinite politeness and modesty, with a great resemblance to Dick Innes and Montie Pollock's children and the Royal Family. His work is no good, but it's bound to be good one day with all this at the back of it.

To a place like this — which no one passes but which is an end in itself, the RAC and AA signs are worse than useless because all we get through them is complaints. Five dreadful people whom I had charged 5s. 6d. for lunch on Sunday told me they would write to the AA about it. Saunders of the RAC, who happened to be lunching at the next table, told me I could tell the AA, if they wrote, that the lunch was worth 6s. The AA did write, and I told them that if complaints of their members embarrassed them they would be wise to take me off their book. Today the RAC man from the Oxford office came to complain that a gentleman had been here five days ago, had rung twice and waited fifteen minutes and never got any tea but went away. I told him to tell the man that he was evidently one of those people who preferred to shout a complaint to HQ to shouting to a kitchen. Kate, as a matter of fact, remembered seeing the man and wondered what he and his dog were doing, as both were apparently inarticulate.

People give me things, their books or other creations. It's a peculiar kindness, making gifts to one who has been already paid sufficiently for his services. Professional men get the same jolly surprises. I asked Rooke Ley why people did this and he said it was 'to pay for that which you couldn't put down on the bill', which ought to disembarrass me. Since in trade giving is illogical one has to make a virtue of taking as next best.

Kenneth Bell

Kenneth Bell brought seven hearties to dinner – himself in proctorial robes, just like him – the first batch of the six-months Oxford course for West African Administrators. These 'Hearty Beasts', as they style themselves, are to found the new tradition there and will think well of Kenneth for not treating them as children at Oxford. During the soup Kenneth Bell asked me if I could put up himself and his family here for a more or less indefinite period. As his family is immense I was rather surprised. After dinner he asked if I had one of those big cheeses that you taste in shops, so I put before him a sixty-two pounder, thirteen months old, and he talked again, now still more earnestly, about his family's coming. So I wrote next day to Mrs Bell and asked what he really wanted, if anything. She quickly replied, saying that she 'knew these sudden outbursts of Kenneth's emotion and was left to deal with the results herself'. Once he walked here to dinner and back, 29 miles, leaving a running

Blue to be picked up by the roadside. Under his savage
exterior he's a tender sentimentalist... And there
came today Guy and Cathy Vaughan Morgan, the
black pearl I call her; and of undergraduates B. Bonas
smiling, Wordsworth ponderous and good-natured, D.
Branch struggling to arrive in wit, Rupert Crawshay
Williams important but pink, Rumbold theological
student with his vast red Cadillac holding only two,
and Favell, he too will make a pretty parson.

The Philosophy of What we call 'Lavatory Work'

It had rained all day and the house had been unsuited
with a soul when two people, a man and a pretty
woman, arrived at about tea-time.
'Will you show this lady the
ladies' room?' he demanded. She
was shown. 'And where is the
gentlemen's lavatory?' He too
was shown. And ten minutes
afterwards they brushed past
Kate and the maid without a
word, got into their car and
drove off. Kate told me just

Curious how large the lavatory looms in this Diary.

in time to look out of the window and take their number, for I thought it rather cool. I have written to X. to
know his name and address . . . X. has sent me the par-
ticulars wanted, etc. – a Brig.-General B———. To him
I wrote, apologising in case I was writing to the wrong
man, recounting what he had done and adding, 'You
were guilty of bad manners, you know it but can't help
it.' The Colonel replied asserting that his action was
allowable in an AA hotel even without taking a meal
(damn the fellow for suggesting that I wanted anything but common thanks), and that I arrogated to
myself the right to lecture AA members on manners
and that he would report me to that Body. I answered
that my short note had elicited just what I really
wanted from him. I explained his position legally,
socially, and as to the AA, and told him that unless he
sent me the AA's reply to his complaint I would
assume that they had put him wise. I added that I
hoped he had no unfriendly feelings towards me and
offered my kind regards. He never replied. I also wrote
to the AA telling them that if my connection with
them meant an open lavatory without thanks to some
hundreds of thousands of their members, I must cancel
it . . . I heard no more. I started this fight for personal
reasons: I continued it *pro bono publicouse*. And this
fellow gives me to reason about the practice of using
an Inn for some purpose for which the Landlord is not
directly out of pocket, or of thinking that they are
making good by graciously ordering a drink. The
drink has to pay for itself, of course, and not for other
amenities. If a stranger uses the telephone and w.c.,
then looks round the garden and asks to be shown the
dining-room because he's heard that it's see-worthy,

and then out of kindness or patronisingly orders a drink at the market price, and sits with it before your fire for 1½ hours till his 'bus comes (his sole purpose in coming at all), and has said neither 'please' nor 'thank you', he has paid nothing for those other things and amenities which cost the owner money and labour. They can be paid for only by charm of manner, just as they would be at a private house, and it is irritating to have people thinking that they can avoid the effort of behaving decently by this inexpensive little trick of buying a packet of cigarettes. Probably the custom arose in the avaricious publican himself who, valuing trade at any cost, preferred fourpence to a guinea's worth of grace. The practice is especially vicious because delightful people also, having by their generous manner put the Innkeeper under an obligation to them, still think it necessary to ask for the habitual complimentary drink, which I try to dissuade them from persisting in. Today's examples are of either sort: the latter, Jack Haldane, brother of Naomi Mitchison, and Mrs Charlotte Haldane ('Brother to Bert', etc.) came to see me and the place for the first time and began by apologising unnecessarily for coming too late to have lunch. Then, after a delightful half-hour in the garden, most of which I spent in quarrelling with handsome Mrs Haldane's factitious prejudices, Haldane, the huge and virile, insisted upon buying a 1*s.* 2*d.* box of Turkish Delight (presumably 'for the good of the House') and left with it under his kind arm. The former sort: a car drives up with two ladies. One of them gets out and I catch her running upstairs and she turns round, 'Oh, tell me, isn't there a beautiful garden here?' (The wording of the question would imply that

it grows there either of itself or out of public funds.)
'Well, I have rather an interesting garden, but it isn't
upstairs.' – 'Oh no, but I heard that there was a beautiful garden here.' – 'If you would like to see my garden
I'd be glad to show it you.' – 'Oh, would you? And perhaps we might be able to get back for lunch.' And so
far the difficult 'please' or 'thank you' has been vigor-
ously withheld. She collected her friend and we
proceeded and she repeated her luncheon threat to
which, knowing it was all rot, I now replied, 'You
don't pay for seeing the garden by having luncheon,
that pays only for itself.' In the yard she asked, 'Is this
a *very* old house?' – 'Well, it's not Roman. Indeed,
judged by some Inns it might be considered modern.'
So I showed them politely into the garden and left
them. They returned almost immediately and drove
off, their visit upstairs frustrated, and didn't return. It
may seem petty to bother about this sort of thing, but
we Innkeepers pay for our gardens and UDC lavatories
and should not tolerate these sneaking attempts to get
privilege and shy refinement for nothing.

E. V. Lucas has written a whole column about this
place in the *Sunday Times* in his best style for these
articles, not naming it but giving a liberal clue. The
only immediate result of this delightful bit of reading
by the public was the coming today of a pleasant old
lady who told me she'd promised her chauffeur 10s. if
he could discover the place and get her there. What
touched me most in Lucas's article was that he was not
afraid to call me a gentleman and insist upon it. It isn't
easy to be one, especially in an Inn, in fact no man can
safely be called a gentleman till he's dead or 80 or has
kept an Inn, but to be *called* one is at least encouraging

in the struggle. Once a man told me, for no good reason on that occasion at least, that I was 'no gentleman', and I was glad to coin the only possible reply to this old cliché, by saying, 'I make no pretence to being a gentleman, so we may continue the discussion on equal terms.' A don-like *tu quoque*.

Mr and Mrs Earle came (Monday) to lunch from London – a dear affectionate old couple who treat me with a cosy cheer. She told me of Mrs Jopling-Rowe's tea-party for old friends, herself 83, about forty of them, including old Sir Dighton Probyn, 95, with an average age of about 80, and all upstanding and getting about. Mrs Earle said her grandfather was still earning a living at 96. And Mrs Budd, another amiable old lady, came from Oxford with a couple. 'Grow old with me' is not a bad sentiment if you can be as nice as these and have as nice tea-parties. Lady Wedgwood, in contrast to this, sent her son and a white-faced, jet-black curly-haired beautiful Scotch girl down to lunch from London.

Some say what a good book *Sorrell and Son* was; the fellow who took a hotel and made it pay for his son's sake. Well, he was out for money primarily – not I. When I find a commodity better and more expensive than what I have, I buy it. It may pay in the end, or it may not, but it's only polite to give good things to good people. It does seem strange, but I think no better meal was eaten in England this evening than ours – with that saddle of Welsh mutton got from Mrs Walker's Lake Vyrnwy Hotel, which you press to the roof of your mouth and it melts into *purée* – yet no one came to eat it, and tomorrow it will melt in the stockpot.

Oliver Baldwin and John Fernald, President of the

OUDS, dined. Oliver has a real heart, but is so wrop in himself that talking to him is merely listening. He sold us for 3*d.* a raffle ticket from some Trades Council, the winner to have a free tour to Brussels and Paris, presumably in laborious solitude. I asked him if he would take one of our 1*d.* Primrose League tickets for a community tour to the North Pole, where they would all be left, Ministers and all, and he said on that condition he would take one.

Gerald Dillon, accountant, came for the night – once a Balliol Scholar – and I should think he will be a great man in this line. Like Humbert Wolfe, he has an amazing repertoire of romances all told in the language of truth, and, like Humbert Wolfe, he believes them. Clever devils. Major Hunter Smith, Instructor at Sandhurst, and his pretty young wife, are lovely in their unaffected ways. As he likes port and burgundy, I am putting him through a course of claret. They must be thought odd at Sandhurst.

John Tailleur and a friend Craig came to dinner – the only gents inside these walls today. J. T. and his friend, Vere Pilkington, when at Oxford, were self-conscious and at effort to converse. Suddenly they have become natural, John Tailleur a thinking talker and V. P. a talking thinker. (Rubbish.) George Ely (Oxford University Press) brought dear old Robert Steele – the Bacon scholar, and Miss Peacock. Steele told me of the 'perfect tobacconist'. – He had occasionally got some Manila cigars at Van Raalte's till, owing to the Philippine War, they ceased, and Steele ceased also to go there. Fifteen years after he went in again, when the tall handsome man at once leant over to him and said, 'We have some of those Manila cigars now, sir.' I told him I couldn't aspire to that as the perfect hotel-keeper, much as I tried, (I didn't tell Steele that no one but a blind man would fail to recognise him again after *any* period with a face like two little bright red polished apples and an eyeglass hung on black silk two inches wide), but the other day a man came to dinner and I said to him, 'You've been here before?' – 'Yes,' said the man. – 'And', I conjectured, thinking hard, 'it must have been some two years ago?' – 'No,' said the man, 'it was at tea-time.' Plimsoll says he doesn't believe the story – but Kate witnesses that I told her of it at the time.

Dr Waterfield, Guy's, came with one of kind Cony-beare's treats to his staff. As he was writing a lecture on astronomy I asked him if he ran both sciences – astronomy and medicine, 'Medicine isn't a science, it's a superstition,' he snapped. Plimsoll and Enid had Thursday till Wednesday, holiday from secretaryship of Middlesex Hospital – they went to Dieppe – got sick of it in six hours and came straight here, impetuous compliment. It's curious to think that this young man is the son of the historical Plimsoll who, I discover, is called in the small Oxford dictionary a nineteenth-century 'agitator'! . . . Impetuosity again in the third generation, for today, six years later, their pretty little daughter, Barbara, brought her young man out here for after-dinner coffee, 94 miles in all.

A new, picturesque and delightful couple, the Camerons – he, Director of Education, City of Oxford; she, 'Elizabeth Bowen' – brought friends to dinner. Their party had (as always since) the bright air of a dinner-party. Mrs Cameron, with a pleasant bite in her looks, behaves as if she'd just been set free from the

pathetic company she writes about so satirically. Edgar
Lobel, the Sappho King, brought his nice folk to dinner from Oxford. He is an epicure, and good to look at.
When I told him of a certain New College wine epicure, he said he didn't know the difference between
wine and turps. When I told him this evening that he
would like Château Montrose 1918 since Wade Gery
had liked it so much, he said, 'Good Lord, Gery has no
taste at all,' and only for an instant it struck me to
reply, 'Now, when Gery was here last, that's exactly
what he said about *you*.' Lobel will argue anything,
even to my pet discovery that 'the sun has never seen a
shadow, and so could have no conception of three-
dimensional form'; he said that I assumed that the sun
was the only light, 'What about the stars even in day-
time?' I replied that there might of course be a man
lighting a cigarette on the mountain-side. 'Yes, that's
just my point,' he said. – 'Well,' I replied, 'and it's just
a Euclidian point.' The other day Lobel came to tea to
give dictionary authority, but rare and antiquated for
his using the word 'exsection' rather than 'excision' as
an act, and I gave him the usual pot of Greek honey
for winning the bet. I told him it was disgraceful for a
distinguished scholar to make profit thus out of ignorant publicans; in fact, it seemed to be his only source
of livelihood!

The blank of no one to dinner for the fifth night running was filled by Tom Marshall and his wife, beastly
pleasant folks and beautiful to look at.

A lovable, charming old gentleman, Sir Sainthill
Eardley-Wilmot, came from Henley with J. E. Farrar,
barrister, and his wife, E.-W.'s sister. Old Sir S. drops

all his '*g*s' at the end of his words, and succeeds at first in making you think he's second-class. Farrar has a different set of mannerisms to indicate the compleat gentleman. The old lady is full of sweetness, and said they would stay here in the winter. The lovable Sir Sainthill is the great authority on elephant shooting! I told him of my late friend John Marshall's unwritten book, 'Our Dumb Friends, How to Kill, Skin and Stuff Them'.

Mrs Haynes

Colonel Freyberg, VC (*bis*), when he comes to lunch, is disappointing, for instead of talking about Gallipoli and Channel swims, he gives me long lists of the vintages of Burgundy and Port that he has. Lady Jekyll,

his mother-in-law, brought a pretty little trio to lunch
– Miss Asquith, Raymond A.'s daughter, Miss Mark
Hambourg, a wonderful sight and Colonel Freyburg's
little stepson. I owe more to Lady Jekyll's *Kitchen
Essays* than anything else, though much to Mrs E. S. P.
Haynes, who has given me some fine things; one a
jelly which I called 'Huxley', thinking that it came
from that part of her antecedents. She heard of it and
wrote:

*I protest, my dear Sir, that I must write to you, having,
in a Letter from my eldest Daughter, now in Residence
at Oxford, and I trust pursuing her Studies there, heard
of the Pleasure that she took in a visit to the Spreadeagle
upon Sunday last. But first, upon one matter that she
writes I vow I will take you to task! To be short, it is the
christening of 'Very Fine Orange Jelly' by the name of
Huxley! No Huxley ever had enough invention to make
a jelly. If he had tried, it would have consisted of the
Bones of Monsters long vanished from our Earth
strengthened by their Eggs found in the Chinese Desert!
No, the jelly was made by my G^t G^nd mother Waller of
ever honoured Memory.*

*It has ever been a Matter of Gratitude in me to
Divine Providence that in this respect I took after my
Father's Family in their gusto for Life, and I have ever
endeavoured to follow the Family Notion of High Living and Plain Thinking, it being surely ordered by
Providence that we should not think, as is plainly shewn
by the numerous unhappy Results of this Practise. Con-
trariwise, the Creation of Animals and the Fruits of the
Earth for the Benefit of Man make it an Act of Impiety
not to use them to the greatest Advantage; as says one*

Authour, a Prime Favourite of mine, 'It were a great
Pity that one or two Peevish Cynicks should put Good
Eating out of Fashion.'

I had meant to write to you sooner upon other Mat-
ters, so important that though doubtless You are already
acquainted with them, I will venture upon repeating
them in Case they have escaped Your usual Penetration;
these are that a Bisk is a Soop with a Ragoo in it; and
that Morils are not a plant but rather an Excrement of
the Earth that grows in Woods, engendred of certain
putrid Moistures, but of a hot as well as of a Humid
Quality. Command me, Sir, I beg if I can be of any
Assistance in sending You Recipes for Puptons, whether
for Flesh or Meagre Dayes, or a Dish of Pleasant Pears
or even a Pig soused whole after ye Spanish Fashion,
and how to make a Saucidge Royal.

Present, I beg, my respectful Compliments to your
Lady and my best wishes for the Health of your Infants
and Yourselves.

Your obedient humble Servant

ORIANA HAYNES

Mrs Gordon-Stables, to whom I wrote saying how we
had liked them when staying here replied that 'that
was a most gratifying testimonial to have'. She may
have been joking – but if not it is rather disconcerting
to think that by holding out for decent people here we
are now in a position to give diplomas to people for
being good hotel guests! Yet if certain hotels are
'listed', why shouldn't also people be listed, appointed
and starred?

Dormer Dillon brought to lunch Hume, an *habitué*
of years ago when at Oxford, an odd couple, and perhaps

still odder Seymour Lucas, whose perfect-looking wife persists in looking too perfect to look the part. Also at lunch were Guy Chapman and Storm Jameson, whose cheer and affection have not ceased for years.

Some time ago a Colonel came to dinner with two very beautiful girls – some suspected them, others were certain, but I maintained that they were all right though I couldn't place them – he gave them the most expensive champagne. A fortnight later he did the same thing with two other most beautiful girls and the same champagne. A week or two later an officer identified him for me as a fatherly and generous man who took out to dinner annually the Infirmary nurses. 'The prettiest he takes alone, the next prettiest in couples, and "the rest" in a charabanc.' So I hoped to be able at least to quote him a price for a high tea for thirty-five but within an hour of this officer's departure I got a telephone from the Colonel booking a table with the same champagne for two! They came and what a wonder it was! At least for the good of the story this ought to have happened but didn't . . . and now, five years later, I'm still waiting for his return in *any* form.

Truly a beastly thing publicity. Guy Chapman (for Knopf) writes for my biographical details for the jacket of what is only a simple, practical piece of tabulating utility, *The Gardener's Colour Book*, and Chrysède Silks Ltd write very politely asking if they may make use of a letter I wrote to them asking them for some odd patterns as being inspiring for my and others' garden designing. I go through it grimly for business' sake.

*

Nothing now disturbs my nerves, not the patronising, nor the third-rater, nor the person who says, 'What fun you must have had in getting it all like this,' or 'I suppose you get a lot of motorists passing through?', when I like to think that this Inn is a cul-de-sac, or, 'If you find a table gone you'll know who, etc.,' or the man who says, when you ask him where he would like to sit, 'It's all the same to me,' when I would like him to be embarrassed for a choice that you wouldn't get at an ABC or the person who, looking round, asks 'Is this a *very* old house?', thus seeming to give credit to the house and not to me for the filling of it because I know now that it's all meant pleasantly, words which are only rather ordinary wings on which good feelings are borne, but only the occasional Oxford lad who brings a shop girl disturbs me. This evening two of them brought girls of that type in my opinion and that of the Bolderos, charming folks, who sat next to them. The lads were rather squits. Before they went I said, 'Are these girls sisters or fiancées?' – 'No, nothing to do with us.' – 'Then I don't think I should bring them here again as they are not in keeping with the place, nor indeed with yourselves.' The lads took it quietly – perhaps rather hurt, but in this peculiar situation, near Oxford, it must be done, and I hate it. After all, we have the respect of dons and heads of colleges and all the best undergrads whilst our sons will go to proper schools: these shop girls must not come and spoil the show. It's one thing or the other.

Barcenas, Argentinian, came to lunch. He used to come four years ago with a young foreign grandee, A. B., whose great uncle, a greater grandee, I used to know in Rome and whose lovely beds, one 8 feet long,

I have slept in for twenty years and have now thrown open to the lucky public. A. B. was quite the most beautiful youth we've ever had, with his almost Mongolian face, knowledge of food and wine, and wonderful manners. He held sumptuous parties here and would afterwards escort them all down to my cellar. — 'Do you like Brandy?' to one, and with a lovely gesture, 'Take three bottles.' 'Do you like Château Yquem? Take four bottles,' and so on, and they exuded loaded from below. He left Oxford and my bill which his mother very graciously paid, mildly reproaching me for letting him have so much credit, which I felt deeply. I replied that I couldn't very well tell him in the cellar before his friends that he shouldn't buy the stuff even if I had known that he couldn't afford it, which I didn't, and so ended my giving credit to undergrads which is distasteful in any case, it's bad enough to take their money at all. Edinger dined. This curly-haired, angel-faced little man when at Oxford a year or two ago billed the town that 'Professor Emil Busch' would lecture on psychoanalysis, took and filled the Town Hall and assuming a beard and a slight German accent lectured in his own manner, to undergrads, dons and heads of colleges, quoting German colleagues who never existed in non-existent Universities at whose mention the dons respectfully clapped, and then the game was exposed in the *Cherwell* an hour afterwards and he was never found out. He and his friends have just come through Gloucestershire and yesterday in a small village they asked the lady standing outside a good and very antique house where they could stay. She said there was nowhere, but asked them to stay at her house and did them very well. The

friend said that owing to the uncanniness of such hospitality, he felt like walking in his sleep on the way up
to the door.

Sweet and Dry Wine

Dr Rouse looks like a ship's captain, not a Don and
schoolmaster. A perfectly charming, kind little man,
and like dons, full of funny stories and uncommonly
secretive about himself. I told him that I thought only
those people who liked sweet wine had the right to
prefer dry and he said he liked this doctrine 'because it
suggested that only those who were wicked had the
right to be good, a consolation for sinners'.

If you want to drink a lot of wine at a meal a dry
wine is the thing, but a good sweet wine is as good and
better if you don't drink much. I got some confirm-
ation of my theory that this dry wine preference is
generally only a prejudice from a girl's telling me that
when she 'came out' her parents said to her, 'Now,
when you are asked what you would like to drink, say,
it does not matter what, provided it be dry.' The result
is that good dry wine is hard to get and good sweet
wine is dear or unprocurable because it has been
turned into dry wine to supply the demand. Fifty years
ago claret and sweet wine were drunk, then, to supply
the demand, the merchants deteriorated the quality so
much that people had to turn over to Burgundy and
Graves – and now the same has happened to these, and
what was palate persists as a prejudice.

The first party of undergrads this term to dinner –
Corpus Christi CC. After dinner I found one on the
roof of the stables and I swore at him so much that he

almost fell off. Then I gave him a lecture on the desir-
ability of keeping this place nice and the danger of
precedents – I told him that I didn't think of undergrads here as undergrads or 'collegiates', as the locals
call them, but decent people like the rest of the folks
who came here. The worst of it is, since Oxford, save
for the dons, is a moving population, I shall have to
keep up this old hen-and-chickens-pedagogue attitude
so long as I am here. The result of the lecture was
that the roof scaler and two others promised to come
here on their honeymoons, not, I hoped, to be spent on
the roof.

Chauffeurs

I went out to say good-bye to two delightful women in
a Rolls Royce asking them if they had fed well. 'Very,
indeed, thank you, but I am sorry to hear our chauffeur has had such a poor meal.' – 'Why, what did you
have?' I said to the tall fellow. – 'Oh well, I couldn't eat
it.' – 'Did you have soup?' – 'Yes, and it looked as if it
had tea-leaves in it.' – 'Oh, that's the Black Soup – how
did you like it?' I said, turning to the women. – 'Very
much indeed – I knew it in America.' – 'Well, and you
had veal – I remember cutting it, the exact shape of it
on the plate!' (I have cut every helping – many hundreds of thousands since I've been here.) 'Was that all
right?' – 'Well yes, but the vegetable wasn't fit to eat.'
– 'I didn't see that – and the sweet?' – 'We were offered
tapioca pudding.' – 'Yes, I know, but that was the stupid cook's fault and it was rectified at once – what did
you have?' – 'A sort of lemon thing – I couldn't eat it.'
– 'That was lemon flummery, an eighteenth-century
dish. – What did *you* have?' turning to the ladies. –

'We had that, and thought it very good,' − 'And cheese?' − 'Yes,' − 'It is an eighteen-months-old Cheddar, I get 900 pounds of it every August − so you see you had exactly the same meal as Madam − now next time you come here I recommend you to go to the ────── Inn where you will get food which you will like.' − 'Yes, I think I should.' − 'That's why I recommended it,' and I turned to the ladies and we all smiled pleasantly at one another − and we all had something to think about. The fact is the average chauffeur is either spoilt or brutalised by a class of people and hotels, who have never had the chance of keeping a groom and learning how to treat him properly. One nice chauffeur gives us more gratitude than six nice people.

Isa Fletcher, niece, very pretty, told me that someone had said that I was getting on so well that I could afford to be rude to people. This is stupidly untrue − it's just the opposite. I was ruder still at the beginning and it is just because I have been rude to people whom I don't like here that we *are* 'getting on'.

Claret Drinking

This evening Beamish, a very young city man, spectacled, modest and so polite, who comes here a lot, brought six other quiet sympathetic men of the same charming modesty to dinner. I think it was an excellent dinner and it was our best old-time claret drinking performance; they sipped away at it long after dinner, till they got up to go. I told them of a wine list of 1850, or thereabouts, that someone had lent me to look at, of the, I think, Waldorf Hotel, New York. There were only two Burgundies, both misspelt, two champagnes, one now unknown, the other 'Cliqot' (not Veuve as now), two clarets misnamed, and then there followed a list of twenty-four Madeiras, all with the most phantastic names.

Sir Arthur Colefax came for the first time with Lady and both lads. He is a remarkable man to look at, and he understands wine. Like his sons, overwhelming, but kind and overwhelming in that.

Champagne Buying

Having bought £1,100 worth of wine last year I thought I must invest also in champagne. So I wrote to one of the best firms asking for a small reserve. They replied that they had completed their reserve list and regretted that they could not comply with my request. I told this story to Charles Neilson, stockbroker and friend, who said, 'That's absurd – write for 60 dozen, enclosing a cheque for it, which I'll give you, and see what happens.' It did happen, and one of the Directors came down (he told me afterwards out of inquisitiveness), a courteous elderly man, and we sat and talked in the garden. The reserve being agreed to he turned to me and said, 'And now, Mr Fothergill, may I give you back your cheque, it will not be due for six months.'

The grandfather of Katie, Phyllis, Bessie and Ella Lomas, our blessed maids, was brought here from Nottingham in 1880 to look after the gasworks. Two years ago, then 75, his life was despaired of by the doctors and we gave him the brandy with which (and not with the doctors) he came to life again. He was told not to work any more by the Directors, now become generous, who gave him a pension. Some months later, having been told that he was still working, I met him in the street, and asked him why? He replied 'I don't consider it honest to take money without doing any work' – and he is still at it all day, and sometimes hard at it. (Now, November 1930, I believe he has really retired.)

Gerald and Mrs Gould for the night, after an absence of four years, once hardy periodicals. I asked him if his *Monogamy* wasn't thought one of the cleverest and brightest pieces of imagination ever written, and he said it was not well received. He told me how once the first poem was written the rest came so rapidly and so pat that it took him just two days to copy them down, tinker them up and finish. I asked him why no one had ever written on the 'animology' of authors, and he said Pirandello seemed to have done so in his *Six Characters*, which he said he himself had turned down in a review as being too dull to read. He said that Francis Meynell told him of his staying at a grand house full of 'County' where, by some accident, it was discovered that he was a literary person, so an old gentleman took him aside, saying, 'Look here, it would be a damned good thing if a good deal more Henty were read nowadays.'

I showed a woman into No. 12 where in a heavy deep frame there is a magnificent Victorian group of fruit in sculptured flannel, polychrome on a black background. 'How splendid!' she enthusiastically cried. 'I wish they did more of that nowadays.' Now, by a sudden access of telepathy I thought I caught a ring in her voice that was neither archaeological nor aesthetic, so I asked, 'Why?' – 'Well, you see,' she replied earnestly, 'I'm an Australian and it would increase the sale of wool.'

After the Commem. crowds it is a sweet undertaking to have for dinner only twenty-eight and give them really nice food in peace and quiet. Of inmates Miss Robertson, very pretty, and a friend, who have come for a week's painting (where even Tonks and Steer could find none though it is true Mark Gerstler painted and sold a picture of the garden). Charles and beautiful Clare Neilson and two others. Of undergrads, Peter Colefax, Alfred Beit and Donegall, Clive, Nog Dugdale, Adam Chetwynd, the constant Grant Lawson, and their little parties; of Catholics, Norfolk, Girouard and Dawnay, and as each of these went out, lovable, they thanked me, as if the great wonder had been theirs and not mine! Oh my God! And this at the end of Kate's birthday – who had issued to us invitation cards to 'tea, games and dancing' at Dinton Castle (a ruined folly on the Aylesbury Road). It is one of the prettiest sites in the district – we took the newly bought wireless box and listened to tales of our glorious Empire and played hide and seek.

A Fine Fellow

A journalist of some repute wrote to me that he wanted to come here and perhaps write about this place. I replied rather deprecating the writing. At lunchtime, today, Sunday, he turned up in the yard with car and a lady. 'I didn't know you were coming,' I said. – 'Didn't you get my second letter,' he snapped. – 'No.' – 'You're lying,' to which I replied, 'Anyhow, it's not worth disputing about.' – 'No, but you're a liar for all that.' (No letter reached me even afterwards.) I sent up his bags and then hinted that I be introduced to the lady, the silent witness of this comic advent.

'Mrs B——' he grudgingly announced. But somehow, though he had asked for 'a room', I began to think that not he alone but both were staying here. 'Is the lady staying too?' – 'Yes.' – 'Then you want two rooms?' – 'No, I said a "double room".' – 'But really you make it very embarrassing for me.' – 'Why?' – 'Because you're not married and I discourage indiscriminate coupling here.' – 'That's not your business.' – 'But it is.' – 'You mean, you think you can ask everyone who comes here if they are married?' – 'Yes, if I want to.' – 'But the law compels you to take me if I ask for a room.' – 'Perhaps, but you'd make out a poor case to the magistrates in these particular circumstances.' – 'Then what about the ——?' Here the fellow descended to implying that I did a fine trade in a very different kind of couple, for which I gave him what the bully deserved. Then I recounted to him the whole interview, everything of which he denied categorically, and I ended with, 'So you're a liar yourself, a cad, and I'll do nothing to help you. I'm only sorry for the lady who's heard all this to her distress.' I went back into the kitchen to carve meat, and I suppose he got back his bags, and took his car away. I felt wounded at first, then I rejoiced that the place had escaped a repetition of the dear old things that the average journalist has written about it, but with a novelty, perhaps, a hint that it was a place for a jolly weekend with a lady friend . . .

'Because of thy raging against me and for that thine arrogancy is come into mine ears therefore will I put my hook in thy nose and my bridle in thy lips and will turn thee back by the way thou camest.' (Job.)

*

C. E. Bennett, KC (now Judge), has just left after being with us for three weeks standing and failing as Liberal candidate. Huge mass of kindness, integrity, enthusiasm and laughter. The chief obsessions of our Liberals here are ham, tea and local option. I couldn't think that Bennett would plump his full rugged soul for any of these things, though he did, and for a time at least this place is safe for him for his bottle of Château Latour.

I would like to know if it increases the value of a Town to have merely its name better known, for how many thousands, perhaps hundreds of thousands, now for the first time know of this place, either through coming here or being told of it or through reading about the place in books and papers.

Being 'Eights Week' we had eighty-eight to dinner, besides our house party, ninety-nine in all. I didn't expect more than forty, so that whilst serving the meal I had to prepare another. People often ask if it isn't difficult to cope when you don't know how many you'll have to feed, and before taking an Inn I used to bother over this problem with hypothetical cases. But in practice it doesn't trouble one. True, sometimes almost all you have is your brains to put in the pots and pans for people to eat.

Leslie Crawshay Williams, whom for his notorious honesty I'm proud to own as a cousin, at least the Crawshay part, brought son Rupert and Morna Stuart and others. Morna is so attractive that I can believe the tale that she's had thirteen proposals, with her black hair, white face and drunken eyes. It's rather horrible that those who used to come so often in our quiet days come again now and I can see so little of them – busy in the kitchen doing the work of rotten cooks. We've given, with three parlour-maids, 240 meals today and not a bloke has waited more than digestion requires. Jock le Maître, who smiles attendance on the First Lord of the Admiralty, Douglas Paton, kind Scot of 6 ft 8 in., W. Waldorf-Astor, Donald Lennox Boyd, the maddest of his brothers four, Nigel Sligh, de Candolle with flashing teeth, Alan Bicknell, nephew, a *drôle*. And of couples, some of our best, the Hugo Pitmans, the Guy Vaughan-Morgans, Lawford and Eldred Curwen, the Ian Forbes-Leiths and the Peter Cleggs. At dinner someone wanted the Cognac left on the table and disputed Katie's computation, who deducted the 3*s*. Moral, if you want a yard of calico, cut it off the roll yourself.

I may be hopelessly neurotic, but when I object to this or that person or class of persons in the place I get no sympathy often from the very people for whom I keep this place and who like it most. They say: 'Why shouldn't they drink whiskey or beer at dinner?' 'Why don't you have a girl in the bar who can make proper cocktails?' 'You can't have everyone highbrows.' 'Personally, I like to see *all* sorts of people; it's amusing.' 'Doesn't the law compel you to give beer and food to everyone who asks for it?' 'Why shouldn't the undergraduate make a noise? He's young,' and so on. But if all these types came in their numbers my ungracious critics wouldn't come themselves any more. The atmosphere would change, I should take no active part in it. I have found that the person who comes all the way here and drinks beer or whiskey at dinner (I except undergraduates of course, and a few legitimate cases), generally wants a chair and 'grub'. I prefer the other kind of guest who says, 'It's a shame to drink beer with this food,' and with such people one hasn't even noticed that they *are* drinking it, nor would one mind if they drank nothing. With good food water runs wine very closely. So away with my friendly critics. I must paint my own picture in my own lonely way.

Old man, Mr ——, of that doubtful age between 100 and 200, who has been here grumbling, dieting, refusing and plaining, all with a pleasant crocodile's smile, for fourteen days, moved off today.

Nice Americans

So far we don't get Americans as such. Three good ones dined here from Oxford, friends of Mrs Kenyon Cox and Mrs Shipman, New York. It may be the German blood that makes the nice Americans so sentimental and affectionate. What makes them so calm, as if they had been landed gentry for centuries, I don't know, save perhaps their having made enough money and the knowledge that their businesses are sufficiently well organised to make them free from care when away from them. Anyhow, these folks exude sweetness, the little man with black specks, the thin man, and the rather beautiful woman. So does Edward P. Larrabee with his old-fashioned pose of 'Mam' to Kate and 'Sir' to me. He's very learned, but goes about modestly deferring to us English as if we must be better educated than himself (in my case, at least, with a little suspicion, I would think) and his little daughter Ankey, a precocious mixture of Queen Victoria and tomboy.

*

Yesterday ten undergrads, ex-aesthete and now the-
atrical, with their long legs, lunched and then went on
the switchback and spoilt the garden air by their noisy
conversation. I feel *de trop* in a garden myself; all
adults are out of place in a garden – save gardeners.
After that they monopolised with their long legs the
little dining-room for tea. Today seven of the same
party came and had tea again and went off without
paying or saying anything. Some time afterward I
wrote to one and had no answer, then to another:

DEAR MR S——:

*Seven of you had tea here three days ago and went
away without paying. The incident would argue a
delightfully communistic spirit amongst yourselves in
that apparently no one enquired or cared who paid for
his tea provided he didn't himself, but I cannot live on
the high ideals of others. I write to you because I think
you would be the most humane and respectable of the
party which very reason makes me loath to write to you.
I would be very grateful to you for getting me out of this
embarrassed position.*

No answer, but a month later S——, ever delightful,
came with a vast family party, and Papa, on his own
initiative, nobly paid.

Kind Young Lady

A sweet little tottie, totsum jetsum, sent for me to see
me – she had already made her way into the kitchen
passage. 'How do you do, Mr Fothergill, I'm so interested in your place.' – 'Oh, that's very kind of you.' –
'Now, I want to see more of it, and have a good look

round upstairs.' – 'The rooms are engaged, and if they weren't one could hardly make a museum of the place. Where do you come from?' – 'From Maidenhead just now.' – 'Ah, from Maidenhead.' By this time I had led her back quickly into the hall to be confronted by her undesirable man and another couple. – 'Ah, Mr Fothergill, you know Mr X?' – 'No, I don't.' – 'Then you know Mr Y?' – 'Yes, I did.' – 'But I thought I'd seen you at the Café Royal?' – 'Well, I haven't been there for twenty years,' and so I shuffled off. This is not funny, but it's hard to have to do it, especially when everything else has gone wrong and seventeen people have lunched when seventy-eight lunched this time last year. Brothers Sitwell dine, two ordinary, stalwart, kind fellows, and so unlike their works which I haven't read. About the most cheerful sight we have had here are the Jackson twins; the Oxford one brought his Cambridge brother tonight for dinner with Roberts, all from Rugby. They are both at physics and at first sight their excitable, fidgety, feminine ways make them look half-witted, till you realise the reverse. Vyvian Jackson has just published his discovery of a nucleus that revolves, which he says has been accepted and much appreciated by the Dutch – why the Dutch I don't know – and no mean discovery, I should think, since no one has yet seen even the nucleus that *doesn't* revolve. The other, Derrick, I overheard at dinner reply to a question whether he liked better Dickens or Thackeray. 'I've read a novel only by Dickens, so naturally I prefer Thackeray.' Larrabee told me about the twins which are, like the Jacksons, split eggs, and always the same sex. He said the best analogy in animal life was the Armadillo who has either 1, 2, 4, 6, or 8 young, which being of one egg are always of the same sex, 'i.e. all little boys or all little girls'.

One of a party from Ascot, possibly a Spaniard, asked for claret cup as she had had it for the first time at the Races. I said I didn't think ours would resemble too closely the Ascot claret cup. When they said how good and different it was I replied, 'Well, you see, it wasn't I who stole the Ascot cup.' Such silly patter is a good enough vehicle for showing people that they are nice and that you like them. How else can you show it?

Kind Spurway

As I went into the little dining-room I saw at the table by the window one of three undergrads flopping over the arm of his chair with his head pointing downwards near the ground and soup just served to them. I asked one of the others to take him out at once; they were silent and immobile and I recognised in one of them a fellow I'd had an altercation with before. Having no effect upon them, I had their soup taken away and their table cleared, before which they continued to sit whilst others were eating, looking, perhaps feeling, rather silly, and yet no response. Then to my grateful relief, a soft voice came from another table, M. Spurway's, semi-hearty, semi-sentimentalist, 'Mr Fothergill, do you want any help?' So we gently lifted the huge fellow, who had brought his drink here inside him, which I believe is not public-house etiquette – hence the alacrity with which a publican complies with the law in declining to serve a man who comes in drunk from the opposite pub and hesitates to comply

when he has made him drunk himself – out of the window into the yard and pushed him into their car under the protest of the characterless youth who really seemed to think they were still wanted on the estate.

Memory plays tricks, and cruel tricks. Miss Dale brought to dinner Mrs Dr Carew-Hunt, whom I hadn't seen for some years. I pointed out to her an uncommon purple pentstemon on the table, and having momentarily forgotten that it was her late husband, the most courteous man alive who had given it to me, and yet being certain that she was in some way connected with him I risked – 'That's the pentstemon your dear old

parson friend gave me,' then instantly knew what I'd
done. We all felt a bit shaken – later when I came up
with an attempted excuse, I knocked her glass of champagne all over the table. I'm sure they did their best to
forgive me.

The Brintons

Mrs Rathbone, mother of the rowing blue, cheerful
and talkative, is always bringing decent people here to
tea. Today she introduced an apparently modest little
man and fine-looking wife as Mr and Mrs Brinton. I
said to him, 'I know two Brintons – Selwyn Brinton,
who writes about art, and Brinton the Kidderminster
carpetmaker.' – 'Yes, those are my brother and cousin.'
– 'And who are you?' – 'Oh, I'm nothing,' then in an
undertone, 'I've only been a master at Eton for twenty-
five years.' – 'And that's a good one for you, Hubert!'
said Mrs Brinton. His daughter is still more lovely.
Hubert Brinton told me he took it down in a note-book
at the time how the verger was escorting a party round
Westminster Abbey, when one of the party knelt down
and prayed: 'Come along, sir,' commanded the verger.
– 'But mayn't I have a few moments of private devotion?' – 'No, we can't 'ave that, or we should soon 'ave
people prayin' all over the place.'

A Colonel and Mrs Stirling, charming folk, came to
lunch. I almost got angry with her because she told me
the salad was tired and had been cut with a knife, so I
said, 'Now you who evidently know about salads will
see that this has not been cut but torn, and it's this very
tearing that makes it look tired, and as for the crisp-
ness, lettuces have grown no hearts this season,' with
which the Colonel agreed out of kindness. In point of

fact they were bad lettuces out of my garden. I knew it, but for once took up the dealer's attitude out of shame. Anyhow, I gave them a lot of good names of plants and the address of a Cheddar cheesemaker, and sent them to Miss Hamersley to see Rycote, where the little church is almost monopolised by two immense Tudor pews like four-poster beds, made for Charles II and Queen Elizabeth to sleep in – who and which, I knew, would make up for a poor lunch.

More Nice Americans

Lady Osler, widow of late Regius Professor of Medicine, lunched, bringing her equally huge and generous sister. The second time they came, they often come now, Lady Osler asked me if I remembered her and I replied, 'Not quite.' She then said, 'Don't you remember telling me you never saw three such big people getting into an old Ford car?' This time she brought Dr Harvey Cushing, one of the world's great surgeons, who cuts brains out, now lecturing in Oxford and Edinburgh. He was excited to meet me as a kinsman of Doctor J. F. in the eighteenth century, the Quaker friend of Philadelphia. He is a dear, keen, emotional little man and it's good to be remembered by such a one. After lunch he said he'd never had 'such a dinner' and shook hands for the third time (twice during lunch) . . . In 1930 Judge and Mrs von Moschzisker with their two lovely red-haired daughters and bright son Michael gave me Doctor Cushing's life of Doctor Osler. More sentimental Americans. The Judge has a curious whimsical attitude towards the horrors of life, like Mr Scott, father of Ridley's pretty wife, of Balliol, another perfect American family. And what better than the enthusiastic affection of Miss Sargent of Newhaven, Conn. and the Joseph Darts of Dayton, Ohio.

Mrs Stirling came back to buy three more copies of the *Gardener's Colour Book* and to ask me what colours went with what in a garden; she sat down, whipped out a pencil, and opened the book to take down the words of wisdom. I told her I thought East-lake had done this and gave her some bits of Chrysède silk to show her that nothing mattered much. She must be a very remarkable person with such energy and deference. It was horrid not to be able to help her.

Odd man Duncan Jones, parson and on the *Guardian*, and Mrs Duncan Jones for the night. Hitherto he has always come with a son or friend, looking like tramps. An affectionate man with a most proper taste in Rhine wine and good stories. When he first came, shabby, unknown, tramping, he told me they were going to Aylesbury for the night in order to walk eight more miles the next morning. But I didn't see why they shouldn't stay here, however poor and needy, so I went and worked out the comparative costs and presented them with a reckoning showing that if we motored them to their destination next day for our own pleasure it would be one and threepence dearer than the Aylesbury scheme, but with much more than fifteen-pence worth of moral and aesthetic advantage to which he agreed at once, and at dinner he surprised me by ordering everything that was most expensive and sumptuous in the place. Next morning we drove them to Sir X. Y.'s, but only to the Park Gates since they had to arrive on foot, a harmless Biblical deception.

And now, as Dean of Chichester, he is the best dressed gentleman in the eighteenth century.

Liqueurs and Bitters as Beverages

Eight people, including two boys and two babies at breast, escaped in here to lunch today, Sunday. Half-way through the man called out, 'Hey, Guv'ner, we'll 'ave a bottle of Chartreuse — one bottle's enough, those four are children.' — 'But you don't want that, it's a strong liqueur.' Then the woman prompted him, 'You mean Soreturn.' Years ago, on a cold lonely Monday, at lunchtime, Katie came and said, 'A young man wants two glasses of Angostura.' She had already tried to dissuade him, nor when she went in again with my message would he be dissuaded, so I told her to give it them — enough to poison the town with. Soon I went in to see this hero — a lad with his girl. He had to admit that the girl didn't like hers and that he had put his own into his coffee. Then he climbed down from his grand position, taken up for the benefit of his girl, and told me that some years ago a friend had taken him into a London club and he could have sworn till now that the drink he had been given was called Angostura. 'But', he asked, grasping at a straw, 'was it *White* Angostura?' — 'Of course,' I said, throwing him a rope. 'That's the mistake people are *always* making,' and he breathed again. But they'd had enough 'liqueur' for the day so there was no need to invent one.

It's worse than a schoolmaster's experience, saying good-bye to lads who have been delightful here for three or four years. A school has Old Boys' dinners and cricket matches, and so on; here we can only wait and

wait on the doorstep and then perhaps not know them
when they do return.

Lytton, who came here on Nat. Savings machinery,
is comical: he said he was going to Wolverton, the ugli-
est of all little towns, but that the natives there were at
least humorous. Of the main street, one side is composed of a dreary row of houses looking like attached
villas with two shops, the one selling what the other
didn't. Down the middle of the street goes a tram – the
oldest in England – which they are now painting like
new, and on the other side is a very long and very high
wall hiding a printing works and the railway shops:
this street they call 'The Front'.

'Misunderstood'

Three middle-class governesses dined and slept in the
yard cottage because we were full up. Next morning
they complained of the charge. I explained sympathetically how they had been charged less for dinner than
everyone else and less than ordinary even for the cottage. They were a little truculent and cheeky. I kept in
good temper and said, 'I'm sorry about this unpleasantness.' – 'It's you who are the cause of it,' said one, and
another said something vulgar which the subsequent
happening caused me to forget but in reply to which I
said, 'Now, none of your schoolgirl nonsense.' – Like a
flash of lightning the young female near me raised her
sharp elbow, caught me a smash across the head with
her hand and simultaneously jumped out into the
street . . . She describes herself, I suppose, as 'fond of
children, good disciplinarian', and what a lot of wrong
practice must have gone to the making of that wicked
reflex action! Somehow I felt as if I deserved it, for I

have been high-handed here throughout. But I felt at the same time a martyr in the cause of keeping an Inn for decent people.

Marcus and Val (sister) Cheke stayed the weekend. Despite his seeming at first to be a play on his own name I got to like him so much and their visit was one of the most welcome we have had. The house seems otherwise to be full of a mass of unable-bodied men and women in twos and ones sitting like flies round the room.

Mrs Kenyon-Cox appreciates our food. When she praised a saddle of lamb today I didn't tell her that I had excavated the undercut of it this morning as rotten and that I had thrown away some forty pounds of rotten meat today. Thus we, not our clients, pay for having in summer properly-hung and not ice chest meat.

Old Miss de Natorp, age 83, is staying here with Miss Gordon, frail and indescribably sweet, more like a very quiet little girl. She lives at Berkhampstead where, after twenty-five years at St Leonards she bought her house. She knows the Quennells, of course, and of course loves Peter Quennell, the ornamental. My father would have thought his poetry was trash for all that he is very clever. I once heard him epitomise half a dozen better-known undergrads but remember only, 'Prince Lubomirski, that pompous little man who goes about as if he felt the weight of the Holy Roman Empire on his shoulders', and one day a dear friend of mine asked why all the undergrads came to her tea-parties unshaved. As none of the undergrads present answered this idle question I ventured that perhaps she had a peculiar effect on them so that they grew beards on the way. 'Yes,' piped Peter Quennell, 'a sort of capillary erection,' which, for the first time in my life, embarrassed me before a female.

Thirteen days' holiday with Kate to Cologne, Ratisbon, and Munich, swindled by the Strike out of some instructive meals at Vienna – came back tired out from the constant noise of trains and towns. Top of Skiddaw next summer. Whilst away sister Ethel (Bullmore) kept shop for us well and enthusiastically. She was as indefatigable for our sane or mainly sane folk as she was for her insane or mainly insane patients in her twenty years of asylums. And today the cook let us down nicely at lunch, having made half the proper amount of soup and vegetables and secretly economised on seven chauffeurs who went on strike, so I could only go in and pacify them, telling them that no one would be charged for. But they were all charged for because I forgot to pass on the news to the maid. Then people waited and went away unfed and other rude things happened, and I bolted upstairs and ejected two tears and came down to have a little kind advice from Sir Vincent Evans to look after chauffeurs better! So back to this sort of business and to find the garden under the weather ... weather that not only makes you more and more irritable but it seems to suit the irritating who rise to greater heights and no one stays for the August Bank Holiday – work goes on as usual upon this old place, carpenter, plasterer, builder, electrician, all here; there's always someone in the yard with a cart or a tool-box. I asked Reg Cox if he could get the hymeneal sow out of the pig yard without walking her over the plants and, with a wan smile, he said there were at least seven men working in the yard to help him.

Romney Summers is without doubt the best and the most intelligent host of his day at Oxford. For one of his parties here he brought his thirty friends over in a fleet of six Daimlers. The departure was not so impressive as the arrival. Though perfectly sober, as, in spite of themselves, all his parties were, they seemed to prefer to crowd all into the first three or four cars so the others followed empty, leaving Romney himself and two friends talking quietly in a room to find themselves without means of transport at about midnight. Having rung up every possible garage, our own car being unfit, I undertook, since Romney was too frightened, to wake up a disagreeable rich little youth at the Mitre who had been at the party and had had his nose put out of joint and beg him to bring his Bentley. He told me it was my duty as Innkeeper to see that my guests had cars to take them away! He arrived and repeated this odd conviction. I told him to be damned and Romney and his friends crept into the back of the car in silence. It wasn't that we charged him heavily, but it was the quantity they ate that made his parties so costly. 'Romney, you are doing us very well,' called out one of them, with *foie gras* as well as caviare heaped like porridge on his plate.

A fat elderly man came and asked for a room saying that he had had an accident outside and was 'compelled' to stay the night. 'Compelled be blowed,' I felt like saying. He turned out to be too delightful, Colonel Cator, late Marines, full of fun, an unspoilt bachelor. At dinner he said he had almost brought his female cousin with him and at the time of the accident thought how lucky he hadn't, and now he thought how unlucky. He sat with us in the office afterwards, bolstered up on the great settee till eleven o'clock, and every time there was a joke he rolled over on his side and on his face, this vast, rather asthmatic old dear, with, but for a big double chin, a very good-looking and childlike profile.

We went to tea with the E. S. P. Haynes family, who have taken Albury Rectory for the summer – an amazing party of beautiful people. Mrs Haynes, more distinguished than and as beautiful as the rest, Mrs Marillier, who has a son of twenty-three, herself prettier than a girl, and three remarkably pretty daughters Renée, Celia, Elvira. The males were Rupert Crawshay Williams, pretty also, and Philip Steegmann, pretty and apparently a coming portrait painter, fooling about in an eighteenth-century suit. The manoeuvres are on and on the drive gate leading to this alluring household is a big placard, 'Breeding stock, don't disturb'. 'Most rude,' I said to Renée ('Neapolitan Ice') Haynes, 'Yes, we thought so too.' They had had a call from a neighbouring 'County' and one of the ladies said to Mrs Haynes, 'Now do go to Mrs Shaw; she has everything you'll want. Very good bromo paper, two qualities, the cheaper for the maids but really quite good enough for anyone.' I told Mrs Haynes that she should have said her family used *The Times*, the maids the *Daily Mail*, and the butler the *Girls' Companion*.

The landlady at Littlehampton wrote and asked Kate to send back the bills when 'she had overlooked them'. How easy to overlook people's bills, even their bigger ones!

Army Manoeuvres

Colonel B. came down to see about the General and thirty Field Officers, Divisional Headquarters, staying here for three weeks' manoeuvres. I quoted him in a letter tonight 12s. 6d. per day for all of their carefully enumerated requirements, i.e. all that a man could want. As I shall have to find rooms for twelve in the town, the profit will not be in ratio to the turnover. Colonel B. seems a delightful person, so good-looking and beautifully dressed . . . Aldershot manoeuvres are upon us next month, and General Ironside, a huge man, stayed here last night with Colonel Fuller, a little man, with a white face, immense forehead, black eyebrows cocked up and blacker eyes glinting. Ironside talks and talks and says he speaks nine continental languages. I doubt if he talks in these as he does in English. An officer with him told me that in the War one quiet morning he saw three Tommies sitting frizzling some nice bacon in a pan over a good fire. As he got nearer he saw that the fire came up through a narrow hole leading down into a sort of dug-out which was on fire with three German prisoners burning inside it . . . And told so seriously too . . . After the big and generous Ironside, the pretty pattern-plate Colonel B., who came with three other Colonels to arrange terms and conditions. I had already quoted 12s. 6d. for the fullest requirements possible, at which price I had written that I hoped to make their man-oeuvre quarters and fare the best they'd had or be ever likely to have. 'Mr Fothergill, you say 12s. 6d., I would like it done for 12s.' I declined. 'But you will make money on the drinks,' so I had to enlighten this innocent soldier by telling him that HQ Staff didn't drink, and that even if they did it wasn't right that the drink should pay for the food as well as itself. (And they didn't drink − not that I wanted them to − save at the beginning when Colonel Grove had an awful cold and treated about ten of them every evening with rum and hot milk in order to cure it.) 'Then, Mr Fothergill, if not 12s., what about 12s. 3d.?' At this I let fly a bit and compared him with the farmers and freemasons which we had had to deal with in the past. At 12s. 6d. I said I would put my heart into it, otherwise nothing at all. 'Well,' broke in Colonel Grove, RE, whose humanity upheld me later on other occasions, 'if we can buy Mr Fothergill's heart for 3d., we are in luck!' and we all felt cooler. As a palliative to this horrible interview, it was good to find Philip Gosse just arrived outside. Looking at it from Colonel B.'s point of view, he was only doing his best to save 1s. 9d. a week for thirty field officers . . . Colonel B. had insisted that the thirty-two officers should come in to dinner punctually and together. This would have been very difficult to serve. Fortunately the Colonel arrived a day or two after the bulk of them to whom I said, 'I would rather you didn't at the sound of bell goose-step into the room all together and frighten any harmless civilians there might be in it. It's not like a mess, so please choose any tables you like and come in at different times,' and all went well throughout, and they looked very beautiful . . .

So far I find the Army undemonstrative. If they appreciate this place, surely a hundred times better than any hitherto manoeuvring ground, they don't say so. They seem to accept it and credit nothing to the maker of it. Probably the nature of their own work prevents their thinking of *anything* as the result of one man's effort and invention. Their army machine is such a vast mass of accretions that they must think that every other achievement is brought about by some impersonal syndicate or evolution. They would view a painting in the same way (though the average picture, of course, and average hotel is just this very community production). Colonel Grove is excellent. When I was feeling rather flat about the inarticulate reception of my best, I asked him if he'd had enough to eat. He replied, 'Well, for the last two courses, I've had to fall back on greed!' . . . This evening a good-looking, curly, fair-haired officer, not HQ Staff, wanted a room 'for this lady', which I said we could give her. He then said he'd like a bath and wanted to go and change in her room. This I deprecated, so he undertook not to. Later, on going up to her room to ask her to tie up her dog who growled at the maid, I found them both in the room. She went out and I confronted him with 'Isn't it a little unfair on me when I asked you not to go into this lady's room?' 'But you make a mistake; this is Mrs ——, my wife.' – 'I am very sorry, but why didn't you say so before.' Anyhow, I'm not at all sure about it yet, for why otherwise would he have made the above undertaking?

Another curious interlude. Gavin Campbell, KR Rifles, Compensation Officer, has been with us for two months, and is one of the family now, purring and smiling every evening with us in the office. He told me that their Regimental Sergeant won the King's Cup last year and everything else possible, so I invited the crack to come and shoot against me at the Fair – a hos-

pitable act, because I am less than mediocre myself.
The champion arrived, with an escort of three officers.
We crossed the road to the 'African Jungle'. I did a
mediocre target; he did a poor one; with a truly sporting gesture I told him his gun was a bad one, made
him exchange, and to my horror beat him again. I felt
very ashamed of myself and my rash invitation, and it
was most embarrassing for all of us. I saw we couldn't
go on like this, dragging the King's Cup in the mud, so
I took them back to the bar. We tried to be cheerful,
and the officers told of the Sergeant's prowess, but
it was all useless till someone had the happy idea of
saying, 'But you should see Sergeant shoot at two thousand yards!' — 'Ah, of course,' we all sighed with
infinite relief, and the incident closed.

Colonel Grove told me that when he was a child his
parents, parson and wife, told him that if he was brave
in having two teeth out without gas, he would get
2s. 6d. a tooth. This he endured and received the 5s.
accordingly; he said he didn't mind his parents saving
15s. on the anaesthetist, provided he got the 5s.; 'That
was fair do!' but he did feel it hardly to be taken
straight to the SPCK shop and to have his 5s. spent for
him on a Bible and Prayer Book. When they got home
his grandmother said she was so sorry because she had
always meant to give him his first B. and P. B. Anyhow, she was pleased to inscribe them with her name
and affection as the donor. So they all felt good and
generous at the expense of the little sufferer who got
nothing.

An officer wanted to know if I would make a
charge if his chauffeur slept during the manoeuvres in
the Dance Room. So I asked if the man would be

sleeping under his tiles or mine, and if I had to pay the rates and expenses here, or he? – in a word, ought one to charge at all at an Inn? I asked the organising captain if all were comfortable and well-fed. 'I personally', he replied, 'have heard no complaints.' This I was assured afterwards by Captain Gibson, RE (human), was the highest compliment, and was very seldom, if indeed, ever given, whether at manoeuvres, camps, barracks, or elsewhere ... I go on jotting down these examples of soldiers' ways because now with a little experience of HQ staff officers, I believe, with exceptions, they haven't the vocabulary of graciousness or praise, in which they resemble children along with their innocence in everything else ... Colonel Grove had been trying all day to get a friend on the telephone. I asked him 'Why not write a postcard now?' – 'I never write postcards and seldom write now.' Colonel Fuller, one of the very human ones, and an Intellectual outside as well as inside the Army, asked me to have the breakfast on their table ready before they came down, as, 'All a soldier wants is to eat or sleep; if you can't feed him you must let him sleep.' When Colonel Fuller was much younger, he wrote a very attractive book on Aleister Crowley (I've since bought A. C.'s memoirs which are disappointing. For all his reputation he reads like a living example of Oscar's man who 'wakes up every morning with bad resolutions and always breaks them') and *Atlantis* on America wherein Colonel F. is witty enough to suggest a novel kind of future for this comical country. He has made me proud possessor of both these books ... I mention in dispatches Colonels Fuller, Rawlings, Grove and Dalby, and Officers Stone, Edgecombe,

Gavin Campbell, Gibson, Lester, Laby, and Meysey Thompson . . . Two months after the manoeuvres . . . being a dark November evening with no one in the place, Kate remarked, 'We never charged the manoeuvres for the use of the Dance Room for Conferences,' into which 50 or 60 wonderful-looking officers would pour twice a week. So I sent in a bill for £2. Colonel M. replied that no arrangement had been made as to paying for this room and that in any case it would be very difficult to get as all the accounts had been settled. Not dismayed I wrote to the uncommercial soldier and told him how every room had to pay its own way and failing that it would have to be taken down or converted into something that did. I added that if £2 was difficult to get perhaps he would find it easier to get for me a more appreciable sum, viz. £32 for the majority of them having left two days before their contracted engagement with me (part of which I had already paid out of my own pocket to the several landladies in the town). The £2 came by return of post. So whilst Colonel M. failed to save the taxpayer £2, I succeeded in saving him £32. Poor Colonel M., it became a morbid pleasure to me, over-wrought, to be hard on one so pretty and keen and dutiful, yet at bottom so petty.

Rowan and Mrs Walker (Mercia Marsh) I took round the garden. This red-haired, shapely, striking figure had a lovely Chow puppy with her. 'Take it,' she said. I protested. 'Take it,' said Rowan Walker, 'she's like that.' It was killed in the road soon afterwards but Joan continues to bless and ornament the place.

The relationship between Innkeeper and his guests is a peculiar one. You don't get or need to know the scandals or virtues of their lives, nor their politics or bank balances, yet along with a good deal of small talk, as between barber and barbed, there comes also a giving and taking of certain personal, even intimate feelings and an understanding that is made easy by each party knowing that he isn't condemned to bother about the other again. I imagine the Greek Oracles were in the same position. They didn't mind what they said to people, rot or otherwise, nor did the inquirers mind what they asked; it was just like throwing stones down a well; it was all part of the day's outing.

Garvin

J. L. Garvin came to dinner with Mrs Garvin. He said that it was their sixth wedding day, and they had decided to come here rather than to the Café Royal. Afterwards they came into the office and talked. The wife tries to organise this, when not working, irresponsible and tireless person, but has no effect on him whatever. They were to have left at nine o'clock punctually and it was after 10.30 when she at last moved him. Just as he writes in the *Observer* long, long articles, which are too good to read, so does he talk, and you have only to listen pleasantly to this semi-foreign, what-is-it? voice, which is sometimes difficult to understand. He said they had had a wonderful evening, but I wondered how, since I lent nothing to the conversation, for Colonel M.'s bargaining has left me deplorably depressed and stupid.

A party of ten very strong Lancashire folks arrived by telephone for the night. I let them come because I

always soften to the Lancashire accent, if strong
enough. They arrived at ten at night after having said
they would be here for dinner, which was now drying
up in the oven. They objected to the two rooms in the
yard cottage, the house being full, though I told them
they were in constant use by chauffeurs, professors,
peers and stablemen. 'Well,' said the little fat fellow,
'our young friend here, who has almost passed his second Doctorate's examination, ought to know,' which
settled it, of course. At 11 p.m. Kate took them down
the street for other rooms and here they kept her waiting half an hour deciding who of all these husbands,
wives and sons was to sleep with whom. 'Jane,' said
one woman, '*you* ought to sleep with George tonight –
you haven't slept with him but once all the trip.'
No one laughed, it was quite serious, and natural and
very late.

Philip Gosse says I ought to keep notes of things
and people here for a book. Aren't I doing it? But how
string it together? Storm or G. B. Stern would make a
wonderful thing out of six weeks of this.

The Physiology of Disappointment

Sunday, a lovely day in the midst of nationally destruc-
tive weather, and, instead of sixty people six came to
lunch; as much of a surprise as when on a bad day last
March eighty-five came. This sort of wash-out makes
one feel flat – it's not the not having made any money,
nor even the loss of it, because one is careless of the
joints once they are cooked, nor the feeling that one is
not perhaps serving a useful purpose, but, having
worked oneself up for an effort, and then not making
it is just as if one had trained, changed, rubbed down

and gone to the starting post for a race to be told that the race was off. All the steam, manufactured for use, is pent up, it can't escape through the natural channel but goes into the blood and bones and poisons.

A. E. Kingham, faithful friend of us, was here for the weekend. He was one of our first lodgers with Gerald Gould and Langdon Davies, generally the only people in the house. Ten years ago, when Kingham was political, he embarrassed me, a nervous wreck, in the RAC smoking-room by wanting to stand up on a chair and inveigh against the harmless members (and non-members) as capitalists. Old Mr Ely of Oxford University Press brought a most surprising beauty in Mrs Chapman and her husband. There never was rough, wavy hair, more brilliant copper. Larrabee brought a beautiful woman also – Mrs Riddle and husband.

All our soldiers are out for the day. J. C. Squire for lunch – he says he's ashamed for not growing scented verbena in his garden for his son even as his father had one for him – Gerald Gould for tea. E. S. P. Haynes dropped in, a sort of modern Shelley in his fight for *Personal Immorality* (Cayme Press), *Divorce as it might be*, *Enemies of Liberty*; his books and perhaps he himself would get a better hearing if he wasn't so unlike Shelley otherwise. He's so hot-tempered, so good-humoured, and Rabelaisian. A. D. Knox for dinner with Mrs Knox. Here's a chance missed for a man who, in such a family, ought to have been a blend of Evangelical, Roman Catholic, and anglo-humourist, whereas he's only a first-rate scholar and father of two disgustingly clever little boys.

'Fat White Lady'

A man brought down in a sumptuous Rolls a very fat bejewelled woman in white flannel who sat at the table with billows of white fat in front of her. She appealed to me, I liked her and we joked. Apropos of nothing, she suddenly asked me in a loud voice before the others in the room, 'And what do you think of me?' It was damned difficult to reply, so I said, 'Oh, you have some style.' — 'But is it the *right* style?' I felt now that the room expected me to give the proper reply, so looking at her streaming ropes of pearls, I said, 'Well, you look like the Maharaja of Baroda out for the afternoon', and, thank God, she was as amused as my remark was kindly intended.

Mrs Angel's pretty little girl, called Heather, came, and a man. I felt in the air something excitable about them. Later at lunch when champagne was asked for, I felt it must be for them, and when I was administering, it came out that they had got engaged five minutes before getting here. How wonderful!

Peter Luling came with his new wife, late Sylvia Thompson, they having now spent all the gains of her *Hounds of Spring* and the potential gains of his painting; a most beautiful-looking couple, like children, unsophisticated and unhumorous. I'm glad to be if only her third cousin or uncle once removed by marriage.

County Tact

During manoeuvres, a county gentleman came to me and said, 'Mr Fothergill, can you get me out of a hole? I want some port for the troops.' 'Yes, of course, how much do you want?' – 'Two bottles; you see, I've run out.' – 'But why should you run out with me so near.' – 'Oh, well, you see, I've got a lot of wine coming down from Town. Fairly cheap port, if you will.' And away he popped, happy, generous to the troops, tactful to me. Will Rothenstein once asked me what my father did, and I told him that he spent most of his time thinking out the proper thing to do and say; surely enough work for two men. Indeed many times since I took this Inn I have felt ashamed of working for a living; such reactionary feeling was confirmed by a sentence I read recently in one of the Upanishads, *'and work, that vile thing'* – for when work is imposed upon you, you get boggled or disgruntled or hardened and behave ill to others and especially yourself.

Basil Murray, who came here four years ago from Oxford with Benoit Tyzkiewicz, came with his newly married pretty wife for the night. They looked so delicious that I hesitatingly admitted them. G. K. Chesterton and three young folks lunched. I said to him, 'You were the first to expose "cheese and biscuits" as a corruption of the cheese. Now, I have made these biscuits with which to confute you.' He replied, 'I'm almost inclined to recant, and on the whole I would say now that to eat cheese with these biscuits is a corruption of the biscuits.' Talking about sauces, I told him how well he himself could write about sauces in relation to the thing eaten with them; for instance, the French laugh at our only sauce, bread sauce, but, when well made, there is nothing more delicious, and no sauce better adapted to its vehicle; but why do we spoil lamb with mint sauce, and give its capers to

mutton? This shook the Château Chesterton to my eighteenth-century chair-rungs.

Montie and Lady Pollock came over with his pictures for our Show. Lady Pollock told me she had said to their new simple Oxfordshire gardener's boy, 'Would you like a watch for Christmas?' The boy replied, 'That'll do.' The same boy asked Montie if he could take some of his apples. 'You see, I could have taken them without asking, but I believe in Honesty's the best policy, they say.'

Manning, with Rivers-Reffold, David Wilton, handsome actor, stayed the night. Talking through the window, I happed upon Manning's Christian names, to wit, Cecil John Edward d'Orellana Plantagenet Tollemache Manning; great nephew of the Cardinal. Apparently, his sister's names are far worse. 'Come inside,' I said, and got it all into my visitors' book. Colonel Grove said he supposed that if he wrote these names vertically on the wall where I measure people he would get the free lunch as the tallest.

Garvin dined with his stepson from Marlborough. He said the farmers were protesting against the parsons for having harvest thanksgiving when the only harvest was mud and rotting grain. 'And I'm with them,' he exclaimed. 'I tell the parsons that perhaps God didn't *want* a harvest and in any case doesn't want to be thanked for nothing. *I* say – Let God alone.' He sat opposite this beautiful and gifted little boy and harangued and disquisitioned to him as if he were a public meeting.

Diccon Hughes

Richard Hughes, not here for two years, turned up with Jay, New College, (now All Souls) looking the same as ever, having walked from Amersham, 20 miles. He has not hung on to rich people, and still likes the romance of poverty, and a Bentley automobile. He's been in Istria, 'with a room in a palace, and an ancient countess to make his bed, all for 4*d*. a day'.

A pale-faced but strong-looking lad from some Colony and Balliol came to dinner alone. During dinner he asked for paper to write a poem on that had just come into his head. When he left his table for a moment I couldn't help looking at the first line – 'I know a land that is full of naked girls.' We shall hear more of this poet, but where?

Marcus Slade gave a dance of 100 to 120 here for his son. They supped in the dining-room between

11.30 and 1. For the first time in these shows I got plenty of staff finding that a pound or two extra is cheaper than using oneself up physically. I think there never was such good food at a dance supper. No aspic, faked cream, polychrome and frilled tasteless viands, nor packet jellies, but everything tasted of food, and each dish tasted differently from the other. On the strength of this I'm going to try for the South Oxfordshire Hunt Ball . . . I did, and all I got was a single ticket for the next supper 'to see for myself how good their own food from London was'. How gracious, but what a sell for me!

Algernon Talmage (Talmache), sentimental, kind fellow, brought, as promised, Lynwood Palmer, the coaching man, to lunch – a single-hearted, four-horsed man, who promises to bring a coaching party for the night in one stage from Hounslow. I promised to be in readiness to meet him as he drove up, with four old men who haven't done an honest or dishonest day's work since coaches disappeared, to hold up what remains of his four horses and to clear all the Rolls Royces out of the coach-house to receive him.

Breakfast 3s. 6d.

What has always puzzled me is the price we and others charge for breakfast – 3s. 6d. – over against a vast lunch of four courses at the same price, and I guess that this exorbitant but very general charge originated in the fact that the proprietor, having once got them in the house, can charge what he likes because they can't comfortably go out for breakfast or without it. But discussing it sometimes with my victims, e.g. Colonel Spenser (Ipswich) and Richard Green (Haslemere) their opinion is generally that the amenities of the place make it worth it. I'm not convinced, but go on charging it.

A very good-looking and delightful couple, married a fortnight ago, he, J. Kellogg, Archaeology, she, *née* Mitchell and Chicago, came for the weekend from young Gordon Selfridge. One could joke and giggle with them exactly as if they were a beautiful English couple. Though staying at the —— in Piccadilly they said ours was the best coffee they'd had since they came away and liked the food, every dish of it, and the walk to Moreton and the drive to Brill. What is the place or the man, but the mood! She looks rather like Mrs Hugo Pitman. Mary Somerville, getting rapidly calmer and less self-centred and always delightful to look at, moon-faced, brought Sylphia Townsend Warner, Charles Prentice and Mrs Raymond of Chatto and Windus, and spent the day here – a delightful four of them. It's a horrible culinary responsibility having nice people coming so far with you in their stomachs all the way (and now as a reward Prentice has got me to make this self-exposure to the world).

Exorcising by Music

David Tennant brought Hermione Baddeley, who looks as if she were one of Oliver Messel's more expensive masks, but the beauty of the meal was Hoyland Mayer's friend, Miss Saleeby, with eyes like two full cups of eastern coffee and a double jet-black curl on her forehead. To dinner came Oliver Roskill to fix up about the concert that I have at last got going for this place; through him it will be better than ever I hoped for. My purposes in having a String Quartet are (*a*) the last finishing touch in the exorcising this place of its last ownership and clientele, (*b*) to have wonderful music in our own home. Roskill and Tom Marshall have now got the programme into shape . . . The programme was: Flute and String Quartet, Mozart, No. 28 D Major, and String Quartet, Beethoven, Op. 18, No. 3, D Major; songs and piano solo. Tom Marshall, leader; O. Roskill, 2nd violin; Bernard Robinson, viola; Olive Richards, 'cello; Anthony Pott, flute; Leslie West, our local musician, piano, and Miss Marshall singer. The noble quartet had practised here for two days solid. I seated the room entirely with sofas and armchairs for sixty and lit it with candles, and when the air had been incensed with dried rosemary, lavender and the pine needles of last year's Christmas tree and all the labour was over and Tom Marshall's marble beauty glowed like the moon and the musical exorcising began, I, like the hero of the *Chartreuse de Parme*, was lifted out of my chair to cook and serve a dinner for Romney Summers with fourteen friends just arrived, one of his regular 'parting dinners'. The expenses of the concert were the same as the takings, so I gave £10 to the Nursing Home to show what we could do.

Dunstan Skilbeck and Roger Campagnac drank a bottle and a half of brandy between them after dinner. He and Campagnac, with his 6 ft 7 inches, swaying, perhaps, ever so lightly, left the room as they came in, gentlemen, though young gentlemen.

Thomas Burke and Inns

Thomas Burke and his bright wife (*Green Fields of England*) came for the night. Two years ago we found it difficult to associate this quaint, correct, grateful, wise little man with *Limehouse Nights*. In his *Book of the Inn* he says we are the only Inn in England that he knows where the meal is not a hotel meal, etc., and why aren't there other places like ours? The requirements for keeping a good Inn are: (1) 14–16 hours a day and few even half-days off; (2) some capital with which to have good food ready and to waste; (3) a mind for the tiniest details; (4) an all-round outlook; (5) an ability to formulate a policy and courage to carry it out; (6) to have had first a good time in life oneself; and (7) a natural, not enforced, love of the job. Wherever an Inn fails in England or elsewhere, it will be, I think, for the lack of one or more of these requirements. This place, at least, has required them all.

Evan Morgan comes with his usual big party to dinner. He pays for the meal and does all the talking. That's not fair. Since becoming politician he seems to have lost the romantic and ascetic that he used to have. He leaves his priceless fur coat in our office and brings all his friends to pile theirs – it's his welcome prerogative ('provocative', as Kate calls it), for he used to come here in *our* simple days as well as his. But tonight when one of them came in to get his cigarettes, I couldn't help asking him if he minded my eating my supper in his cloakroom.

Manners, Low and High

A telegram came asking us to reserve a room for Mr and Mrs —— of ——. I had guessed from the name and address that they would be exactly what they were, good commercial. But he was a very fine, big, clean-faced, good-looking, honest, respectful man, and she remarkable with a shock of hair. As soon as I had greeted them in the hall, the fine-looking man said, 'We've heard so much about your place from a friend of ours that we determined to come and enjoy it – You have some very good furniture – We have not yet signed the register – A double gin and vermouth and a pint of beer for me, please.' This timid peroration, prepared beforehand and got off so rapidly, he had probably curtailed, because, thinking that I had come only to take the drinks, he got down to business. I never saw them again, even when they went away two days later, and yet this sort of people makes one want to change one's policy and run the place for the good and unsophisticated; it makes one feel very ashamed and cruel. He came and said good-bye to Kate with many big, slow bows; he didn't presume to ask for me. Oh, it is very beastly, very snobbish! Let me not be thought snobbish. They don't mix. And let me be as gushing to them as I might easily be in all sincerity and on common ground, viz. the heart, they wouldn't come again. They don't want it or me. *They* don't blame me – why should others or I myself? But what bad manners Bloomsbury have! And I've had a good many experiences of them. Bad formal manners as well as those that should spring from an ordinary sensitiveness about one's place in creation. They have invaded that fortress of Victorian gentility, of the serviette, sugar tongs, fish knives, not passing on stairs, hat-lifting and not licking your fingers and have learnt nothing from it. I once heard Will Rothenstein say that Bohemianism was essentially vulgar, so is Bloomsburyism. But for the sake of a few, like the very gracious James and Alix Strachey, Clough Ellis and David Garnett I forgive them. The other day a car drove up or, rather, not up but in the middle of the road outside, which was inconsiderate of the traffic, crowded with four Blooms-bury, two of each sex. One of the males ran in and after introducing himself as coming from a dear friend of mine asked how much I charged. 'Six shillings a room.' – 'It's rather a lot,' he said. 'Well, it's about the same price as charged by places which, not like mine, are run at a profit.' – 'I'll go and see,' he said, and ran out and I followed. 'What's the price?' rang out a lady's voice from the car in the middle of the road. I approached and said, '6*d*. more than elsewhere.' But in spite of the expense they came in. Later, at dinner, a voice rang out to me the length of the room, 'Mr Fothergill, is this the sort of pub where you can have second helpings?' I wondered afterwards if they would treat the ordinary Innkeeper like this and, if so, what he would do, and I concluded that it was an *ad hoc* manner invented to 'amuse' me. 'Keeping a pub must be so amusing.' . . . These ones have certainly made good since; besides, they weren't at their best on that particular occasion, I believe. Apart from Bloomsbury it's difficult to under-stand why good manners should be the property of some and not of others unless manners be like all other urges expressed by human nature, e.g. music, mechan-ics, drinking, gardening. Ordinarily you allow a bad-mannered person through without taking offence, just as you don't expect everyone to paint good pictures, but it's trying when a person, county or literary or political, imposes upon you a product that is faked or insincere, cubist or academic or patronising and expects you to swallow it gratefully.

*

Philip Steegmann, whom I saw first and photos of his pictures at Mrs Haynes's when at Albury, and was rather staggered by their bright, almost brilliant imagery, and commissioned him at once to paint Michael, is coming down shortly and has sent a lad, Tim Brooke, to stay here. Brooke was at Exeter and is writing a book (*Mad Shepherdess*). He is not artist, aesthete, highbrow, lowbrow, nobrow, hikebrow, sex, hearty, or any coterie, merely commonsense, and is the best teller of a story I ever met.

A good-looking, very nice lad, 6 ft 3 in., with red, curly hair, Sandys, came with a girl to dinner. I was at Oxford with his father — funny to keep a public and not an open house for your friends' sons. I've had several of them; I don't like it, but I like the sons.

—— told me a very young and bad story of having held a pistol to his head and fired, but nothing happened because someone had unloaded it that very afternoon. Much better the story Oscar told me of how, when he'd paid the blackmailer £400 for a packet of his letters, 'I threw them into the grate, and, in order to punish the hands that had written them, I held them close to the bars, and they grew quite cold because there was no fire in the grate.'

Tim Brooke took my side against Mary Somerville and Kate in objecting to allow people to 'see the rooms'. I say that those people who have once seen me or Kate or the little hall and then ask to see the rooms *ipso facto* disqualify themselves as fit to stay here.

Young Lords —— and ——, who used to be at Oxford, came with six to lunch, took away £5 worth of gin and vermouth and oranges, drank it all and came back ten to dinner, with four or five little girls —

Oscar punishing his hands at a cold grate.

whether they were aristocrats or chorus girls, who knows? I don't suppose they knew themselves, since plainly each of these classes must irritate the other into imitation when in London. But they all said 'Thank you for having us', etc., which was very charming, and they liked the food, which was very good.

A. C. Russell had a twenty-firster, with thirteen from BNC, a very courteous lad; he and four others wore kilts which we filled with haggis.

Martyrs

Alan Bicknell brought Bentley, Mrs Bentley and two others to lunch. To this timid little man I said when seeing them off, 'I suppose you get the pick of the

batch for yourself,' to which banal question he gave
the equally banal reply, 'No, I always get the very
worst.' – 'Like me here,' I said, 'you've had a lovely
meal and I've just lunched off a bit of chocolate tart
left on your plate,' – which reminds me of witty Sally
Cobden-Sanderson's Boat Race Party where they had
1,500 sandwiches and sausage rolls for the invited and
uninvited, and 'My own food for the day', she said,
'consisted of half a sausage roll which I retrieved from
under Jane, our spaniel.' I told her that it was no
longer necessary to plant a row of dark blue hyacinths
as well as light down the path leading to this annual
fiasco, but to a Cambridge man I did my best for
Oxford by telling him that they had long since given
up rowing there and that this year, merely in order to
be social, they had, in fact, hired a boat from Cambridge for the day.

The kind-natured, genuine D'Oyley Cartes came
with their usual big party. It differs from other parties.
It has as much noise as the jazz type, but it's laughter
and not scream, running water not gin, ripple not
tipple ... People must have been funny and happy
sometimes in the well-bred Victorian days without
either sex or good clean fun, and this party must be
an echo of it. Having seen the map Hoffman did for
me they had him do one 6 ft long for their house at
Brixham.

I accepted Mrs Ball's invitation to criticise the Pang-
bourne Art Society's Exhibition. I arrived when fifty
people were already seated and as many pictures, and
sweated. Mrs Ball is a very extreme example of the
type to be found in every community beating up shows

and finding local genius. Kate and I went to a most exquisite luncheon beforehand at her fairy cottage in the wilds of Bucklebury Common, with Heidsick *circa* 1896, quite flat yet a strong, most delicious, almost oily drink of darker colour than today's stuff. After lunch there came round in the tiniest, thinnest glasses I've ever seen, a liqueur. I didn't know what it was and kept silent, but the others began to ask questions. I had a prevision that someone would ask me as a wine merchant, and from my dear friend, Lady Pollock, of all people (probably to advertise me) it came – 'Now, Mr Fothergill, what is this wonderful thing?' Rapidly deducting from the exquisite food, wine and furniture that it could be no other than 'Imperial Tokay' which I'd never seen before, I said so and I was saved.

Lately I've had no trouble from half-knowledged people asking if it was oak under these panels, but today passing up and down the dining-room I heard a party of four deciding who was to bell the cat. – At last the spokesman said, 'I suppose you will soon scrape off the paint your predecessor (letting me down lightly) has put on to these panels.' So I was cheaply disingenuous, and suggested that common deal might look rather poor, and that one ought perhaps to stick to painting them as they had been when they were first put up. And once an old lady assured me that they were oak. I told her they were deal – 'Of course that's oak,' she said, and striding across the room, charged the wall with her umbrella. 'No,' I said, when the metallic clang had died down, 'that's an asbestos sheeting partition I put up six months ago.'

A pretty and clever lad, Alan Pryce-Jones, came to tea, and amused us very much by a wholly invented story of his adventures in France amongst the castles near Tours – how he wrote to one duke, dragging in one or two princesses' names and what they had said to him, by way of credentials, how he was met at the station by a Rolls for himself, another for his hand-bag, and another for a footman, and got changed in time to meet a house party of forty in the hall before dinner, and didn't know when or not to kiss the women's hands and how he stayed a fortnight there and so on with three or four other castles. Volatile, catching.

Couples

Last night, owing to the fog, four nice people who were to have come didn't, but instead at 10 p.m. came, owing to the same fog, two young men with two handsome girls of the bright young highbrow type, on their way to Burford, asking for food and sleep. We gave them in ten minutes a full-course dinner of great goodness. They asked for double beds and fires. In the morning, I said to the young men, 'Next time I hope you will get through to Burford. Last night, of course, the fog rather threw you at us, but we are not good here at mixed couples.' When they took this quietly, I added, 'You see, you might tell of this place to people not as nice as yourselves and they again to others, and so we could quickly degenerate into any old thing,' and we parted very pleasantly. When we had been here only six months, a neat Cockney Jewish lad came for the night with a pretty and domestic little female friend. They made a sumptuous dinner, the first such we had ever served, and retired. I didn't like it but said nothing. On the following Saturday, the same boy and girl brought another couple, the spit of themselves, and fared still more sumptuously and retired to bed. I now felt that I ought to get busy, and had a bad night wondering how I should put it to them. After breakfast I inveigled into the office the ringleader, and put my policy before him in a nervous speech of some fifteen minutes' duration, and then begged him not to come again. 'It's quite all right,' he exclaimed, 'I quite understand. It was just the same at the Swan at Xton!'

The difference between the place now and what it was lies in this. When we came here, like our predecessors, we had to stand and wait for our custom, like every other country or seasonal Inn. We depended upon the weekly visitations of the farmers, the freemasons, the Grammar School biennial dinner, race meetings, the local bar, Rent Audits, commercials, people held up by fog. I can't describe what an anxiety this dependence was, because if these failed through weather or foot-and-mouth disease or other cause there was nothing. It was at best a limited unexpandable trade, a blind alley job, and worse. We had to put up with all sorts of treatment from our paymasters. In our first days a party of artistes had been lodged here by a local philanthropist for his annual concert. There was no one else at dinner, of course, and half-way through I came in and saw one of them standing on an eighteenth-century chair, making foolish. Rather timidly, I asked him to get down and not endanger the chair when one of the others called out, 'Now, me man, none of that!' And one baking hot day the son of a local 'County' came in and asked for a dozen syphons. As there was no man in the yard, I had to carry this impossible load all the way down myself. When I came out of the archway, I saw in front of me, perched high in a Ford car, the hard pergamene face of the lady herself. Though feeling like to drop, I forced up a little wan smile as I struggled near and looked up at her – 'Put it in the back,' she ordered in a sepulchral voice, and I was glad to drop the smile and the syphons. And now what a relief to make our own trade.

Mrs Trouton came with her young brother to lunch and buy wine. They are Norwegian, the brother has now come up to Cambridge. I asked her to put her name in our book because she was beautiful; she did it. 'Do you want this?' she asked, pointing to the brother. 'You may not like his name very much.' – 'Of course I like your splendid names resounding of the fiords,' and down went 'Albert Bugge' (hard '*g*'). He told me the Dons at his College had had a dinner especially to decide how his name should be pronounced in Cambridge, where, I think, it came out as 'Budge'.

Staying here is Miss Horniman, founder of the Manchester Repertory Theatre; she who was one of the modern women of the world, now the very dearest old maid. The cigarette in a holder, but only after meals, is all that remains of her hardihood.

John Pilley, of unique manners and appearance, wrote hoping we were having a 'prosperous Christmas'. I replied that only ten people had been here in eight days owing to the cold and impassable roads; it was, as the French would say, a state of 'maroon glacé'. Eight big cars thick in snow were left in the garage over Christmas, and ten days later their owners returned to take them away with the same snow on them that they had come with. It makes me think of the letters that we and other similarly affected trades have written to their creditors promising cheques after Christmas. And yet 'prosperity' is a bad word, it smacks of grabbing from others.

A man with a very pretty baby wife were lunching. He rose to introduce himself. 'I am —— of ——.' – 'Oh, yes, that's good.' – 'This is my wife, not bad for four children, is she?' – 'Has she really? She's wonderful.' – 'I wish you would come to tea with us this afternoon. We live a long way from here, but I'll bring you back.' – 'But I haven't time.' – 'Oh yes, you must. You see my wife is angry with me at present because she thinks I am carrying on with someone else, which is all rubbish; so I promised to devote today to her *solely* and *alone*; so do come with us.' I did, just to help him.

'...*not bad for four children, is she?*'

1928

Nice, fat, laughing, appreciative Conway, barrister, came with lovable wife and Sir George Someone. He said he had been to two dances since the Slade's here, and had talked about our supper all the time at both. Save for lapses like this Conway is one of those rare people who make an effort to keep things humming round him, like Ellis Roberts (whom I used to take for Mark Hambourg, and now Ellis Roberts tells me he has been taken for me, so who of us three beauties is the most insulted?).

'Are these biscuits a home-made effort? I like them so much,' said a luncher, with the dish empty and his mouth full. I told him they were not an effort but an achievement, and I might have added that his was both.

Some Hunting Folk

——— came to lunch on Sunday looking very much a sportsman having just become joint master of one of the big Hunts. I told him this was one of the greatest sporting events that had happened to us here. A hunting man had epigrammatically told him that 'if, instead of inviting the farmers to drink his champagne, he would go and drink some of their beer he could do what he liked with them.' As for our own sporting experiences we were told to 'look after the hunting men and they'd look after *us*.' So, when hounds met outside we put bowls of gingerbreads on the bar and they came, men and women, and ate up the gingerbreads, and women went up to the lavatory, and as soon as the gents discovered my new lavatory in the yard, there was the thin red line to and fro. For me to have objected to these little acts of trespass would have been thought as heinous as if I had gone and eased myself in their own back yards; and once I found a dandy in the Common Room in his shirt-sleeves vehemently brushing a very dirty coat on a rosewood table in the middle of the room. But the yard was full of horses and red coats and yellow waistcoats and violet buttonholes, mounting and dismounting, and I used to give Reck (short for gypsy Reconciliation), the old man with the old red coat on foot with old terriers, the double rum 'he'd always had', and to the hunt servants sometimes drinks and smiles, and all looked bright and busy and ye olden time and I tried wanly to feel part of it for an hour or two till the fanfare sounded, and in an instant the place was cleared with 2s. to 3s. in the till, and not a penny to the yard boy or even a nod to me.

This morning, as in bed we heard the pleasant clatter of hoofs coming under the archway, Kate suggested that we ought to put up a notice – 'Hunting folk are invited to continue making use of our poor accommodation without asking, and free of all charge as hitherto.' I told one of the hunting people about this arrogance and rubbish and she said that it was an abuse and complaint common to other districts. This is sport; it's the old game: huntsmen, artists, priests, politicians make it their business to gull or frighten the multitude into thinking they are fine fellows and into thinking, or pretending to think, that they themselves enjoy and have a part in the game in order that the huntsmen and so on may have the good time they

want and use the multitude to do it with. Who but
a lounger or gulled person, if he had no money or
leisure, would stand round on a pouring day and watch
these bright folks meeting in the market-place? Once a
young sportsman booked three loose boxes; the horses
arrived. 'Oh – er – I never made an agreement with
you as to the charge for our three horses, the straw and
the groom, two meals and sleep. Well, at Wheatley we
paid ten shillings.' – 'Ten shillings for what?' – 'For
what I've just said, and of course I shall be bringing a
lot of other hunting people here as this is a good
centre.' So I made him listen while I totted up the cost
to me of all this – 'It gives me a *gross* profit, then, of
2*s*. 4*d*.?' – 'Yes, that would be it.' – 'Well, that doesn't
seem very much for me, but I'm thinking of those
other people you undertake to bring here.' – 'Well, I
don't guarantee, but of course I shall do my best, you
know.' – 'Yes,' I replied, 'that's just it – I tremble to
think of it.' After trying to explain to him that to clear
out and litter three boxes for an occasional horse and
lodge and feed properly a groom was not worth while
for 2*s*. 4*d*., I suggested his going to the other Inn. Here,
he told me later that he'd got the whole thing for
8*s*. 6*d*.! A nice lad and all that, but they must try to pay
a little better and so avoid obloquy.

A major, of a smart regiment wrote, be it recorded
to his everlasting memory, booking his groom and
horses. He didn't turn up or write it off. I asked one of
his subalterns, a charming fellow, if the major often
did that sort of thing, and he said he didn't know. –
'Well, would you please tell him that he does.' So I
wrote to him with a bill of 7*s*. 6*d*. to include extra
straw and a day's work clearing a stall of bottles, etc.

The major, having first written from a grand house in ——shire, now writes from one in a smart London Square, saying that he had passed his stall on to the subaltern. I wrote and explained that the subaltern had booked and paid for one independently. A letter now from HQ saying that he didn't wish me to be out of pocket and enclosed 6s. So I wrote (I'm now very ashamed to say on a postcard) saying that if he found satisfaction in sending me 6s. instead of 7s. 6d., I was glad to think it possible and the matter dropped. It's all very silly this, but a lot of it tends to brutalise and make Innkeepers what they often are. Yet, it's absurd to be bitter about them, the unpleasant ones of them, the spongers, the hangers-on. To be on a proper horse after hounds is a revelation, a new life and perhaps the only true one. I hunted sometimes with the East Sussex, but was unpopular, chiefly because one wet day, since they used to hang about gorse bushes so long after mangy foxes or none, I brought out an umbrella and opened it to good effect. Moreover, I dressed like a Daumier man. But now, 1930, this horse-play has entirely ceased, for us at least – only one gentleman comes and leaves his cardboard hat-box in the hall and his groom paces up and down the yard till evening when they go home. He never speaks to me as he changes into the other hat, I wouldn't discourage him – this little reminder of old days.

I said to Mitchison that it was rum that young X., now in his father's financial office, should be a communist and he said that G. D. H. Cole says that all the dull sons of rich coal and oil parents come to him to learn labour-lore, and he tells them to go home and think it over. Well, that sounds very pretty and paradoxical and superior and idealistic, but I wonder whether G. D. H. Cole or the Labour Party or any other party really refuse either the rich or the dull.

A foul, cold, windy wet day begun by an hour's investigation with the police sergeant into the disappearance of a leg of mutton from the archway. Then I had to give the town a full daylight display of my running powers in chasing the biggest boy, sportingly chosen, of a gang of six whom I saw puncturing the wheel of Lucas Scudamore's Rolls right outside the door with a new galvanised nail, and after a quarter of a mile of dodging and running I got the real culprit's name from the exhausted and frightened runner.

A handsome, black-haired woman came to dinner with a rather distinguished-looking man. She had been here before; he and his huge Daimler not. They came from London to dine at 'my famous Inn'. But when I complained that two squit undergrads had just brought two nice girls with them, and, by a trick the parlour-maid had watched, were trying to make them drunk, the man started the old argument that 'I couldn't pick and choose and the law compelled me, etc.' I told him that it was a little ungracious of him who liked 'my famous Inn' to argue a policy for me that would make it infamous. I've had this attitude before and don't understand it. In any case, this is the young man's only chance of being chaste in his life and he ought to take it. Even as it would be difficult for me now to stop the flow of decent people that I have encouraged, so would there have been a very different picture here had I not discouraged the indecent. It would have been far more human and jolly, perhaps, but troublesome.

Pritt Wit

Day after day passes, and it seems a waste of cellar and desire to put it in order when not a dozen bottles go out. I am hoping that this time next year will see a change when my new 'stunt' of selling by post to people who live in flats with flat purses even one bottle at a time, though I would profit only 2*d*. on the single bottle, has had its chance. I recognise that a cash trade is hard to make; it would not be possible in Oxford and hardly in London. In a little notice I have printed about selling wine in detail, with a mahogany coloured cover so that you don't see them tho' lying about on every table, I give a list of wines ending with 'each of which is either drinkable or remarkable'. 'Mr Fothergill,' called out Johnny Pritt, KC, in his nice loud voice before everyone at dinner, 'what should I do with a bottle of wine that is remarkable but not drinkable?' But the sight of Mollie Pritt put me at ease.

Togo Maclaurin and Mrs are here for the weekend. He is a fat, innocent-eyed, beautifully mannered lad with lovely teeth. She is immense and fascinating. In the Office after dinner I was sitting opposite her whilst she was showing above her beautiful silk net stockings at least 8 in. of the inside of a smooth white thigh. Maclaurin was sitting beside me too when suddenly he said, 'Darling, your dress has gone wrong.' Instantly she pulled up a bit of shoulder that was falling. The old pudor changeth yielding place to new. Fifteen years ago I told Will Rothenstein that I'd met at a

party a beautiful lady whom I would ever remember as Lillah McArmpits, and he said that the dressmakers were at that moment deciding which part of the female body should be exposed next.

Big Show Risks

John Fernald, President OUDS, came to talk of my doing their supper of 150 in the Town Hall. If I do it, and they have now asked me, I should owe a debt of gratitude to that gracious and charming youth, who still says that the week twelve of them spent here doing a film in July was the best time he ever had in his life. It seems absurd to owe such an interesting experience to a lad of 20, I being 52, but if at that age he is so discriminating as to ask me to do the job, it puts him onto a plane equal to that of a man. Against

the profits of all big outside concerns you have to consider the risk of something essential going wrong, by
which you will lose a reputation, especially when you
are not doing them regularly. Here, for instance, two
years ago, by a mistake of mine the band didn't turn
up from London for a big dance we'd advertised, so
they threw the sugar about the room till I got one at
midnight from Oxford, and at the next dance the band
came but, owing to the fog, the dancers didn't, so we
presented the thirty that did with the champagne supper ordered by those who didn't. One of the assets
which we paid for with this Hotel was the catering for
the big Agricultural Show, 500 lunches and so on.
With no experience and a job lot of hired staff we
suffered badly. The carvers gave helpings too big for
eating, the food was too good, and the loss on the drink
too awful. As I was taking away the stuff in the dark, I
saw a man take a bottle of sherry under my nose from
the cart, and push it under a sack on the ground. I was
too tired to bother about him. So I gave this privilege,
for which we had to pay £10 each year, to Gargini, an
Aylesbury caterer, a competent man with a permanent
staff, who takes the thick against the thin throughout
the summer, but I heard that the people of Thame
were angry at my doing so, 'sending the money out of
the town'. I felt that I'd sent enough of *my* money out
already. It was easy to see that to do one show in the
year was like having one big bet. In our back yard
are still stored some thousands of plates, etc., cold
reminder of the dismal failure we made of it the last
time we did it.

Gypsies

It seems to me that the average actor takes to the job because he has the call of the wild. Sometimes they have lapses into humdrum, bourgeois lawfulness, they contemplate a little home with little parties and gardens, get engaged and married on Saturday, and are off on Monday. This is an instance: a famous actress telegraphed here at length wanting rooms for herself, her lady friend, maid, chauffeur and big car for the weekend. We sat up till 3 a.m., they arrived and went to bed. Well, they came down at 1.30 next morning, empty of breakfast, and a man in another big car took them away without their even saying 'good-bye'. Why had they come? The little vagrants had had the bourgeois idea of a weekend in the perfect country and they couldn't stand it, not even in bed till 1.30; they'd even brought tennis racquets! The maid came and paid the bill and said the reason why they went was that it wasn't sufficient country for them (even in bed). This was strange because they sent the maid to find the bathroom and she returned to say that it was too far away to go there: surely a countrified enough condition of things! Or does the 'too far' point back to their gypsies' origin of living in the constrained area of a caravan. Bourgeois and simple again they became when they had ordered a big breakfast which went up looking wonderful on a huge eighteenth-century mahogany oval tray, but when they saw it, back to the wild again and they asked for it to be taken away and the curtains re-drawn. How good to be so natural but how expensive!

*

The fact is, sixteen months without sunlight is telling its tale on all of us, tonight it's howling as usual with wind and no one came to dinner to eat what would have been no food because the cook had spoilt it all when I had to be out of the kitchen for an hour. Moreover, we have with us a disagreeable stayer who hates us — very rich and still stingier — whom we call 'leather-face', but she's going on Tuesday. We have had this hate of females before who, having the whole house to themselves, and all the kindness of our servants, can only sit on their behinds and curse us inwardly. The only consolation is that in other Inns they would curse outwardly.

The dinner, though there were a heap of delightful folk from London and Oxford, was spoilt for me by two undergrads, one a nice the other a very unpleasant looking fellow, bringing two girls, almost certainly Oxford hacks. I told them we hadn't a table, and then I said the truth was the ladies didn't quite go with the furniture of the place. 'Are they relations?' — 'No.' — 'Undergrads?' — 'No, but if it's any use to you they've both been presented at Court.' (!) Ultimately I told them to come in if they liked but under protest, and they didn't. This may appear quixotic and absurd — not everyone thinks my way, and how I hate it when it happens.

G. A. Wright, a gentleman, soon to be a parson, had twenty to dinner — repeating his twenty-first birthday dinner of last year. He got his party away so quietly that I didn't know they'd gone. He told me he thought it better so, since in Oxford undergraduate noises were not thought anything of. I told him that the spirit and way in which he could influence this

his first congregation promised well for the future.

The OUDS dinner in the Town Hall was 100 strong. The cook spoilt the black soup completely, curiously enough they all swallowed it – evidently they had sat down believing that the dinner was to be so good that this prejudice was strong enough to carry them through at least the first course of brownish salt lemonade. The next four courses were exquisite and the savoury sloppy. I was so disconsolate that I didn't dare to go through the screens into the room, though afterwards several of them, including Diccon Hughes, always generous, came round and thanked me for the best OUDS supper and the first where they had had enough to drink, which was clear. In the middle of A. P. Herbert's speech, when he was touching upon the coming Revolution, fifty of my best plates were dropped on the top of the fifty marble steps just outside the room, and as they clattered down with intermittent crashes he made full use of it, getting the laugh of the evening at my expense, though I admit that I myself thought of Southey's 'Falls of Lodore' at the same time.

Furber, charming person, OUDS secretary, came with Shepherd of *Punch*, his wife and daughter to lunch on Sunday. He said that once after a fancy dress ball he pulled a policeman's whistle out of his pocket thinking he was a fancy-dress policeman. Then I told him how two years ago an uppish bobby here suggested, or rather repeated the then sergeant's improper suggestion of the day before, that I was selling liquor after hours – for in those days they couldn't understand how otherwise a pub could be open after closing hours. So I rated him outside the house and in my

anger caught hold of his tunic about waist-high, when suddenly the whole thing flew open, disclosing an expanse of grey shirt. Realising at once that this was a crime equal to the debagging of a king, I climbed down into a humble apology, and, indeed a sincere one, for although the buttons were so loose that a soft wind blowing across them might have done what I did, the sight of the grey shirt I felt must have been humiliating to him.

'Vogue' and Victorian

Pritt and Mrs Mollie Pritt brought Mrs Settle, editor of *Vogue*, very 'vogue' herself, and T——, handsome and heavy in Labour Party corduroys, and Mrs T——, heavy again with her own habitual form of labour, lolling about, smiling, pretty and natural. The 'Vogue' wanted to see the place and I showed them round. 'This is the bedroom I've put all my Victorian truck into, here is the great walnut toilet altarpiece and before it on this beadwork mushroom stool you sit and do your plaits, and then on this *gros point prie-dieu* you say your prayers, when, decorously climbing into that Albertian bed . . . (ribald laughter). Here is a beautiful oval wool flower-piece given us by two charming people who, sleeping in this room, were nabbed for co-responding by the detective who was not expected till they got to the next and better adapted hotel. This is a sampler of Ann Annall, Aug. 20, 1806, aged 12 years, with the verse:

Fragrant the Rose is, but it fades in Time
The Violet sweet, but quickly past its Prime.
White Lilies hang their Heads, and soon decay
And whiter Snow in Minutes melts away.
Such and so withering are our early Joys
Which Time or Sickness speedily destroys.

– Joseph Gordon MacLeod discovered in this a transla-
tion of lines 28–31 of the poem *Erastes*, attributed to Theocritus with the last couplet emended for refined consumption. It should be:

The snow is white: melts where it had been frozen.
Beautiful, a youth's beauty: but it lasts not long.

See his *Ecliptic*, a beautiful but rather too beastly eru-
dite poem (Faber) –
'And here in maple frame, but they are all in that, is a picture of the Queen and Prince Albert tripping a polka by Jullien, charmingly tinted with the very young Queen looking for once really happy, and a

china bust of the young Prince of Wales on top of the
fiddlewood wardrobe. A faded super-lodging-house
bedroom, but it reminds me of those seaside rooms
commandeered by our thirteen headed family fifty
years ago. It was a delightful party?'

And not to be able to help him!

A young man, ——, came to arrange for his twenty-
first birthday dinner – this for his Oxford friends, for
his other friends the dinner was to be given at the ——
Hotel in London. There would be, however, 'one or two
regular soldiers at this party, and possibly an attaché of
the —— Embassy'. The entire afternoon was taken up
in making the arrangements, because he had to inter-
polate between each suggested course what a grand
person he was and how a nephew of Lord ——, and I
agreed to take something off the price of the wine . . .
The dinner was a very noisy one for neither the regular
officers nor the attaché were present, and he offered to
send a cheque next day . . . Three weeks have passed
and no cheque has come, so I write my disappointment
to him . . . He replies that he hasn't been able to get
here because his car has broken down (and presumably
the post) . . . Yesterday, at last, he came and told me
how in a brilliant palace at a dinner-party in France
(General ——, a famous Frenchman, was there) he
was sitting on the right hand of his host and how, after
a toast to De Guise, there was a toast in compliment to
himself, viz. the King, to which he replied in French,
poor French, he modestly confessed, and then we
retired to our humble Office to receive the belated
cheque. He produced the crumpled bill on which I had
made a reduction of fifteen shillings (besides that on

the wine) and at that point I felt I must leave him to Kate. 'I suppose Mr Fothergill will give me 2s. 3d. – My bankers don't like uneven cheques.' – 'Of course,' said Kate, from the fireplace, thinking he was overdrawing the cheque by that sum to make the pounds even and wanted the change, but no, he had omitted the two shillings and threepence and drove off in placid self-satisfaction with some to unlearn.

We had the 1927–8 Rugger team here to lunch and dinner on their way there and back. After dinner the sixteen of them sat in the Common Room where I gave them sherry. The game had been an amusing one, the RAF got thirteen goals in the first fifteen minutes and were beginning to be kind to our team, saying, 'Now, come on Oxford,' so Oxford came on and got nineteen goals to their thirteen. I told them that when they wrote threatening to come here I expected them on arrival to demand a leg of mutton each and then chaw up the eighteenth-century furniture (loud laughter), but instead they were fifteen mother's boys (howls of laughter); then I asked the slightly built lad at my side – Mallalieu, I think – what part of the field *he* played in. 'Scrum back,' he replied. 'Really? you don't look as if you could play at all!' (Yells of laughter and a fifteen-stone Forward shot from the sofa into the air and across the room.) These delightful people told me that the Rugby team had dropped the traditional 'beating-up' nonsense.

Tom Best-Dalison

T. Best-Dalison whom, not only for his lovable nature and manners but for his always having come with the late young Lord Pelham, equally perfect, I remember perhaps best of all our past undergrads, came to dinner with a friend, whilst on a holiday from the diplomatic Mission in Vienna. I told him it was ugly work feeding one who was straight from Vienna, but he said he came here as being the only place in England where he enjoyed his food. Almost too diplomatic. It's so easy to put me in a fool's paradise here because I never leave the place.

It was the same old rush of eighty to ninety to lunch, the rats coming out of their holes in the fine weather, and all our food seems very loathsome and the waiting bad, though it can't be bad in comparison with other places. These crowded Sunday lunches are hateful because I can't see anything of the nice people or do justice to them or myself – the penalty for having done my best for them in the past. And that must be the way places get spoilt in spite of the fellow's efforts who runs them. They merely get beyond him, his original people fall away and he finds himself merely making business and money behind a counter from an alien crowd.

The First Clean Guests

Henrietta Bingham, daughter of Judge Bingham, came for the night looking entrancing. She and Mina Kirstein were the first decent people who ever stayed, coming here as the result of a friendly 'puff' from Grant Richards, and over against the farmer element that we seemed doomed to for life, Kate and I will never forget their beautiful faces and clothes, and air of love and baths and comfort. No one would understand this feeling of ours who hadn't lived amongst the people and in the atmosphere that we took over here, with certain exceptions still with us, e.g. Mr Bull, Mr Boughton, Fred Edden and Mr White. It wasn't yokel and honest farmer, of the earth earthy, but of the dirt dirty with arrogant and grasping half-breds.

Sir Bertram Jones brought his son and nine or ten others to lunch for the son's twenty-first birthday. He is about 6 ft 3 in. high, and absolutely huge. This vast man, who ought profitably to be utilised in moving mountains, spends his spare time in microscopy! His main business is laughing.

The Marquess of Graham (Angus) is, I think, the most beautiful youth we've had here, besides being 6 ft 5 in. high. He has a pink face and lovely teeth and a calm wise smile.

If you make the disasters of life, and its difficulties and irritations the real and interesting things, they will soon cut out in their joy and beauty the more evanescent joys and beauties commonly thought real.

It's a horrible thing to be a fanatic. I saw a girl, rather a nice girl, on a nice undergrad's knee in the Common Room, so I attacked the four of them like a fury, telling them to go out, never to come again and to tell their friends not to. One of the youths, an American, apparently not quite an undergrad, came to me afterwards and showed complete sympathy with my views and policy and we parted sentimentally. How much better and more penetrating if I had sat down and slowly and kindly talked to them! This conduct of mine is going backward. I have learnt nothing. It's awful. I hope the same sort of thing happens again soon to give me another chance.

A very pretty girl, Joyce Handley-Seymour, under-graduate, and young Bicknell came out to meet her mother and Mrs Patrick Campbell here for lunch on their way to Oxford to lecture at the English Club, which is surely the right spirit. We fed them well. It was rather pathetic to hear Mrs P. C. whom I last saw as Mrs Tanqueray say she was 'looking for a job now that all they want on the stage is flappers'.

Wine Drinking and Wine Talking

Two days ago three lads didn't like, when they had drunk half of it, my well-known Château Neuf du Pape 1919, and the bottle was in good condition; so I gave them instead a pint of another sort, which apparently had the effect of improving the taste of the Château Neuf, which also they finished. This was as it should be, but what of the following? One evening, a modest undergrad asked me for the best bottle of white wine in the cellar for his friend and himself for their parting dinner. I opened a bottle and a more foully corked one I have never smelt, left it on the dresser and opened another, a perfect one, and left that there too, for we were very busy, and I never saw him again. Next morning, however, I discovered that Katie had given him that frightful bottle by mistake, and we found it amongst the empties outside, drained to the last drop. I didn't know his name to write to him and indeed, had he come again, could I hurt his feelings by telling him of it? But Kate suggested that I should thank him for his very courteous act in drinking it. Sometimes stupid, made-up and unconvincing stories about wine one puts up with smiling. Yesterday a man said he asked the waiter at the ——— Hotel, Brighton, for a Burgundy he could recommend, and he brought what purported to be an old and expensive Chambertin. After tasting it he called the *maître d'hôtel* and said, 'Look here, I may be off my taste, but is this the correct taste for Keystone Burgundy?' The *maître d'hôtel* tasted it and answered, 'Yes, sir, that's perfectly correct.' . . . Well, it pleased him to tell the tale.

Two rather stodgy underbred folks came and asked for a room, adding, 'Can we see it?' I explained, as usual, that it wasn't necessary to inspect my rooms unless, of course, one was going to stay some time. 'Then we can go elsewhere', rang out the harsh voice of the woman. 'You can', I said, 'and so relieve the situation,' and out they went. I'm rather tired of this unpleasantness; next time I shall ask them what price rooms they would like to see, stick it on, and so make them pay for the inspection. Once, in one of these periodical altercations, the man said he 'always looked at the room first, even at the Ritz', to which I replied, risking that he knew as little about the Ritz as I did, 'That would be silly seeing that they are all the same there.'

The House Public

Practically all we got from the race meeting at Tetsworth was a row of three girls descending from a Lancia and going straight past me upstairs to the lavatory. I called out to the hindermost, 'Are you wanting lunch?' No answer. So I waited for them. They were inferior females got up to look grand. 'Did you leave anything upstairs for the housemaid?' and the front one began fumbling in her bag. I said, '*I* would have done so if I had rushed into *your* house without even

asking your leave or saying "thank-you".' — 'But *is* it
your house?' — 'Of course it is. I am licensed to sell beer
here, and not to give water-closet accommodation to
passers-by.' — 'They don't say anything, anyhow, at the
Ritz and Berkeley.' — 'But those hotels are quite different and you would go unnoticed there.' — 'Yes, and
they give you good manners.' — 'In return for bad,' I
replied, and they got off.

Borden

Geoffrey Hart, a nice little young man, with only two
Isotta Fraschinis, brought to lunch the three daughters
of Mary Borden — Comfort, Mary and Joyce, little,
short, short-necked, round, fat-faced, pretty, vivacious
wild things, of ages quite impossible to guess. I
thought from 14 to 17, Kate from 16 to 18, and very
clever and taking. I thought how pleasant it must be to
lunch in that little room with that foursome at the
next table. Hart asked for a nice claret, 'A good children's claret?' I suggested, and we decided on Château
Latour 1908, and after lunch they sat, each with a doll
or teddy-bear in one hand and a double port in the
other. 'Look, sir,' said one of the maids to me, startled,
'those children are now drinking port!' Long after
lunch, they were alone in the little room, all looking at
the same book, and some people came in and said, 'Is
this a private room?' — 'No,' I said, 'it's the nursery, and
we keep a male nurse.' — 'We are pleased with your
description,' said one of the gnomes, 'but regret that it
should be so temporary a state of things,' and they
never seemed to say anything ordinary, and having
stayed on to tea they left me wondering whether they
were precocious, clever, precious, cunning or angels . . .

(two years later) Mary Borden came for the night and within ten minutes of her arrival was up to the neck in paper and a new novel in the little room where H. G. W. had written. Evidently she has the egg urge like E. P. Warren who, when passing down a street in Boston turned suddenly into an unknown grocer's shop and without a word, I followed him, started to write out an 'A. L. Raile' poem on the counter. Anyhow, she has undertaken to write a story for my *Omnibus*, and I heard her telephone to General Spears that 'Mr Fothergill had just given her a job!' How different it would be putting out to sea in a boat with eighteen women novelists from with as many women politicians!

Public Services

They asked me if I would stand for the Urban District Council, so I assented very reluctantly. After having been posted up, a deputation of two men, one himself a councillor, representing a 'number of people', perhaps mythical, perhaps only the Councillor himself, came to me in the garden and asked me if I, who was the only candidate, would stand down and so save an expensive election (technically wrong, I believe). I got them to admit that their mission implied that they thought the possibility of my replacing one of the present Councillors was not worth £25 to the town, even once in a century. I told them to go back and do an honest day's work ... I'm glad to have got in ... Finding that their meetings are held at the time our dinner began I have resigned, and by way of redemption decorated the Council Room worthily of their work.

We've had lots of honeymoons and have been the

field of at least three engagements, but more touching
than these was when Curtis Brown and C. B. Fernald,
having suffered from a mutual grievance and silence
for many years, made it up and came here for their
feast of reconciliation.

'Gastronomic Specialities'

The place with its *spécialité gastronomique* is at least
one better than the place with none, but you can't
make a meal of *écrevisses* alone, or Grasmere ginger-
bread, Rouen duck, Edinburgh rock or Westminster
school pancake, or *pâté de canard d'Amiens*, especially
as, in these speciality places, the rest of the food is
extra meaningless. But where is it, besides here, that
you get intention in *everything*? When I took this
shop, I thought round for all the things I had found
best wherever I'd been and sent for them. So Kate pays
regular bills for food stuff in Athens, France, Norway,
Jaffa and Italy. And of English things we have daily
from three bakers three different kinds of bread made
from flours that I have forced upon them, besides the
breads we make ourselves, cheese from East Harptree,
salt from Malden, mustard from Leighton Buzzard,
sausages, after a romantic search all over England,
from Glenthorn in Thame, books from the Book Society, bacon, found by accident, from the International
Stores, (for their ugly branch here they tore down part
of the most remarkable building in Thame, the Bird
Cage Inn: an obscenotaph to Lord Devonport), and
despite the trouble, the net result upon the patient is
that he is alive to something very different in the food.
Real food *is* a surprise, and simply because the gastric
juices fly out to it, whilst they hold back aching at the

aromalessness of synthetic, poor or adulterated products. Surely this is better than buying all your stuff
from a 'Hotel Purveyor', making out your quantities
required on a big list — butter, coffee, coal, caviare,
paraffin, all tasting the same and all wrapped up in
Marie Stopes paper, even the coal. Surely this is
better and more difficult than having one *spécialité
gastronomique*?

Konody brought a big party to tea, including Sigmund
someone, Hungarian painter, who did a quick drawing
of me, and be it now on record that I have, in the last
five years only, become ugly and rugged in face, and
the top of my head is nearly bald. Such a rapid break-
up could only be expected after five years of this place.
Thank Heavens, Kate doesn't show the same. Fifteen
years ago I was the best-looking and worst-mannered
gentleman in London, and now I am the worst-
looking and best-mannered thing in Thame. 'Don't
you know John Fothergill?' said Robbie Ross to someone, twenty years ago. 'Why, he's the worst-mannered
man in London, but when you know him well, he's far
worse.'
    Sometimes I get badly sold when fishing for conso-
lation. But this lonely evening I felt I had the right to
expect some little expression of comfort from a man,
apparently a Cambridge don. He had push-biked 75
miles and was in for 70 miles to Cambridge the next
day. He had had a very good dinner, and was sitting alone before a big fire in a big very pretty pink
drawing-room, so I said apropos of nothing, 'How did
you come to this benighted place; had you heard of
it?' — 'Oh just convenient.' — 'Well, yes, I suppose it *is*

exactly half-way.' – 'Yes, it was either this or Oxford, and I dislike towns,' and there I left it, feeling small and uneducated.

This evening's grandee to dinner was the Prince of Baden. I must say the three or four high Germans we have had here, he, von Berthold, Baron von Halem (6 ft 6 in.), and Baron von Dörnberg, (6 ft 9 in.) are remarkably lovely people, and, I think, more sympathetic and delicately mannered than the average titled English young gentleman, and they look cleaner and healthier. E. P. Warren agreed with me about this, but he thought the rest of the Germans infinitely inferior to *our* rest.

An Evening at Corpus

I dined with Ned Warren (Hon. Fellow) at Corpus last night. Towards dinner time you stand in suspense near your open door till the bell goes; then you have to rush feverishly downstairs into the quad, where you join a row of dons, old and young also running, as if greedily, in the darkness. I can't think what would happen if you were late. Ned was always frightened himself. Apropos of something or other, I asked Dr Schiller at what juncture the old lady *did* cease to lift the calf over the gate. 'I suppose', he replied in thin mandarin voice, 'she went on until the animal lifted *her* over it.' After dinner (and *mind* you bring your dinner-napkin under your arm) you stroll back through the quads to the Combination Room. Here, in horseshoe form, pretty Regency chairs face a roaring fire with ugly little light oak pedestal tables in front of each couple of chairs with two pretty green Swansea dessert plates for your biscuits and wine. You take a fresh partner for this,

and alongside, not *vis-à-vis*, you sit with him, 'perhaps
a friend, perhaps a jealous foe', monophilously till the
end. At dinner one doesn't mind being glued to one
person, but over port and smokeless it could be rather
trying. Fortunately, I got kind Professor Clark, who
years ago gave me his genial treatise on the Latin
cursus in English prose and tonight some wonderful
claret. He told me of the Paris restaurants he knew, e.g.
the Brasserie Universelle, 'noted for its number of *hors
d'œuvres*, but if they omit to bring the *pâté de foie gras*,
you must ask for it, "*Garçon, pâté, s'il vous plaît,*" and
then they bring various cheeses on a board – very nice'.
Professor Clark knows all about wine and buys it for
the College, and whatever you say to him is always
slightly wrong and requires correction or a gentle
warning.

A highly respectable Scotsman, Mr Paterson, of
Beaconsfield, dined with his beautiful wife and two
good-looking daughters. I told him that with his immense car and every possible gadget, he had only gone
back after all this evolution to the snail state by taking
his house with him, but I asked him if Company's
Water was laid on. 'No,' he said, 'I think we have each
our own private supply.' I smiled doubtfully, but looking back through the glass door I saw him having
a good rude giggle over it with his wife and family.

Two altercations today on a busy overworked Sunday: (1) a Jew boy of most horrible appearance is to
report me to the RAC for my treatment of him for
coming in off the road and using the inside lavatory
without asking, and (2) a semi-drunk Oxford tradesman is to do the same for my telling him not to sit on

one of his two tarts' knees in the Common Room . . . The Jew boy didn't report, the other did and regretted his trouble.

Cruelty Last

Talking to mild-natured Robin Skirving, who is so tall that he leans elegantly with his elbow on the top of the 6 ft 6 in. office door, we deplored the necessity of sending sensitive children to school to see or to be submitted to injustice. The child is born with no thought of injustice – once he sees it he is shocked and might ever afterwards expect it everywhere, but he says nothing about it nor complains. My own experiences illustrating this were: (1) When five years old my stepmother told us a little canary had told her we had been seen rolling on the pavement in Leamington, which was a lie. (2) On my first morning at prep school, aged 10, I read out 'Horatius "Cockles" ' and the HM, whipping the cane out of his desk, sprang up and gave me three across the back, with 'Enough of this silly old joke!' (3) As little boys we watched this fellow, taking turns with the cleverly invited father of a boy, a townee aged 17, cane him terribly (the HM took a run each time) for some not heinous offence against some of us, and the boy never uttered a sound, and not one of us sickened little spectators, I am sure, ever reported to our homes this vicious assault. Robin Skirving's was, I think, the only letter that *The Times* published in connection with the recent Public School suicide that wasn't either 'hearty' or vested interest. His was mild, mine wasn't. Some time ago a man – I wish I could remember who – surprised me by saying, 'One day, I imagine, there will be no cruelty.' I have since thought what tremendous scope there would be for a 'Kindness First' or 'Cruelty Last' movement, not only for schools and homes where they dare to touch the skin of a child because they are too stupid or bad-tempered to teach his mind, but in so many other directions not covered by legislation.

G. B. Stern came with a party to lunch, simple, sympathetic and handsome. She seems to have the kindness of Storm Jameson and Clare Neilson. D'Oyley Carte has just given me her racy *Bouquet* in her inimitable woman's style, with nothing but bottles of vintage wines for a plot.

Eight up-to-date obscenobitic types of eight sexes came to dinner, and luckily they came very late when most of our diners had gone. The loudness of their stupid semi-drunk innuendo and stomachic guffaws was too much for me. I asked one of them to keep them quiet. 'Why, is there a service on?' asked her semi-female neighbour. I replied 'Yes.' To save their ears I withdrew Lord Clonmore, Hughes and two other quiet little theological students into the little dining-room, and had to leave the three remaining lay undergrads, Best, McElwee and another to take their chance, but these told me afterwards that they hadn't noticed the loud party, having been deep all the time in a religious argument! whilst the young theologians perhaps felt like ladies sent out of the room after dinner. As soon as the house was empty four apparently quite nice people arrived, recommended by Sir ——— ———, and took four single rooms, only two of which they quickly monopolised with a deal of mixed bathing. I never looked at them again for the rest of their two days' stay till one of them said to me, 'Mr Fothergill, you know we are going this evening?' and I replied 'Yes, good,' and made off, for once too bored to argue my convictions.

Dr A. H. Church, Director of Botany, Oxford, came the other day to tea with his daughter and now sends me his volume *Succession of Wild Flowers in Oxfordshire.* In spite of recording his appalling knowledge with the mind of a Blue Book writer he has the light green soul of a gardener and with the help of his living photographs the book *is* the countryside; wherever it goes you have your nose on the ground; lawn and water plants, weed heaps and hay fields rush past you in their course from Spring to Winter with their Latin names.

It's their bloody dog of an Alsatian which has got between me and the Adam Chetwynds who are really as nice as could be. Chetwynd was telling me how admirable our staff was, how even better than private house staff. May Stratford and Gladys Lindars have all the charm and goodness of the Lomas family, and I here and now bless them all for being what they are, leaving us free to trouble about the twopenny difficulties and problems of every little matter. How did two rather nice Irish people come here for ten days? Mrs Tullock and Miss Eason, daughter. They were in the Times Book Club and asked about hotels of one of the assistants who said she had heard this place was very fine. So, she told Chetwynd, she telephoned here and all she got was a man's voice saying, 'Good God, I can't hear a word, I wish you'd write instead.'

Beazley and Mrs Beazley arrived for ten days, never

having been here before. She brings a dog, so we have two in the house now and this one barks when anyone passes her door. Mrs B. more voluble and kinder than ever, B. more than ever abstracted. He went to London today to buy Greek vases, and Mrs B. sent him a telegram to Sotheby's sale-room to remind him of his train home. I was told that in the Judge's Lodgings, which they have, there is no overflow pipe to the bath. So Beazley goes into the bath with four books, and, nicely timed, Mrs Beazley goes in and turns off the water just before it runs over the top. It's nice to think that Beazley should fundamentally have upset sixty years of German archaeology in Greek vases, and Furtwaengler wrote for thirty years with both hands and a sewing machine they used to say.

An AA Member's Complaint

A man with three others came to Sunday lunch and with champagne, his bill was £7 10s., waving which in the air he ran into the hall to show me. 'Look here, Mr Fothergill, what is this 24s. for four lunches – it's an imposition.' Somehow I felt there must have been a mistake, but his suddenness put my back up. 'Well, it's worth 6s. isn't it?' – 'It's a try-on, and I'm going to report it to the AA,' waving the little green book in my face, '3s. 6d. is quoted as your price.' – 'It's worth 10s. as compared with the meals of other hotels. I shouldn't report it if I were you.' – 'Yes, indeed, I'll have it out with you through the AA.' – 'Oh, please don't do that; you see it's Whitsun.' – 'That's simply a try-on – probably because my nephew hung his cap on the electric-light bracket?' (I had indeed asked him to take it off as it didn't harmonise with the scheme of decoration.) –

'Oh, not at all, I assure you. But I beg you, really, don't report me to the AA.' – 'That I intend to do, it's an imposition. I shall go through with it.' – 'But don't.' – 'I shall.' – 'Because I have no connection with the AA whatsoever.' – 'But here's their book and here you are.' – 'Yes, but I severed my connection six months ago because of my inability to provide their multitudinous members with water-closet accommodation free of thanks.' Thus flummoxed, I held out my hand to him saying I hoped we parted as friends; and so we parted, I'm sorry, apparently for ever. After that it wasn't necessary to find out what the mistake had been.

Academic Good Taste

Charles Plumb and Birley, of BNC, had last night a most charming party of seven – four scholars, after their finals, and three dons. I gave them our best china and silver. Plumb, three to four years ago, was a trying person, now he is an urbane and distinguished young man. Birley I'd never met before, he is splendid. When he came again he endeared himself to me at a very crowded time by saying, 'This is the only place in London where you can lunch decently on Sunday.' Maurice Platnauer, epicure, was one of the dons.

Miss Harbottle, the gay, good-looking bursar of Lady Margaret Hall, whose fellows are having dinner here at their Jubilee, told me that Oriel kindly lent them all their records of their Tercentenary doings, at the end of which was, '. . . the Provost and Fellows went to the Spreadeagle, Thame, where Mr Fothergill gave them an excellent dinner'. It's nice to think that this archive will exist for another 300 years, though not I nor this place.

After having served breakfast to 150 people in the previous 1¾ hours, sitting down to our own breakfast – I with a double-brandy – it seems like a nightmare from which we have just woken up to find everything in the house quiet and in order as ever. We have had eleven hundred dinners in the last thirty days, with the same establishment that does an average of three hundred.

Oliver Baldwin came to dinner with four. He often comes and always is host, and always brings nice people. Today I deprecated Socialism to him, having just had a slang at a kitchen boy for 'disgusting, culpable negligence, a sly, sulky, evasive, plausible, shamming, slippery type'. – 'Then he must be a Tory,' said Oliver; 'I'd like to speak to him.' – 'I'm sure he's not,' I said, 'he's the sort who would be Labour and betray that side too.' But Oliver said that this type will be still worse off under Socialism but, of course, they would be accompanied by a lot of the now rich worthless people who, I submitted, would be in such a minority that no appreciable change would have taken place.

Young Eyres-Monsell has been staying here. He is an imperious noisy lad with a soft Chinese-eyed graceful nature. He has recently got notoriety by having a duel at Oxford in Victorian costume, and being fined by the Proctors. He'll get on very well.

In Oxford I saw old Mr Jones of Franklin and Jones, Estate Agents, one who would have been a success elsewhere with another upbringing. I've not seen him for three years. He was sitting in his Austin Seven alongside of his chauffeur outside Frewin Court. I went up and said, 'How do you do, Mr Jones?' – 'Pardon me, would you be so kind as to tell me who you are.' – 'My name is Fothergill.' Then he turned over to his chauffeur and said, 'Robert, this is Mr John Fothergill, of the Spreadeagle, Thame. He has, with his great knowledge and exquisite taste, transformed that old place into all that is most beautiful and desirable, he has etc. etc. etc., and now he wishes to bid me good day,' then, turning back to me, 'Good day, Mr Fothergill,' and off they drove.

Shrub Hunting at Pendell

Lady Pollock had a lovely Irish father who one day invited the elderly Sir Thistleton Dyer and Sir Theodore Hooker to Pendell to choose whatever of his trees and shrubs they liked for Kew. After having fared very sumptuously at dinner and slept well, Sir Thistleton Dyer and Sir Theodore Hooker went out into the Park after breakfast, replete with tea and toast, to inspect and make their choice. 'That's a good *Sambucus nigra pyramidalis*, Thistleton,' said Sir Theodore. – 'Yes, Theodore, but look at your old *Sarcococca Hookeriana Digyna.*' – 'Well,' interrupted the kind Mr Bell, 'take the lot, if you want them.' – 'We'll do our best, Mr Bell,' they exclaimed in duette. – 'What a splendid *Salix Babylonica ramulis aureis*, Theo.' – 'Yes, I wish we could grow them like that at Kew. But I bet you don't know that, Dyer.' At that moment a hunting horn was heard over the trees. 'Gentlemen, hounds!' exclaimed Mr Bell. 'Yes, indeed, Mr Bell,' replied the gentlemen. 'Yes, Theodore, I do know it, it's *Rosa omeiensis pteracantha*, and what wonderful red translucent spines!' – 'Gentlemen, won't you come out with the hounds? It's a splendid morning.' – 'Ha, ha, Mr Bell, I'm afraid not. Theodore, do you think we could move that *Prunus Laurocerasus parvifolia Hartogia capensis* to Kew?' – 'But', broke in Mr Bell, 'Sir Theodore and Sir Thistleton, I promised to hunt today. Won't you just throw your legs across a horse?' – 'Ah, Mr Bell, thank you so much, but when did you graft your pretty little *Thuya orientalis rosedalis compacta?*' But between the little party and the stables there was a collection of that most remarkable of Wilson's and Edwin Beckett's discoveries, the *Viburnum rhytidophyllum Aldenhamense*, and by the time Sir Thistleton could say *Thuya orientalis rosedalis compacta* Mr Bell had dodged round the *Viburnum rightyo-phyllums* with their bold wrinkled shining leaves and their once brilliant scarlet fruits, now turning black, and was never seen by them again. Mrs Bell had already started for town, to which the distinguished botanists also returned after lunch.

The Siren of Pasadena

An American, living in Paris, Mr Keen, came to lunch two days ago and suggested our going to Pasadena to run a restaurant. He gave me an introduction to a friend. 'If you have children leave this damned old place – excuse my expression – and', waving his hand down the dining-room, 'take your whole joint with you!' Today, he, Mrs Keen and his pretty daughter, Mrs Ellis Roberts came for the night. Like the daughter he is brimful of kindness. Kindness is not an English virtue, E. P. Warren used to say, and told how when he and a cousin of mine were shaking hands good-bye after Oxford, the cousin said, 'Well, Warren, whenever you are passing, do come and see me,' and gave him his address. E. P. W. discovered later that it was on a moor in Westmorland, nine miles from any human habitation, and there were no motors then. A German professor once told me kindness wasn't a virtue at all.

As to how we could sell out and go I consulted Colston Bush, our accountant, a scion of generations in this town. He's a generous and delightful fellow, extremely clever and up to date, but also a good demonstration of how a town like this remains as it is for centuries. He won't think outside it. When we had been here for three years he used to write me warning letters in official phrases as to the urgent and immediate need of drastic economy in expenditure. I used to argue that I was only spending money in order to make the place capable of earning it; I went on spending and he warning. Tonight he brought a balance sheet showing a profit for the first time. I asked him what chance there was of selling this Hotel. 'Well, you are certainly the best hotel in Thame.' – 'In Thame!' – 'Well, let's say in the district.' But this was a great concession to my vanity, for the 'district' to him includes as much as all the surrounding farms and villages. (I believe he has expanded to London since.) It's this obdurate insularity which makes and keeps the countryside sound; only the restless, the crook or the conceited leave places like this for London or America, not sound people like Bush; and here in Thame these nice, polite people work without ambition and almost for nothing. After the war, it must have been a wrench to them to have to double the prices because they couldn't double their labour. The farmers' ordinaries here, including our own, are still the same price (2*s*. 6*d*.) as before the war, and in one place even less.

A good little American with whom I had discussed old Boston families that we both knew put into my hand 2*s*. 6*d*. in the hall after lunch. I almost ran after him to ask about the pathology of this kind action. Harrington Mann, the artist, is an amusing and generous person, who gets more portraits than he can do in New York, spends five happy months in London and the country, gets pictures into the Academy, and has a lovely family of girls and their lovely friends – the all possible for an artist. He says I should not uproot and go to USA.

Punctures

Two dear friends married today, arrived for the night after a 100-mile journey, preceded by the telegram, 'Delayed by puncture; dinner late' – then another telegram, 'Punctures, still pushing on', and indeed it's amazing and gratifying that the poor things ever got here at all.

Sunday. A complaint from two people at a very crowded *prix fixe* luncheon objecting to paying 3*s*. 6*d*. for only fish, curiously cooked, proper cheese and the rest. The arguments for discouraging these little *à la carte* meals are (i) in a country place you don't get people eating at all hours as in the town, and since a turnover has to be made in a limited time and space, snacks have to be discouraged, especially as the snackers sit as long at the table as the *prix fixers*; (ii) being near Oxford one has to be careful not to establish this precedent or we could fill up every night by people drinking a tankard and cheese whilst perhaps others, at busy times, are waiting outside for a full ceremonial meal; (iii) it is not what you eat that costs so much as the upkeep, the atmosphere and the time you spend on it. Here these last are especially costly. In short, cheese and beer, in the dining-room at least, doesn't pay. One has to risk being thought mean or grasping.

Three Kinds of Cooking

I define three kinds of kitchen:

(i) The French, where the food doesn't taste of what it is, or ought to be, but tastes good;

(ii) English hotel, where the food, when even it is food, doesn't taste of anything, or tastes badly;

(iii) Our kitchen, and the true American, where the food is food, tastes of it, and tastes good.

Kate has made nine hundred pounds of jam this year herself.

A Joke

To some people talking about the idle rich I said, 'Well, it's something to be able to put square meals into round holes, isn't it?'

Three perfectly lovely American girls came to dinner with their Daimler hire. The leader was Miss Charlot, I think, 30 miles from New York, and the love, sentimentality and gratitude that they expended upon me was very touching and I was sorry that Kate should be all the time doing accounts and not so enjoying the fruits of our labours.

'... *square meals into round holes* ...'

Visitors' Droppings

Five poems better than the ordinary visitors' book variety:

(i) Written by E. V. Knox upon a map drawn for me by Spencer Hoffman of the district, 'showing the hills, villages, churches and the houses of the Great and Good, within some seven miles ...':

> The village of Brill
> Is built on a hill,
> When you stop
> At the top
> The great thing to do
> Is to look at the view
> From the mill
> That is marked on this map
> Produced by a chap
> Called John Fothergill.

(ii) Left by Humbert Wolfe on a piece of our writing paper:

> The paper I am writing on
> Is not as reticent as John;
> The little picture at the top
> Is not so obvious a fop;
> The thickness of its texture is
> Not half so durable as his;
> And nothing I can write upon it,
> Chant Royal, virolay, or sonnet,
> Can even imitate the art
> Of classic balance in his heart,
> Or catch the cool antarctic thrill
> Of great Queen Anne in Fothergill.

(iii) By young Parson Beevor, left behind him after lunching:

> Oh, that skill of Robert Herrick's,
> Honest praise without hysterics,
> Were vouchsafed to modern clerics;
> So might I, a motoring metic
> Hindered by no qualms ascetic
> Duly hymn your wealth claretic.
> Me vocant iniqua fata
> Ad Swindoniensia strata
> Ave, et vale, aquila lata.

(iv) Ewer sent this by Helen Gosse, vast, exultant, long-legged, beautiful, aged 19, looking 24, with a lion's mane for hair; if you were with her in St Peter's you'd find it a crush:

I have not been to Thame,
I live among the Chiltern Hills
Yet have not been to Fothergill's.
People went and people came
But no, I have not been to Thame.
It is no distance there and back
But there I might meet Bacarach,
That is not any gain or loss
But then of course there's Helen Gosse.

(v) By Johnny McNaught (Canadian) after three weeks of awful weather and dull emptiness:

L'ECLAIREUR DE THAME

Journal du Syndicat d'Initiative Thamois

26 juillet   No. 606

MONDANITÉS

LL.AA.RR. le Prince et la Princesse Odol de Bouche Propre ont traversé aujourd'hui la Route Nationale B 6301, qui n'est eloignée que de cinq kilometres de notre petite ville riante; LL.AA.RR. ne sont pas arêtés, ayant rendezvous ce soir même à Londres.

La population de Pékin est, suivant le recensement de 1846, 2,345,678.

Le ferblantier connu, M. Ernest Hodge, 23, rue Haute, était parmi l'assistance au *Cheval Noir*, à l'heure de l'aperitif ce matin. M. Hodge était accompagne de Mme. P.-P. Snooks, sa belle-mère, qui portait une des dernières créations de Penistan, en gros coton de léssiveuse, et qui est restée en dehors pour échanger les potins de rigueur avec sa connaissance pendant qu'elle dégustait une pinte de la délicieuse bière Worthington, *spécialité de la maison.*

CHRONIQUE

Le temps superbe dont nous jouissons ces derniers jours continue; on peut parler de Nice, de Rapallo, mais ou, dit M. Fothergill, le savant genial si bien connu, trouvera-t-on un climat pareille au notre? X ... Y ..., le journaliste spirituel de Stony Stratford, a designé notre coquette petite cité, dans un article docte et harmonieux, comme 'le Lido de Monsieur Fothergill'; louange fort merité, d'ailleurs, puisque chacun sait la valeur, pour notre renommé, de cet ami des fleurs et de la bonne chère (si nous pouvons nous permettre aussi une phrase hardie).

MADAME SMITH SAGE-FEMME DE 37me CLASSE: MASSAGE SOUS L'EAU

(Communiqué)

Happy thought! go back to the Lake District and extract materials from the Hotel Visitors' Books, and write historical, social, comical, tragical and pathetical treatise upon this development of mural exhibitionism, and so pay expenses.

Commercial Love

Mr Fonseca, cigar-maker of Havana and New York, whom I've never seen save on the box, with his big, black beard and fiery regard, replying to me who thanked him for his very handsome gift of cigars, writes: 'Our American friend (an American dining here who first told me of his cigars) has been the missing link between us and dear Mr Mould (his London agent) the party through whom we have been able to create a mutual devotion and I promise that I will do my best to perpetuate it. Life without friends is not worth living, and I admire those like you who plant the seed and take care to make grow the plant that bears the most sublime flower: LOVE!' Hot stuff and indeed rather a staggerer to get in the way of business, but I'm convinced that it's good stuff. There can be and is a sort of love between good maker and good dealer because like mother and child they depend upon one another for, if not their happiness in the struggle at least the means of getting it. Some such love must be the origin of a firm's calling its clients 'friends', and a commercial traveller's habit of trying to shake hands with you. In my few business dealings with Americans I've found a commercial generosity and affection that I've found rarely in England. Soon afterwards he created for the Barcelona Exhibition a real cigar, eight feet high, and never lived to see it

erected. In my time I have made two contributions to the bad cigar series of jokes. A man kept trying to converse with George Kennedy and me as he sat opposite to us at the 'Horse Shoe'. His last effort was to ask us, 'Do you mind my smoking this cigar, sir?' – 'Not at all, if *you* don't,' I replied. And once I said, 'Never put a gift cigar in the mouth.'

Bank Holiday and Lavatory Work

A man led from a big car a good-looking ill lady limping into the house, and pushed past me in my short white steward's coat, and three other people. So I followed up and asked them, it being three o'clock, if they wanted tea or lunch. 'No,' said the lady, 'the ladies' room, if there is such a thing.' The absence of a 'please' and the suggestion that there was no indoor sanitation in the house irritated me – so I waited on the doorstep. They returned and pushed past me again. When they were back in their car, I went out, signalled to the chauffeur not to start, and asked, 'Have you had *everything* you want?' — 'Yes, thank you.' — 'Ah, yes, it was only that "thank you" that I was wanting.' She looked confused towards the big man, who sat speechless and then at me, 'But I *did* say "good afternoon".' This she hadn't done in any case and she began to look more ill and distinguished than ever. 'No, you didn't, not even that — you were thoughtless,' I replied, as kindly as possible, 'like other people you think a public-house is kept up by no one for the public use; I only wanted a "thank you".' Then I turned and went back. I heard a plaintive voice calling 'Waiter'. For an instant I wondered whether I should answer to this ridiculous title, but I turned round and held up my hand once more to the chauffeur, who had already started the car. As I got up a thin delicate hand held over to me a shilling, 'Please take this.' — 'No, thank you, I'm not a waiter,' then sweeping my hand across the whole nine-window length of the place, 'I — I own *all* this; I *really* don't want it; I only asked for a "thank you". Sometimes nice people like you do this thing, and I get irritated' — and then she looked sweeter than ever. 'But do take it, I *must* do something — it was horrible, I see it was horrible.' And the fool of a man who ought to have done all the work for her in the first instance sat tight. 'No,' I said, 'thank you ever so much — please don't be angry with me — I see you are ever so nice — please forget it, good-bye.' And I retired, sad but still convinced that people mustn't go walking into other people's lavatories like this.

360 to Lunch

For three reasons I shall always be grateful to the discriminating Ernest Beare, Sec. Govt Hospitality Fund, for whom I took on the job of lunching 360 International Congress of Orientalists, for three reasons, (i) it seemed in our line to feed 'The Wise Men of the East' as the public called and expected to find them, (ii) in Christ Church Hall and Kitchen, of all privileges, (iii) it would be an act of courage with our little kitchen staff. As function food it might have been a surprise, for there were dishes, salads, ingredients, and a quality that never get into these wretched meals. But, owing to a mistake, the thin coffee at the end, here where it ought to have been extra strong, and the hearing that the President, Sir Denison Ross, didn't get enough Cognac, has washed out for me all memory of what might have been good in the show. I only remember working in that hypaethral kitchen and the swift grace of their second chef who helped me. He cut cucumbers with the rattle of a machine-gun. The other day when I was standing outside the magnificent Hall a party of six expectant tourists from America came up. 'For seeing the Hall', said the Chief Hall porter, before opening the door, 'there is a charge per person of 2*d*.'! I'm sure I saw these 3,000 miles travellers catch their breath at such an anticlimax.

Dear old Miss Paget, 'Vernon Lee', was brought here by Miss Price. Over 70, but still with a male stride and a downright manner, one more of the last remaining promontories of the 'nineties to come here. I showed her the rock garden and said, 'Don't you think that's a good design?' – 'I don't like rock gardens, so I don't mind *how* they are designed' – rather silly, I thought, but thirty-five years ago I knew that style so well. We all had to do it; for instance, I remember myself saying once, 'The professor was so inaccurate that it was a positive increase in one's ignorance to listen to him,' and how I felt a little ashamed afterwards, though I knew it to be in the correct manner.

Cyril Barnardo, a cheerful, witty lad of over 40, told us after dinner an amazing story of how he went to America with some money, spent it all and began again at the very bottom, from navvy up to waiter when he offered to help an old professor in a restaurant to correct examination papers, and through him became a high-rank schoolmaster all in a few months. I think he works on the Charity Commission. Today, after he had been eating tea for some time, I asked him to come and see the garden. 'When I have finished tea,' he said. – 'And when will that be?' – 'In about an hour,' in his funny, sharp voice.

Johnny McNaught's Enthusiasm

Three people, a youngish father, wife and very pretty boy of 10 dined here and took the fancy of the McNaughts. Johnnie McNaught said they ought to be broadcast as the 'perfect family', so I told them this in front of him as they issued out of the dining-room. McNaught told them he felt more embarrassed than if he had said something dreadful about them. When we discovered that the latest and best Bentley outside belonged to them, McNaught said, 'These are evidently God's chosen and God went to Bentley's and said, "I want an extra special car made for some people I know."'

*

To two maiden ladies who enquired of the price-to-be of everything, and who asked what we charged for an Austin Seven per night, I said, 'If you care to take it up to your bedroom, there will be no charge for garage.' I would like to have added that it might also be of use if they attached a handle to it.

As the Sultan of Muscat is to dine here on Saturday, I ought to write to all the journalists I know to have it well advertised. Why don't and can't I? It may be vanity or pride that prevents decent people shouting out their wares, or it may be merely confidence in the good wine and bush adage, or it may be that one is primarily and always preoccupied with *doing* the thing and having no time or mood to advertise it. Finally, with regard to advertising, I feel that each decent person who comes here feels more or less, or ought to feel, that it is his own discovery or property, and that for him to see it publicly advertised would be to put him off and make me seem disloyal to him. The Muscat came with his Arab ADC, Bertram Thomas, Prime Minister, and Ernest Beare and others, including a perfectly good black slave, in two double-six Daimlers that swung down upon us like great racing locomotives with little flags fluttering in the bows. We had them in the little dining-room looking most excellent with real silver and china, a fire (being summer) and incensed air. Katie heard Thomas say he would rather dine here than at Claridge's, whilst the Sultan, had he come here at the end of his two weeks' tour in the British Isles rather than at the beginning, might have welcomed the event as a relief from the other places. We gave them eleven courses, and I doubt if, chiefly by reason of the Fair being still on, there has ever been so big a crowd to see an individual in Thame as what was waiting to see that Sultan off . . . Beare writes that it was the star turn of the tour.

Being frightfully hot today I descended upon a rich and pompous old stockbroker type who came from London with his friends to lunch with 'What a treat it must be for you to come out into the country after playing half-naked in those hot slums!'

A conceited young man shouted out to me over his shoulder when I was half-way down the room, 'Mr Fothergill, come and tell us what shall we drink?' On the way there, I asked pretty Mrs Raymond Greene how one could answer a person like that, and she said 'poison'.

Three Poets

A delightful trio to miss when we were away was
Gerald Gould, Humbert Wolfe and Garvin's daughter,
who came out to dinner. This will have been one of our
most desirable dinner-parties, and now left to the imagination only. 'How sorry John will be to have missed
me,' exclaimed Umbo upon entering, to the assembled
room. Farouche, Leith-Ross called his appearance, and
I find it frightfully attractive. And I feel that for some
reason or another Umbo has never dared to write what
he really feels and, instead, must be clever or funny
and pretend to be vain. At the dinner we gave to Will
Rothenstein, I told Umbo that he ought to reply to the
toast of the 'Unknown Guest', which I thought was
even funnier than anything in his own speech later.
Gordon Bottomley came during the same absence, so I
sent him a copy of Plantin's sonnet *Le Bonheur de ce
Monde*, printed in his studio in Antwerp, as the nearest
most appropriate thing for this exquisite master,
'printed as nobly as poetry should be,' as he wrote from
Silverdale, 'I enclose a little canticle of me by way of
rejoinder. I would that it were finely printed too, to
make it better worth your having . . . This has been a
miracle of a December for sun and light and wind; it
has taken us more than once to the rocky shore that
you knew as a boy, on mornings of golden creamy haze
over the miles of water and sand.' This is not Innkeeping – it's getting too much for nothing.

Two Actors

Nicholas Hannen, Athene Seyler and Hazel Kennedy,
two actors and sculptress, have been for the weekend.

The actors seem to wear no sign at all of the stage or the actors' vagabundity, their charm, modesty and deference indeed were so great that it even seemed insincere. But Hannen once was a pupil under Lutyens. Moreover, the following was above suspicion. At lunch today, Mrs Kennedy said, 'I would like some coffee.' Then Hannen bravely became spokesman, 'Mr Fothergill, do you disapprove of coffee being drunk after a meal?' – 'Why, of course not.' – 'Because after lunch yesterday we overheard you calling to the waitress "Three cough-mixtures over there please," and we thought you were contemptuous of it and we haven't dared to ask for any since,' which from three very talented, popular and successful people is indeed Christian humility. This evening I telephoned a message to Hannen that I missed them badly.

Another Austin Seven

We were standing near the archway entrance whilst a most awful noise of motor-car was going on inside, then a sudden and complete silence, then out shot an Austin Seven and I quoted the dear old *parturiunt montes . . .*

The Doll's House

Mr Doll, a most handsome old gentleman, who designed the Russell Hotel and a heap of other things in that neighbourhood, told me the story of his family home in Sloane Street. His mother was born in it in 1811, died in it, and his eldest brother took it over. When the ninety-nine years was up, his brother was allowed by the agent of the Earl of Cadogan to renew it for fourteen years at the same rent on condition that

they built on another storey. When the other storey
and the fourteen years were up, old brother Doll, now
almost 80, asked for a renewal, and he was told the
rent would be just nine times the old rent. So this
Mr Doll here wrote personally to the ancient Earl of
Cadogan saying that his old brother was living on his
pension, and could not afford that rent. Lord Cadogan
wrote back at once saying that their connection with
the Cadogan family had been the longest in its record
and possibly anywhere in London, and that he would
like his brother to live there to the end of his life,
which he hoped would not be for a long time, and that
he could have it at no rent or at any figure he liked to
name, and that his solicitors would submit the papers
to him to fill in that sum or none at all. They made it
out for five years in consideration of his age, and just as
the expiring lease was being renewed the old man,
aged 85, expired also. But how move the ancient
widow? It was the new Lord Cadogan now who wrote
that, having read the history of the case, he would like
the widow to remain there so long as the house was
standing. All the others have gone and this stands
alone between two houses that were not pulled down
because that might endanger the Doll's house, but
were transformed into grand flats, and the top flat of
one of them is held at a fine old price. This story could
be worked into a moral for or against Socialism.

Four bright young persons went out after dinner and
kept me up last night till a quarter to two a.m. whilst
they just ambled round the country in the warm night
with their terrific car. On their return there was no
suspicion of thanks or excuse but one of them said, 'It's

more than five years since I was here last.' – 'Well,' I replied, 'and it does seem just about that length of time that I've been waiting up for you.' 'But haven't you anyone to hel— help you?' he murmured. 'Now *do* you think it would pay me to keep a night porter here for you to come and do this once in every five years?' And so the thing passed off pleasantly. Nice young people, no doubt good at heart and certainly good at car, but what b—y manners!

Four becowled monks came early to dine from an Anglo-Catholic monastery and sat like four black pyramids round the table they were to dine at two hours later. When the girl came in with my own make of incense to stink the room out I said to them, 'Please do not think this is meant in imitation of one of your own attractions, though I imagine we each of us have the same purpose in using it, viz., that people, when

they come into our places from the common street, should feel at once a very different atmosphere, hence an appetite for something exquisite and different, whether or not they will get it.' Two days ago Blackie, a master at Bradfield, a very nice man who had stayed a night here once, wrote to ask me where he could obtain this 'burning material', as they had a 'dirty puppy' in the house which had to be counteracted, to which rather tactless enquiry I gave my receipt and told him not to waste it on a dirty puppy.

Michael Scott, undergrad at New College, had a big party here with Czernikoff and Eric Marshall previous to his conducting the London Orchestra at Queen's Hall. Kate and I went to hear him and were mightily taken by this slim and agile, almost 'cat-like' youth displaying all the movements of the old and tried, but with a wonderful grace and quickness. I don't know if he has ideas or pleased his players. To me it seemed that First Violin smiled rather too sweetly all the time. If he has ideas, it must be a change for these rather worn-out looking musicians to play to a young undergraduate. 'Anyone can take over that orchestra for the hiring of them,' said someone to me. Yes, but who's got the courage? . . . I don't think M. S. would have the courage now, 2 years later, because he has been learning the job in Vienna ever since.

The Rev. A. C. Iremonger, wonderful good fun, late editor of the *Guardian*, sent me a bottle of Château Lafite 1858, comet year, the greatest wine of the last century, and interesting as being the first claret mentioned by George Saintsbury in his *Cellar Book*, which has now as much material appeal as Pausanias's descriptions of works of art that no longer exist. The bottle has a double coat of arms, probably the Duke of Bedford's, stamped on it, and the label was written by hand. He bought it at the sale of the Foundlings' Hospital. The wine was not only drinkable, but delicate and aromatic.

Charles Evans, a hardy periodical here, for gossip, sweet-natured . . . he also agrees with me about the beauty and lackadaisical fascination of Mrs Hugo Pitman. His sister-in-law Esther is one of our best-looking and nicest patients.

An attractive lad who used to be at Oxford wrote from Paris for a good double room for the weekend. Apprehensive, I wrote that I'd be 'delighted to see him and his wife, or was it a male friend?' So he arrived, and, before the lady came by a later train from London, I discovered that the relationship was a temporary one and explained that such trade wasn't ours, so they passed on to another hotel at my suggestion. I thought that if a lad, who, though he may be thoughtless in his choice of a hotel for his amours, couldn't take such a direct hint as that which I gave him in my letter, he deserved a little discomfort. But he turned out to be not so thoughtless after all; he told me that my remark had given him to think a bit and in the end he had concluded that 'if Mr Fothergill hints at a male friend surely he wouldn't mind a female one!' And we parted friendly.

Love Me, Love My Pub

Evelyn Waugh gave me a copy of his *Decline and Fall*, inscribed to 'John Fothergill, Oxford's only civilising influence', by far the nicest thing that has ever been said to me here; and against this Mrs Rita Atkinson,

Humbert Wolfe's sister, who has turned into a cheerful and generous Yorkshire lassie, writes to Kate that next time they'll bring a Radio of great power and other things and loose people with which 'just to brighten dear John's ideas for him a bit – bless his simple outlook on life'. The fact is, though my objection to indiscriminate couples is perhaps a conventional one, for respectability's sake, I never did care for the idea of specialists here, hunting men, golfers, hearties, and card fiends, and aren't indiscriminate couples specialists also? I like people here primarily for this place, rather than they should come for irrelevant obsessions.

A wet Sunday and with seating for 60 we lunched 103, plus eleven chauffeurs. Evan Morgan said he'd never seen so many people in so small a place. He didn't make it any better himself by bringing down his Australian crow which ran amok and pecked girls' ankles, having first laid an egg upstairs on his dressing-table.

A modest, good little man called Billam brought Maurice Child, Eric Dean and a lot of other Anglo-Catholics to rather a good dinner. Curious thing this power of Maurice Child over young men and old ones, appearing himself so rosy and comfortable, albeit he has the quick, bright eyes of a mouse. Iremonger said he was very fond of Maurice Child so long as he didn't turn up to breakfast without warning, which he will do at a country parsonage in England, having dined the evening before in some gloomy castle in Austria.

Almost all separately and by coincidence we have for this weekend Guy Chapman (author and ex-publisher), Storm Jameson (author), Bertram Christian (author and publisher), Oliver Simon (Curwen Press and publisher), Humphries (Country Press), James (architect and author), Geoffrey Toulmin (writer), Margaret Lane (on the *Daily Express* and very pretty), and their wives. After dinner, these heroes of the three interdependent trades who from their offices and homes have for long enough done one another down, each man knowing the other's business, now confronted one another in a neutral drawing-room quite speechless. Oliver Simon asked Guy to play Bridge, but Guy wouldn't, so Simon gave it up and came down to the Office; then others broke loose and went into other rooms. Ultimately they all got upstairs together again, and things, I believe, went well. Colonel Freyberg, Mrs and their little boy from Summerfields came to lunch, nice people who treat me with affection. I asked the boy if he liked school. 'Oh yes,' he replied. 'Good Heavens!' said Colonel Freyberg to this brave effort to say the right thing, apparently knowing the contrary. Then I told them of the Gibbons' sons at Stowe. I asked one of them, 'How do you like Stowe?' – 'Oh, as much as I'd like any school.' – 'But it's a very good school, isn't it?' – 'Very, I should think, yes, very,' was the abstracted reply as if he was quite dissociated from the place; and, indeed, how should a boy feel otherwise even about Stowe School with parents and tastes and a home like theirs.

Anthony, aged 7, who has recently made a fetish of me, said to me this morning, 'Oh, you've a lovely face!' – 'Do you call that lovely?' said John, who, belonging to the opposite camp, is unprejudiced.

Prevision and John Fernald

John Fernald brought Mollie Kidd to dinner and announced their wedding and their coming here for a twenty-four hours' honeymoon. J. F., though he is modest and delicate and grateful and sweetly mannered, convinces me as one who will do very well. He has obviously a very clear prevision of what he intends to do, viz. play producing. He was precocious enough to make the OUDS do Rostand's *Fourteenth July* and to produce it and in his quiet, quick way he will go on. He seems to have his knife and fork into his bit of future. To explain the success or failure of people I have always thought that each man is his own clairvoyant: foreseeing his future, whether a success, muddle or failure, he makes for it with no digression. In my own case, in this Inn, for instance, I can look back on certain wise decisions taken or things done (even the very taking of it) that are now so in harmony with the present state of the place, which, since I had no materials or experience to go upon, must have been a consistent series of flukes unless explained by clairvoyance. It's the same with failures. Last Christmas I asked a loafer who used to hold horses and now holds automobiles, to get me some port bottles. He knows every empty bottle in the town, and I promised him three times the price he would have to pay for them. 'I'll do my best, Mr Fothergill, I can't say more than that, can I?' He never got me a single bottle. He foresees failure and idleness in which he is a genius, and to digress once from this line might start the bad habit that would make of him even yet a Henry Ford, no less a genius in his way. Look at Beverley Nichols (you couldn't look at a nicer thing), and I never met a young man with a clearer prevision of his future; if he hadn't foreseen that he was going to be sometimes greatly witty and even thoughtful, how could he ever have written *Twenty-five*? And if the public hadn't also foreseen it how could they have bought the book? It was merely a step in his, to him, clearly marked path, he really couldn't avoid it.

Well-aired Beds

Thank God, we don't get people here now who ask if the beds are 'well-aired'. I had a stock method of dealing with these. I began with the Socratean method, 'What do you mean by "well-aired"?' 'Well, have the windows of the rooms been opened or has anyone slept in the beds recently, and all that sort of thing, I suppose?' – 'Well,' I would reply, 'I imagine the dampness or dryness of the beds is that of the surrounding atmosphere, and even if you do shut the windows on damp days sooner or later the house and beds would become damp in spite of your efforts, even if you had all the beds in front of the fire every day. As for your other point, I would submit that after a bed has been slept in it is wetter than it was before by the amount of moisture the sleeper has exuded from his person during the night.' After this there would remain the choice of risking our beds or going somewhere else where the obsequious and stupid answer comes quickly: 'Yes, sir, our beds are all thoroughly well aired, and in constant use.' The preoccupation, or rather prejudice, about well-aired beds must have some origin, however, and this perhaps in a period when the washing was dried with difficulty in wet weather. But now in the modern laundry, the few shreds that survive the washing are at least dried to tinder in a perfectly efficient apparatus.

Three Jokes

At lunchtime I saw a don going upstairs, I called him down, 'The man's lavatory is outside in the yard. You see, I have to try to segregate the males from the females,' to which, in the appropriate thin high drawl, he replied, 'I hope – you – may – succeed – Mr – Fathergill,' which, of course, discourages my anti-biological world-mission. Sydney Wood, Ministry of Education, told me that his namesake in the same Ministry, who comes here with Jock Lemaître, was staying with one of the Percy family, and, looking round in church, and seeing nothing but Percys in the pews, Percys on the walls, and Percys under the ground, was surprised that the parson didn't begin with 'Almighty and most Percyful God' . . . which was as nice as the shy curate's dream (in perhaps similar surroundings) that he read out 'To God the Father, the Son and the *Morning Post*.'

The Little Red Dog

A dinner-party of old-timers — young Oxford bloods returned — host, an American lad now writing a book on the American in Paris, a quiet, lovable person — guests mainly peerage — delightful ones. They were rather noisy, on little, but good, wine — they picked their food. Katie told me that the beautiful Lady —— got on to the ground somehow and that they left her there. Anyhow, it wasn't the noise of Maidenhead and you knew that it wouldn't end in beastliness ... (Later, 1 a.m.) The silly part of it is that Lord H—— has left behind him his little red dog and we have now got the poor beast in our bedroom, much complaining, and they haven't even telephoned about him ... The American told me that he began his 500-page book because he had told his parents that he was going to write one, and up till the third chapter he hadn't the vaguest notion what he was going to write about, when it suddenly cleared up and he had now only to write away ... (1.5 a.m.) Lord H—— telephoned 'Have we his dog?' — 'Yes, quite happy.' — 'Do you mind if we come back for him?' — 'Yes, do come.' ... Presumably they are in Oxford still and will be back in half an hour ... (2.15 a.m.) It gets cold hanging about and I feel simple to have imagined that an English aristocrat would have started out at once instead of treating me as a night porter, or would he like to remember *me* if he could forget his dog? And yet my memory of his grandfather and his grand face gives me confidence in the peerage ... it strikes 2.30 and I feel that of all feats of service since we have been here (soon after we got here I opened the door at midnight to two bookies, one

of whom was sick in my face), this one is the rottenest –
unless they have broken their necks, as Kate suggests,
in rushing to our and the little red dog's release. And
yet . . . I've nothing to say . . . I get back into bed . . . I
get up again, bringing my 'Tired Note-book' with me
down into the Office . . . (4 a.m.) I put a notice on the
front door '4 a.m., DOG will wake me if you knock
HARD' . . . I go to sleep . . . (8 a.m.) I wake, no one could
have knocked . . . (8.30 a.m.) May Stratford announces
that a chauffeur has come for the dog. 'Was nothing else
said?' – 'Nothing.' At 11.30 Lord H—— rang up and to
Kate answering it asked, 'Would you please send on a
lipstick in a little red box if it has been found about?'
And so ended the story of the little red lipstick and the
little red dog, which were left behind, here and elsewhere, and I wonder who had to wait up with the
lipstick! But Lord H—— is getting on in years now.

Geraniums and Calceolarias

When someone told me he had had a very good lunch
consisting of asparagus, lobster salad, *crème brûlée* and
herring roes, I first thought depressedly of my own
meals of odd things. But to cheer myself up I analysed
it. Asparagus, whether ex-tin or from Evesham, requires no cooking or costing, nor does lobster, and
mayonnaise could be taught to anyone in a day or two,
and the herring roes, as herrings are out of season,
must have been poured out of a tin. Then why does
that Oxford college keep a chef? And don't my odd
things, different from what one gets elsewhere, taste
better than this rigmarole? I believe they must. Once
in our early days an entire dinner for twenty-five was
brought over here from an Oxford college, including

the cook. I supplied only the soup and the sweet. All
the rest, save the saddle of lamb, which was foreign,
came out of tins, even the smoked salmon, and I wondered why they kept their white-hatted man when a
good tin-opener would have done just as well. Another
time I brought a bottle of claret to a man in mistake
for Graves and at the same time his fish course arrived
– 'Oh, that claret will do well,' he said, 'I only ordered
it because I expected salmon mayonnaise.'

The Vending Machine

'Are you the proprietor?' asked the commercial traveller. – 'Yes.' Then he made as if to shake hands, but
knowing this habit that they are taught I avoided it.
'Well, I invite you to take this little thing on for me; it
is', showing me a photograph, 'the only chemical
vending machine on the market.' – 'A *what?*' – 'A
chemical vending machine.' – 'What a horrible word,
and a wrong one too! You mean "selling machine".' –
'No, sir, it's a proper word.' – 'It isn't, it's an obscene
word,' and I made for a dictionary. Unhappily the
word was there but, as I told him, used only legally
and certainly not chemically. 'Well, sir, I suppose I'm
wrong.' – 'Then I hope you'll tell all your business
friends in London not to come out here with such an
awful word in future. Anyhow, I'm afraid I've no use
for it.' – 'But it sells quinine and bromide, aspirin . . .' –
'No, it would be no use here and wouldn't suit the
place.' – 'But, sir, we make them up so far as can be
reasonably demanded to suit *any* place. Here, for
instance, is a copy of a contract – we allow 33⅓ per
cent off the takings.' . . . The contract was for the ——
Inn at Nettlebed. 'But', I said, 'that's a tiny little pub

and in that village *everyone* has headaches.' – 'Ah, yes, but you have a much bigger population in Thame. Do you pronounce it "Tame" or "Thame"?' – '*They* pronounce it "Tame", but they don't come into this Inn. When I first came here six years ago sixty farmers used to eat a 5*s*. 6*d*. dinner for 2*s*. 6*d*. in this room here, and *then*, perhaps, I could have vended some of your vomit', and I pointed to the red-baize dining-room door, 'at this very hour – come in and see them now', and I showed him into a completely empty room with a big fire. 'Oh, yes, what a quaint room,' he said, 'but you are on the main road from Oxford to London, the AA gives it.' I took him to the map and convinced him of the reverse. 'But', he tried again, 'people coming from Aylesbury to Oxford would have to pass through here?' – 'No, they would slip through at the back of the town, Thame isn't even on its own road; besides, no one would stop at Thame even to cure a cold or a headache.' At that moment, I had to go to the telephone, and the poor vending machine took his opportunity to say 'good day'.

Katie came and told me that a couple who had had tea wanted to stay the night. I asked her if they were married, and she said 'the very pretty slip of a girl' had a ring, but as *she* had asked *him* whether he liked Players' or Wills' cigarettes, and *he* had asked *her* if she took China or Indian tea, and as he first asked for a room, then for rooms, and then for a room with a double bed, she didn't think they were married. They stayed on to dinner, saying no more about rooms. A delightful person, I should think, but there are other places for 'slips' of this kind.

Loved only Locally

It is a curious thought that I, who am known to so
many hundreds of nice people, males and females, and
like so many of them, must be thought of by them
only as a character who keeps an Inn, just as I myself have known and liked Innkeepers. Perhaps they
wouldn't want me in their own houses or think of me
as even possible there? But aren't all people esteemed
as filling a certain role, and unable to fill any other?
You like the actor on his stage, the doctor in his revolv-
ing chair, and so on; after all, don't I have towards
many of these nice people the same purely local
and temporal feelings, giving them a defined rôle as
patients? Perhaps indeed this most inclusive and interesting of all trades or professions gives you the chance,
if you have it in you, of filling a more varied rôle than
any other, and, in return, of liking more people and in
more different ways, though still in the same rôle,
as patients. It goes even further than that: doctors,
lawyers and accountants are visited for temporary ail-
ments and needs, priests and county folk only in
morbid circumstances, but Innkeepers for eating,
drinking, talking, relaxation, sleeping and all that's
good.

Two lovable fat people; Lord Elmley and Togo
Maclaurin. Togo is for the moment full of Compton
Mackenzie and his passionate fight for Scottish
independence, where he now passes, I believe, for a
reincarnation of Prince Charlie; Elmley equally romantic as a Liberal MP living in a Lighthouse.

Horrid Couple

I saw going into the little dining-room at breakfast-
time a big man with thick coat, hat and cigarette. I followed him in where there was a fire and breakfast
laid for two parties staying in the house, and a woman
in a thick fur coat already there waiting for him.
'Waiting for a trunk call.' I explained to them quite
decently that it might be unpleasant to the imminent
breakfasters when they came down to see people in
greatcoats, hats and cigarettes in that little breakfast
room. They were evidently what are commonly called
gentlefolk. 'Then where the devil do you want me to
go?' sharply rang out the woman, who had the nastiest
face imaginable. Rather staggered at this onslaught, I
explained, 'In the Common Room off the Entrance
Hall.' – 'But there's no fire – do you expect us to go in
there?' – 'Well, the Post Office or AA boxes don't provide fires,' I politely replied. – 'Oh, it's that, is it?' said
the man, turning on me a very brutal face. – 'And
now', I said, 'you're suggesting that I grudge your tele-
phoning because you don't pay for the accommodation.' – 'Not at all,' he shouted. – 'Then what did you
mean by your remark?' – 'I won't stop in your beastly
hotel,' yelled the woman, and bolted out of the house,
followed by the big brute. Ten seconds afterwards
their call came through. I ran after them and stopped
them just as they were going into the Black Horse to
abuse that also. 'Hi, do you want to take your call now
or pay for it?' The man brought out a handful of
money from his pocket, but thinking better of the loss,
followed me back, and the woman went into the Black
Horse to share *their* fire. On the way back, I told the

man I was sorry about this unpleasantness and tried to explain my point again. 'I don't agree,' he answered, and he said 'I don't agree' to everything else I said. When he had taken his call and actually put through another, and was waiting, I went up and said, 'Look here, I insist upon your understanding the situation and upon being treated properly by you. If you came to what was my private house six years ago you wouldn't have behaved like this, therefore why should you now, because I am in a public-house and care to look after the people staying in it?' But his irrelevant or evasive arguments to everything I said showed that he was a bit ashamed of himself and being a cad he tried to carry it off by fiercely shouting and looking at me with a foul expression on his loathsome face. I left him now for good. Later I found (*a*) that he had rung off a trunk call of our own for which we had to pay, and (*b*) had got Katie to send our cook out into the archway to interview them whilst we were having breakfast, and (*c*) worst of all, he didn't take the cook away with him. And this fellow gave me to reason about the common practice of buying a drink with which to compensate for having used the house for a purpose for which the landlord is not directly out of pocket, e.g. his telephone or map or w.c. or waiting for a friend. If a man uses the telephone and the w.c., and then looks round the garden, and is shown by the maid over the dining-room because he has been told it's see-worthy, and then asks for a shilling drink, he has only paid for that drink at the price paid by everyone else, leaving the amenities still unpaid for, amenities which cost the owner money and labour. These can be paid for only by charm of manner, or plain 'please' and 'thank you', just as they would be in a private house, which is an unfortunate fact for those who are unable to ask a favour and pay for it in this sort of coin. Perhaps the ungracious client and the commercial publican have between them brought about this silly and vicious practice. How often I've had to decline to give this complimentary drink to charming people, who have already treated me frankly and properly for services I've been too glad to render them!

Wade-Gery, scholar, appeared with his new wife. She, well wrapped in a rough inverted sheepskin, he, on a freezing day, blue-nosed, shivering, in a thin sweater and perfectly gigantic fur gloves with a tall speechless friend. I've had pleasant talk with Gery before, but today it seemed difficult, so I compensated by feeding them as well as I could, for which they gave thanks.

A Bad Debt

From a society woman, with an address but, I've been told, no credit, who booked rooms for her party of seven, I got a telegram three days before Christmas, saying 'Plans all changed, must come another time', and no letter followed. But there won't be another time . . . The worst of it is that the house being fully booked by her engagement, we had since refused more than that number of delightful people who had to go less comfortably elsewhere and this woman's rooms were empty all the time. She has in fact picked my pocket of the £35 offered me by these good people, whom she has also discomforted. I wrote to her but had no answer, so I leave her to answer to God and her other creditors. Almost certainly, as the result of this woman's telegram, I dreamt last night that a man picked my pocket of one shilling and I said to an Italian I was with how damnable it was, because I had no redress at all. 'What can one do?' I asked. — 'Why, go to the station-master, of course.' — 'What could *he* do?' — 'Why, slap him on the face.' — 'But that seems so unjust. He didn't take the shilling.' — 'That's all right; that's his job.' — 'How do I do it? Do I get behind him and bring my hand round on his face or face him and do it?' — 'Face him, of course.' I don't remember doing it, but soon after I was with this Italian again who was watering the garden with an enormous hose-pipe; as he was climbing up a little mound, he looked back and said, 'Here, hold the hose, will you?' and so saying he turned it full on in my face and kept it there for quite a long time, long enough to make me feel how unjust it was. Afterwards, he told me he was an Italian, and I said, 'I wish you had told me that before because I should have much preferred speaking in that language to French.'

Six days ago I asked Mr West, plumber, if he could make me a new bathroom by the end of the week; and for five days his two sons and two workmen and my own carpenter have been at work, seven of them, in the tiny room, buttock to buttock, and this evening the bathroom was declared open by John Michael in bursting asunder a barrier of toilet paper stretched across the door. So no more of 'those Bethesda mornings' as Mrs Hogarth described our one-bath condition to Lady Raleigh.

A County Supper

We had to do a dance supper in a lovely house a
longish way from here. An hour and a quarter before
embarking the eighty suppers, I found the shrimp
cream was almost solid in salt so I collected all the fish
in the house and town and all the cream, and it was
still uneatable. At the same time, I found we'd forgotten the bread rolls so urgently wanted. Rita Atkinson,
who is staying with us, vivacious, Humbert Wolfe's sister, bright faced, showing thirty-six teeth when she
laughs (which is always) undertook to make them for
us, which she, like her compatriot of old, miraculously
did, and I think they were the best part of the supper.
It made me sweat helping this salt cream and sending

it into a superb, late eighteenth-century dining-room,
30 ft long and 18 ft high, with a quarter of it coming
out again. Then there was a shortage of chicken. A
choice of at least five meats had been asked for, so I
had food for 160, and fifty out of eighty wanted
chicken. The amusing relief to all this agony and
shame was below stairs. There were some fourteen to
sixteen servants in the house, mainly Irish and Welsh,
and they seemed to care nothing about our taking possession of their kitchen — they were doing nothing
tonight, running about, screaming with laughter all
the time, being dragged about by odd men servants,
belching loud and their talk was exclusively obscene.
It gave me an idea of perfect happiness in an over-
staffed medieval establishment. Years ago at Lewes,
talking about our cook's complaint that the servants
were not behaving with the boot boy as they should in
a gentleman's house, I said to Osbert Burdett that I
should have thought that only in a gentleman's house
they *could* go the whole hog. 'No,' he replied, 'not
unless the gentleman himself be the whole hog.'

Yellow Paint

A gentleman in to lunch, looking like blood pressure
and irritability, and seeing a good many people in the
room said, 'I didn't know you were so famous.' I didn't
reply, because he seemed hurt not to have all the room
to himself. 'Why did you put that horrible yellow
paint outside the house?' I didn't answer this either.
'Doesn't it drive a lot of people away?' — 'Yes,' I replied, 'but it *sometimes* fails,' after which we became as
friends.

Time, Space and Professor Jeans

The book *Eos*, a thriller by Professor Edgar Jeans, is strangling me by its atrocious exaggerations of the universe in which we live, and, he says, are the centre of. Dear A. H. Fox-Strangways sent it me, I don't know why, perhaps he too is being strangled, but Tom Marshall and I have agreed that this horrid little book ought to be exposed, either by a parody by E. V. Knox, or by a scientific confutation. Why, the professor says that when the entire firmament has gone out in gas this world will roll round alone, lifeless and lightless immortally! I cannot find the sight of a beautiful landscape compatible with this monstrous state of affairs, much less all human relationships. Tom Marshall says it has made him believe in God, not science. I wrote to Iremonger that the conception of God was plain sailing as compared with trying to apprehend Jeans's computed size, age and future of the universe. It's a wrong-eyed conception of Eternity, this going on for ever of something, Heaven knows what, and so must any conception be simple-minded that involves time and space. How the idea of Infinity ever arose was a mystery to me even when a boy. The nearest I can get as a substitute for this dark and frightening doctrine is that infinity of time is really infinite timelessness, and infinity of space infinite spacelessness. For not only by intuition but by deducing from certain visions and previsions that I have enjoyed, I cannot conceive time or space or how ever they could be. Since there can't be any present and since the so-called future, whatever, if any, there may be of it, can't be known till it has been experienced, i.e. relegated to the past, there is only past left for us to live in. But how talk seriously even of the past when that too is all gone and done with? Our existence is timeless therefore and seems more like a pile of plates, a unit with each plate moving upon the other and the whole moving and wriggling within itself. But I can't explain what I feel. The idea of time; when did it start and how? Aren't there still happy savages as well as animals who haven't invented this oppressive doctrine? So let mechanics like Professor Jeans and his colleagues, even the gentle Dr Waterhouse, of Guy's, go on timing one another with their imaginary speed-nebulas, 'travelling' at 10,000 miles a second; they are only hurrying on the final crash after which something less silly or sickening will be found to discover life and nature for wondering mortals. The other day nice man Groom, zoologist, told me that the aeroplane constructor Dunn had written a book, *An Experiment in Time*, wherein he used dreams and visions, so I got it, hoping that he would formulate my own vague feelings. But like all scientists he soon gets into geometry and I shut the book, and await the coming of another Bishop Berkeley, to think and say in nursery language what Einstein and other calculating boys are incapable of thinking and saying. These multi-dimensional explanations of time and space are, for practical purposes, *lucus e non lucendo*. So I am content to try to think of life, i.e. myself, people, history, earth, air and all their manifestations as a mere point or unit without time or space. Less difficult and more interesting this to puzzle about than the picture of a stream rolling for ever from a source that has no beginning!

1929

People praise me for running an individual and yet decent place. To me there is no secret in it, though others might not be able to do it so well. It's only hard work and a lot of thinking, and sticking convincedly to a policy once rather blindly formulated. But I'm discontented. Our Inn cannot hang on the walls of galleries or be read in winter evenings 200 years hence for others to enjoy as we have enjoyed it.

The Commercial's Handshake

Commercial travellers, poor devils, are taught, apparently, to shake hands on arrival as one of the means of ingratiating themselves. Some of ours have had very big and damp hands, and they're offered to Kate as well as to me. But Kate some time ago invented an excellent smoke screen. When the good man is seen coming in, or when called to see him, she plucks up an

'Sorry that [our] hands are full...'

armful of books or the week's washing or any other embarrassment and marches to meet him, 'sorry that her hands are full'. Today, I saw Messrs ———'s little man coming, of 'good address', and a nice young man, but he *will* shake hands. So I warned Kate and in he came. She, with a sheaf of letters and papers in each hand and I a cardboard box in my arms containing nothing at all, advanced so to meet him. But the comedy turned instantly pathetic, because he found no hands of ours into which he could press the little Christmas offering presented by the Firm, an enormous handkerchief box in black velvet, Japanese landscape stamped, containing a dozen handkerchiefs on a false bottom pushed up from below by a high collar of cardboard and glue.

Harold Acton and Evelyn Waugh

Harold Acton for the night. He gave me his *Humdrum*, which Storm Jameson says is very witty . . . I find in it, as in his talk, a care of words and rhythms that no one has now. With the innovations of face-lifting and cocktail, it might have been written by the young author of *Dorian Gray*. Being great at Oxford is in truth beginning at the bottom of the ladder, and it's a wonder that he has come anywhere at all so soon. Evelyn Waugh, wasting his time at Oxford on himself rather than on others, with his shy propriety rapidly came through with *Decline and Fall*, the wittiest book of all time, a copy of which I keep chained to a shelf in the lavatory marked 'Private Sitting Room'. Angy Hannay (sister) has Law's *Serious Call* in hers.

Yesterday to lunch were three fourth-year undergrads,

Colin Lampson with one of his very pretty girls and a man and his wife. When I went in, long after they had all finished lunch, Lampson was arguing about the spelling of 'holiday' and, being an undergrad, would have it with two '*l*'s. I ragged him a bit and we made some harmless noise. At three o'clock the stranger woman observed to me that it was a pity people couldn't behave properly, and I said, 'I'm afraid I was really to blame.' Then in the hall we had a little talk about Clifton College, where the man had been, and I introduced him to old friend Hoffman, a Cliftonian, and away they went with several thanks for a good lunch. This morning I got from her an anonymous letter from 'London W1', saying, 'We have always looked forward to our visits to your beautiful Hotel when going West and East, but after the conduct we were compelled to sit through today it will be for the last time. We do not care for the modern style; surely it would be better for you to cater for the other.' So the woman gets me in the back. Such people make suspicious or brutish Innkeepers and shopkeepers who would otherwise be decent and sensitive.

The Heights on the Wall

In 1924 I measured David Plunket-Greene on the wall, 6 ft 8¼ in., in a lavender-coloured frock-coat. Since then only five have beaten him and taken the threatened free meal, to wit:

	In boots.	Reach.
Lieut. P. Huxham, RASC	6′ 11 3/16″	9′ 0″
Major W. T. Hay, Black Watch	6′ 11″	8′ 10″
C. T. Maslin	6′ 10 4/5″	9′ 2″
G. E. Sieveking	6′ 8 ¾″	—
Baron von Doernberg	6′ 8 ½″	—

Of women the tallest are Evelyn Pritchard, Lady Lettice Lygon and Violet Wallis, all born to blush just short of 6 ft 2 in. But the real wonder of this collection is unfortunately not in it. In reply to my appeal (see below) Mr Hill, of Hunstanton, very kindly sent me a photograph of his handsome daughter running on the beach with a friend – Evelyn M. Hill, 6 ft 7 in. in her shoes, measured by Mr Hooks, schoolmaster, Pinchbeck, Spalding.

In August 1931, thinking that this list might become after all an unofficial record of the tallest people in Britain of today – no government forms, not even the Census, demand your height, though every other detail about your person and purse is demanded – I got through the help of my friend, Reginald Harris, a front seat in *The Times* Personal Column for an invitation 'to the tallest man over 6 ft 10¾ in. in socks, in health of body and mind and preferably doing a normal citizen's work'. Lieut. Huxham was so good as to appear in response. He told me that having reached Thame but forgotten the name of the Inn to report at, he and McClellan left their car far down the street and walked, expecting to know it by a queue of giants fighting outside for a free meal and presuming that the townspeople were all waiting for him he was never so self-conscious about his height and his free meal errand when they had to go into the Black Horse and make discreet enquiries as to where he might be wanted!

I don't know that the temperament of tall men has been investigated. It would be easy to invent that, having been laughed at and perhaps kicked at school by small fry whilst their consciousness of their reach and often power has made them afraid to use it, they have become humble and yielding. The fact is these tallest men are all gracious and modest, some womanly or feminine, despite the brave efforts of Douglas Paton and Ben Greene, for instance, to appear hearties.

After having manoeuvred and measured into a space of 18 inches square over 2,000 people, distinguished for their altitude and, or, charm (a woman once asked me if it was the record of a dinner-party) I had to frame it over to spare the names as well as myself because X. Y. was seen rubbing out the names of those people he didn't like. Cotts, who likes him as much as I do, told me that if I wanted another long list of names I ought to put up a paper inviting all those who would like to erase X. Y.'s name to append their signatures. One day in the middle of a crowded dining-room there was a party lunching of seven ex-undergrads all between 6 ft 4 in. and 6 ft 7 in. – an aspiration to see these seven rise in a body and file out. Unfortunately, I never made an exact record of the event at the time, though I think five of them were the twin Wards, Lord Stavordale, Lord Weymouth and Alfred Beit. I owe Major Hay to General Charles, whom I invited with other soldiers and wives to eat the last free meal that I should probably have to give under the contract. General Charles, the Director of Military Operations, War Office (now Ordnance), is so mild a gentleman that he couldn't direct the operations of a mouse hunt.

Major Hay told me that once he went to France to learn the language. One day a little Frenchwoman came quickly round the corner charging him navel high. She looked up, then higher and higher, till

finally reaching his face up there, ejaculated, 'Mon Dieu!' Hay, quickly with his new-won French replied, 'Non, Madame, vous vous trompez.'

Christopher Ford, 6 ft 7 in., said that once when he got well inside a big restaurant in Germany the hundreds of people went silent and stared at him, then, too, the band stopped playing, so there was nothing to be done but to proceed boldly up to the band and shake hands with the conductor – so German and so English!

To this monument of industry, this wall garden of human species, Canon Macdonald, himself almost 6 ft 6 in., has given a finishing touch with the record of his having measured the 'Magdalen giant', the late Brian

Piers Lascelles, 6 ft 10⅝ths in his socks (7 ft in boots), adding the Pompeian couplet:

> Admiror paries te non cecidisse ruina
> Qui tot stultorum taedia sustineas.

Farrar translates it:

> I wonder, O wall, that your stones don't fall,
> Bescribbled all o'er with the follies of all.

The tallest dogs are Jane Pauling's and Diana Guinness's wolfhounds, Michael and Pilgrim, 3 ft 7 in. and 3 ft 6 in. on the tops of their heads, both very lovable creatures in spite of their hounds. Jane Pauling's remarkable father wrote in his memoirs that one morning, prospecting in the mountains in South Africa, he and his two friends breakfasted on a thousand small but delicious oysters and about eight bottles of champagne, adding, 'There is much virtue in a good appetite so long as one is able to foot the bill.' Once when I was making a facsimile of Miles and Beth Tomalin's names, which, for a peculiar reason, I wanted to bring inside the frame, such a kind young lady was looking on and said, '*We* know a "gentleman" who is 6 ft 8 in.' – 'Do you,' I said, 'if he were that height I would call him a man.' Then, looking down at the Epstein, Augustus John and Albert Rutherston portraits, she asked, so graciously, 'And who's the artist in the place?' And I, rather proud to have something that wasn't local to show to this kind young lady answered, 'They are not in fact local but done by artists called Epstein, John and Albert Rutherston, who live in London.' Then she, half turning, turned to go and, with her head still unbleeding and unbowed, told me I had 'quite a quaint little place here'.

And now, sometimes, it seems to me a mad thing to have spent so much time and care upon this patch of wall, yet it's a world of people and memories to pass constantly before my eyes. Only this evening G. St L. Carson, Morse and I have stood a full hour beneath it whilst it seemed alive with gossip and associations.

Three staying ten days here now are a girl called Dora Joan Leighton, petite but very handsome, and her young fiancé Kennedy, a romantic Scot who hopes to make agricultural history in Ireland, and their gooseberry, Miss Crawford, a charming youthful trio, all looking so cheerful and hopeful in contrast to a poor washed-up lady just gone who stayed indoors reading, or leaving about D. H. Lawrence, and believes that people's sexual relationships are not open enough; hence all these tears. I wish my book, *Faded Fig Leaves*, sold as well as Lawrence.

Peter Knox gave a dinner of ten serious people including Edgar Lobel. He did the host so well. It's a pity he spends his money and time often on stupid people. As he is eaten out with asthma, this clever, too generous piece of elegance, is wise enough to have as good a time as he can.

Self-mortification

At almost ten this evening —— drove up. He runs a beautiful old Inn himself. He said, 'I've so often been told of you that I thought I must really get clear of the charge of not having been here, so I've come. Could

you possibly give me something to eat at this hour.'
Flattered and delighted I led him in and, wondering a
little why he didn't say anything about the look of *my*
dining-room, got started a lovely meal and sat down
with him ten minutes after whilst he ate it. As he said
nothing about the foaming white soup I apologised for
it. – '*No* matter,' he said, 'I'm hungry,' and continued
to tell me about his beautiful old Inn. Then the delicious omelette – I interrupted him with, 'Rather a
rough and tumble affair, I'm afraid,' and was glad that
he didn't take it as referring to his Inn. But from that
moment, realising that he was a wholly self-centred
genius, I set to work to abuse and apologise for everything else of my own, the steak I'd cut from a ripe
sirloin, the Mavrodaphne trifle which Kate had just
made extra good (she has made every trifle since we've
been here), and was rewarded for my orgy of self-
abuse by his telling me as we said good-bye that he felt
'lucky to have got anything at all at this hour.'

The Oxfordshire yokel doesn't pronounce the 't'. I
heard today 'A(t)s bu(tt)er ea(t) i(t)', which takes some
doing. John has invented a good one in, 'Skates' and
Brainies' aý'fi'ers' for Scouts' and Brownies' outfitters.

   A young man said he had drunk recently some
exquisite sherry of 1834. I asked was it very expensive?
'Twenty shillings a bottle.' – 'Now, if it had cost origi-
nally two shillings a bottle, what would it be worth
today, I wonder, at compound interest?' He proceeded
to work it out beautifully and rapidly in his head with a
very fine two-lobed forehead, 'About £8 10*s.*' Then I
told him of another philanthropic grocer in Oxford who
was selling brandy labelled '1811' for forty shillings.

'Dragging-in'

To him who might collect what we call 'draggings-in'
these might be useful. When finding myself talking
'servants' to a lady of antecedents, parts and obvious
substance staying here, she said, 'I'm so sorry for my
youngest son – poor lad – he's *so* troubled because his
butler *will* quarrel with his second footman.' Many
years ago my hostess at a dinner-party was saying she
usually had her timid governess to dine with them as
being good for her, when up spoke a pretty little thing
from the other end of the table, 'My French governess
always dines with us, but my German and English
governesses dine upstairs.'

The Law Courts

A man and woman came for the weekend. The following evening the lady announced herself as the sister of
a friend of mine, and that they were on their honeymoon, which I said was obvious, and we made friends.
There was also for the second night a single man,
elderly, of a class that puzzled me – not commercial, not
Colonel. He tried to make himself nice, but in doing
so said all the wrong things. – 'You must be busy on
market days.' 'Many tourists pass through in summer?'
'Where were you before this?' 'Is the house very old?'
To all of which my answer was 'No'. I was rather
startled when next morning he and the bridegroom
met me outside and introduced themselves as ex-
Scotland Yard inspector A. B., now private detective,
and the bridegroom as not married but having been
tracked down and caught as co-respondent. The detective told me afterwards that having noted her shoes on

her feet in the evening and then outside their door he went into their room in the morning when they were in bed and introduced himself. Would there be no counter-charge possible for this most damnable intrusion by an unofficial civilian into one's lawful privacy? The couple were very nice about having let me in for this; they plainly didn't know they were being followed yet, and they gave me afterwards a delightful Victorian woolwork picture, which now on the wall looks down upon the scene of their discomfiture. We had to give evidence in Court later, and in spite of the dreariness of it all I must confess to have felt rather small fry as proprietor of a country Inn over against a well-known London hotel where, so big is their business in this line, that they would seem to have a specially constitutioned man who works as porter by night and attends the Court by day. He was up and down in the box most of the time with the identical story. On that day a man prayed for and got a divorce from his wife, having discovered after twenty years that she was his aunt, though an illegitimate one, and the Prayer Book was produced and cited in his support.

The Anonymous Letter Writer

I have received a letter from a woman telling me that after lunch on Sunday she saw my pigs in the yard and that they were in such a filthy state that she is wondering whether to report the matter to the Sanitary Inspector or the RSPCA. Poor pig herself because she writes anonymously and doesn't give me the chance of explaining and for having had my good meal here and not telling me of the pigs at the time. But there's a funny sequel to this – any day after giving this mean busybody another good meal I may be taking her round the garden, giving her plants, and we pleasantly looking at the pigs together, and again and again. To publicans and other owners of public places who receive this vulgar cruelty I would recommend what I have thought of too late: viz. to frame and hang up the letter for the edification of the writer's friends.

X. Y. telephoned to me this evening, 'You may think us very silly but we decided nevertheless to tell you that when at —— (a certain government Institution) one of us overheard a man conspiring with four others to go to the Spreadeagle and give you a nasty time of it at the bottom of your garden.' I felt cold and horrid, their bravery seemed so impregnable, and asked, 'Why?' – 'Because of something you had said to or about a woman the fellow brought to dine with you.' – 'I don't remember anything of the sort though I'm sure what I said was right. Should I report it to the OC?' 'Well, preferably not, as we were guests there. But you'll easily know it if an awful little worm, you can't possibly mistake him, turns up with four others wanting to be pally.' . . . So for a fortnight I kept indoors and then confided my ugly secret to one of their colleagues dining here, a charming scholarly person who said the worm was shortly to leave for a very distant country . . . and later, that he had gone there, 'chased away as a vision of the night' . . . Two years later I said to two others from the same place that only delightful people came from there save one and I told them of the worm: 'Oh yes, we got to hear of that and he was ducked in our pool.' I felt so grateful and touched by this undeclared benefaction.

*

Mrs Burrows (treasurer) and I (chairman) of the
Thame Art Society have been collecting stuff for a
Decorative Art Show, which we thought would miti-
gate the asperities of 'Thame Shopping Week!' Mr X.,
County, declined to lend out of his storehouse of good
things because he was afraid he might be asked to do it
again. I thought of sending him a text, 'God bless our
home, for no one else will'. Major Aubrey-Fletcher, on
the contrary, who has a set of the finest eighteenth-
century chairs I have seen, would have thrown the lot
at us and anything else. Having seen Steer and
Behrend, when painting at Brill, A.-F. got on to Steer's
work and now owns some – uncommon conduct for
County. Generous also Colonel Sam Ashton, one of the
few people round here who smile. I took an open lorry
on the record coldest day and got the worst cold of my
life collecting some £2,000 worth of furniture. From
good-hearted Mr Aubrey Wykeham's house, stocked
with portraits of Pembrokes, Wykehams, Wenmans,
bishops and beauties, I carried away two samples of
eighteenth-century mahogany shell-back hall chairs
with the Bull's Head Arms done in high relief in the
middle of the backs – apparently ye olde waye of
impressing your dignitie into the spine of your guest
when waiting for you in the hall, and with the motto
below, 'Manners Makyth Man', a grim pleasantry
which I'm sure Mr Wykeham has never noticed.

Professor and Mrs Richardson came to dinner, he
exuberant, bubbling, staccato and inexhaustible as
ever. 'That's a fine table, Fothergill. 1810, worth £100
easily.' – 'But I have three of them!' – 'Yes, £150 the
three.' – 'What date do you give this table?' – 'English
Empire, you could get £85 for that any day – side-table,

carving-table.' — 'But it's the same at the back also; I think it might be for the centre of a big hall.' — 'Possibly, yes, I think you are right. Those there are amazing chairs, Fothergill, not as late as you think!' when I hadn't thought at all, and so he dashes onwards, right and wrong, exciting and inspiring, with his pretty and long-suffering wife. When the three of them came for lunch six months ago, very late and hungry, 'Look, Fothergill,' he said, getting out of the car in the yard, 'I've started drawing interiors, Tonks is wild about them, remarkable, look at this one, this — this —', spreading them down all over the yard till it was littered, and then I looked at his wan family starving round and moved him firmly inside.

If ignorant wine talk doesn't come from wine merchants with which to gull their clients, where does it come from? Yet how could wine merchants invent such nonsense as talked by old clubmen and young conceits? Dear old ——— ———, who came to lunch, lectured me on Burgundy and Madeira for half an hour. When I brought out some tip-top Madeira that had been sent me by a Madeira lover, he said he didn't like it and he ended his Burgundy talk with 'Yes, there's nothing like a good Château bottled Burgundy.' When I told him there was no such thing, he shifted off on to brandy, a still more fertile field for luxuriant rubbish, and I paid no more attention. Of wine descriptions this is the best I've heard, told me by Billy Coster, an American, who has divided his time for four years between Oxford and our dining-room (where does America get this element of almost Scandinavian freshness from? And he doesn't talk, he warbles). He was with some Dons at Balliol when they were trying out some wine. There were also there two pundits from Cambridge who were invited to taste also. Said one of the pundits with deliberation: 'It's rather broad.' — 'Yes,' said the other, 'but, mind you, it's a clever little wine.'

Ernest Gye, Foreign Office father of all the Consuls, came to lunch with Jim Baird, soft-hearted, soft-mannered people. They have been hardy periodicals here for six years, starting by staying here a fortnight or more when our food must have been very inferior to what it is now, for which fidelity God bless them, and I hope they are now rewarded.

Micromania

That horrible little book *Eos* has got on my nerves and given me micromania. At this time of life when hope is beginning to go and fear beginning to come, when you can't be a pleasant sight or sound to your wife, and a damned school takes your children from you one by one, you wonder what you are or what is yours and find little or nothing. But to compensate, the freedom that responsibilities once made you fear to enjoy and which you hated to give to your wife and children you now give to them with a liberal hand along with the responsibilities. You can now see ill done with equanimity, saying, 'All's well, let others push the world round.' So, with hope and then fear having worn out, stripped of everything I shall die peacefully. Like our old landlady in Cornwall last year who, when Kate went into the kitchen to ask if supper was coming, met her in the doorway, candle in hand, and said, 'I can't help you, my dear, I'm off to bed.' She rose again in the morning and may yet live to hear that these were my own dying words. And very soon after that, thank God, no one is the loser. Tonks deplores that nothing now is remembered longer than a day. The best and worst on record may happen but next day it's forgotten for something else. But Tonks will be remembered as long as Queen Anne.

Bone and Dodd

This place is getting popular, forty-one to dinner on a cold April night is a sign that there are plenty of folks who like this sort of thing. There came to lunch a live little American, Hallé, and his sister Mrs Scheffer, who told me that her brother had transported a Tudor cottage to USA, and 'erected it inside an apartment house'! He buys Epstein's latests. When he told me he had some Muirhead Bones, I went into the other dining-room and asked Bone and Francis Dodd, who are staying here, if I might introduce to them an admirer. 'We should dislike it very much indeed,' said Dodd, 'but we always like to meet our patrons,' and Bone said, 'That would be most unpleasant, Mr Fothergill, but thank you so much for your kind invitation and please bring them in.' So in they went and the seven of them sat round the table very happy till tea-time.

An old lady came into the hall out of a full-sized Daimler. 'Do you serve lunch?' – 'Oh, yes, certainly.' Then she went back to her old husband – 'Yes, it's all right, there's luncheon,' and the old man went back to talk to the chauffeur. Meantime, the old lady sat down. There were seven people eating in silence. 'What have you got?' – 'Very proper soup – mutton and cottage pie.' – 'Any sweets?' – 'Yes, castle pudding made from real castles and a good jam tart and some remarkable cheese, twenty months old.' – 'I'll have dry toast and tea.' I staggered out of the room feeling a fool, and when the old gent came in he demanded, 'Mutton but no vegetables.' If you *must* have such an odd meal why adopt a still odder method of approaching it?

Three lads, Mathew the KC's son, Twining and Simpson dined here tonight because they are soon all to go to separate parts of Africa. I think it was almost the best dinner we've ever built up. At about 9.30 o'clock they had iced lager beer, and told me afterwards that the four at the next table had taken vocal stock of all they had eaten and drunk and that they had severely criticised the drinking of the lager (they had had *inter alia* Tokay). Personally I would approve. During dinner they asked me who was the Greek god of food. I didn't know, but I went to Professor Gordon and H. V. Routh and threatened them that if they couldn't give me an answer I'd apply to the next table with two Balliol dons, Rodger and Ridley. Mrs Gordon suggested Ceres, who, I said, was the goddess only of American food. Routh said there *was* none for such a material thing, but Gordon said, 'If they could cook, then Flora and Fauna in combination would meet the case!' This pleased the Balliols, who could put up nothing better than Zeus Xenios, which I suppose means merely a shake-down.

Curious experiences peculiar to every trade would be worth making a book about. Take the second-hand bottle trade. Mr Walker, of Kentish Road, who has worked up from nothing, I should think, into an eminently respectable man, has seventy workpeople and at least two million bottles on his premises. He has just given his best employees shares in the business. He told me that once something happened to the lorry and the packing so that bottles were dropping out thick and fast for half a mile before they discovered it, and they had to go and buy all the brooms in the place and sweep up that half-mile trail! This man not only supervises but still helps in the lifting away of the bottles from places – he will take seven thousand from here next week. I told him how I admired him, even as I told Mr Harding the yeoman farmer at Chepstow and Mr Runge, in that they were all like myself. A sort of vicarious self-admiration.

Albert Rutherston in the throes of taking over the Ruskin School of Drawing Mastership is an example of the eternal youthfulness and meticulousness of his family. Though he has had two or three drawing schools and numbers of masterships, lecturings, editings, and exhibitions, he's been here four days and can think and talk of nothing else. The account books, the little notices he's had printed and sent out, the easels and donkeys, and a mass of similar preoccupations – Albert comes to every new job or event in his life with this same excitement, importance and youth. What a fuss this beloved-by-everyone little master will make over his funeral! Years ago he and Humbert Wolfe started to write an epic life of fastidious Albert, which contained these lines:

> But do not grieve, my little hero;
> Your mother's *not* a Trocadero.

The Coming and Going of the Garden Club

The English Speaking Union is sending twenty American Garden Club to lunch here on the 15th of June. As Mrs Shipman and Mrs Frances King both talk about my garden in their lectures these people will expect a lot. Anyhow, we can lunch them well. It's a novel experience getting ready a garden for a certain day ahead, one that must be felt by the gardeners of those places which open to the public for hospital and ostentation. (In the twenty such in this district, I don't suppose there is really much to see save a little expenditure.) . . . The Garden Club came. After lunch I had to explain that I had a little garden at the back with interesting species and outlay and sent them there, unwilling it seemed. In five minutes I followed them up, only to find them all trooping out again, so I ran past them, collared the hindermost and made her go round with me. I felt a little ashamed afterwards of my importunity, felt that I was getting like my sister's father-in-law, Dr King Bullmore, who insisted upon showing everyone who lunched there his life's work, his incomparable collection of mahogany night-commodes.

One hundred and eight for dinner, the product of Eights Week, fine weather and London; we might have had seven more to supper later at 2.30 a.m. and to stay the night, but the Countess wired in the evening in these gracious words 'No rooms wanted', nor was the ordered supper mentioned which we'd got ready, and we filled their places by a pretty little French couple Spitzer, a Dutch couple von Mühlen, brought by the ever-youthful dandy Harry Melville, who offered me a cigarette twenty years ago, and when I said, 'That is a nice cigarette case' – it was quite an ordinary one – he said, 'Yes, it's gold, silver-plated'! And Lord Furneaux, who had just come down from Liverpool speaking for a candidate friend, where he had had an overwhelming reception, especially by the women. He is so charming in manner and face that it's difficult to predict a splash for his future. Too modest and well-proportioned for it. Besides Harry Melville, milestone of a past culture, another one, Mrs Charles Hunter who came to dinner with nice grandchildren, B. Williamson, just down from Oxford, and Elizabeth. Mrs Hunter, in place of Sargent's hard portrait of her in the Tate, with harder black velvet V-shaped low-necked dress, now looked like a soft grey mist in the corner. I was very touched to see this beloved friend of Tonks who has spent Christmas at her house from time immemorial and for whom, Tonks or Mrs Hunter, the family used to act charades. Against these, on the same day, the novel youth Cecil Beaton, Bryan Howard, and others stayed the night, which makes life worth cooking for, because that's about all I do now.

Doris Chapman

A most pretty and remarkable tall girl, Doris Emerson Chapman, with hips up to her armpits, upon which she rests her hand, walking or standing, was brought here to lunch by one of the odd Pete Brown family, where she paints curved-backed shire horses, in face herself rather horse. Her theory is that children needn't be told by their parents what is right and wrong, because they know it themselves instinctively, 'I knew perfectly well when I was being mean or loath-

some long before my parents told me. All a child wants
is sympathy.' Let her at once drop the shire horse and
start a rare and happy stud of her own.

Nice Everything

When I got back from Oxford Katie Lomas told me
Captain ——— had rung up as he was bringing four
people from London to dinner. – 'What will there be
for dinner?' – 'I don't quite know,' she replied. –
'Would you ask Mr Fothergill?' – 'He is out.' – 'Then
Mrs?' – 'She is out.' – 'Then the cook?' – 'She is out
also.' – 'Well, is there to be any poultry?' A horrid term
and, as philosophy don Morris of Balliol said, 'Poultry
is never dead.' – 'I don't think so.' – 'How can I bring
people all the way from London unless there is some
poultry?' – 'There's some nice lamb, I know.' – 'What
do you charge for dinner?' – 'Six shillings.' – 'That's
rather a lot; you could have dinner in London for that
– and with poultry.' – 'Yes, sir, but it's all very nice.' –
'What else will there be?' – 'Soup, fish—' 'What sort
of fish? Hake? Any old sort of fish?' – 'No, sir, nice fish
– quite nice.' – 'Everything you say is nice – nice
everything. Then the meat?' – 'I said lamb – our meat
is always very nice here.' – 'Nice again, what sort of
sweets?' – 'Oh, nice sweets.' – Katie said that by now
she couldn't help it, the bullying idiot had got her into
that state. 'And nice again, I see. Well, I shan't come,
and tell Mr Fothergill what you have told me and
he'll be very angry. I've been there dozens of times.' –
'Well you know what it's like then.' This was Katie's
only score. At dinner-time he arrived, and I
reproached him for giving a good girl such a bad time
on the telephone, to which he replied, 'I was not at all

rude to her; I couldn't have been, as there was someone else present.'(!) He's a good little hardy periodical,
and apparently can be as contumacious as I was
myself before I took a pub.

Sir Lionel and Lady Halsey, Miss Bruce and others
to dinner. We giggled and laughed in the garden,
everything seemed funny with these delightful people,
and after cooking and serving a dinner for eighty-
three, which they enjoyed immensely, as all honest
people would who keep Rollses and Minervas and eat
at the Ritz – their jolly mood was the greatest gift.

Existence is a Mood

Fifty times a day I puzzle about existence; I cannot
even begin to ask the question why or where or for how
long because existence itself is a question. I see people
all round laughing and smiling and sitting, apparently
comfortably, on their bottoms. This must be because
I'm overworked, for existence is no problem, of course,
when we are at par. When we are normal we don't
trouble about God, subnormal we bother, and when
supernormal our souls and bodies are reduced together
into a sort of jelly of utter thanksgiving.

John Gielgud cheered me today by saying he knew
no hotel in England that approached this within
measurable distance. It's true, of course, but you don't
expect people to feel and know that as keenly as I do
myself. Bless him!

Entertaining Adventurers Unaware

A bright yellow Rolls with chauffeur and footman in
fawn livery with coronet came and deposited two
ladies and a lad. The fawn liveries paced up and down

the yard in formation after lunch. As the three sat down to lunch they asked me if I had a Russian cook, which I denied. Then in the garden, 'But did you take this place from a Russian professor?' – 'No.' – 'Are you sure?' And so they had got it wrong somehow and the meal they had come 60 miles to have was an ordinary one and not good at that; they had expected Russian fireworks. It was the even now very attractive Annie, Viscountess Cowdray, whom Will Rothenstein had told of the place. These long-journey disappointments are horrible, especially as one could quickly extemporise a lovely meal, but, with a set meal going, one sometimes just misses the initiative. Late one evening long ago, when almost everyone had dined and gone, a tiny little man in smoking jacket, with a big head, followed by a beetling tall woman, came in to dinner. Knowing that we had no food left, I naturally hated the sight of them, so, saying to Katie, 'Two zoological specimens to dinner,' I went up and put them at a table. The little man said their car had broken down *en route* and they would be grateful for anything at all and that they'd come here on a journey of great inquisitiveness. I was tired, I was always tired those days, so I took for once the 'can't help it' line and produced cold mutton, which they tried to warm up with the most expensive wine, brandy and cigars. Reggie Higgins, friend and lodger all the summer, told me it was Barrie, so I went up to him and said, 'I think you must be Mr J. M. Barrie' (having quite forgotten that he'd been knighted). 'You were not *far* wrong,' he replied slyly, and this is the way I, as Innkeeper, treated him whose plays purge the sentimentality in me till it splashes over my knees and onto the floor.

Dating the House

Today J. A. Gotch brought thirteen distinguished architects to tea. I put them on three tables with old Worcester and silver and, besides honey as eaten by Pheidias and another honey eaten by Petrarch and rose-leaf jam by Apollonius Rhodius, such a vast spread, and they themselves were so charming that, thinking it silly to charge 1*s*. 6*d*. a head, I gave them the choice of paying 10*s*. each or nothing, and in return for the latter I handed each a slip that I'd printed beforehand asking them for the approximate date of the room. One gave 1600 (signature fortunately not clear), Gotch, Wimperis, Guy Dawber, Newton, Caroë, Edward Warren and Norman Evill varied between 1680 and 1780, just like so many doctors diagnosing a simple case. The novelist, R. Straus, was far the most intelligent of the lot; he gave three different dates. On the whole, *circa* 1700 seems to have it.

Harmless Inventions

Of domestic and uncommercial inventions I claim to have made and adopted here a few, including (i) a simple apparatus for removing instantly and efficiently

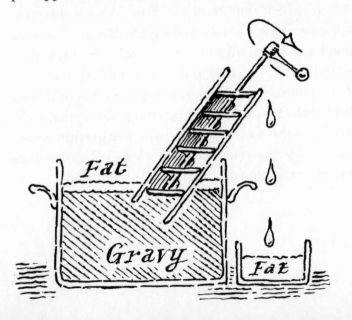

grease from gravy or soup, i.e. by pulling the liquid by a plunger and Archimedean screw up a cylinder, so that the grease falls out over the top till nothing but gravy is left; (ii) enhancing the illusion of distance given by a tapering path or avenue by planting the flowers in atmospherical perspective, viz. hot to cold (I've just been told that Miss Jekyll has anticipated me, though where I don't know); (iii) painting a building in the yard that, facing you, doesn't recede like the rest of the buildings, with two groups of cubist mountains so that a hole seems made in it; (iv) graduating the colour in the painting of the three-storied façade of this house so that it gets lighter as it goes upwards, which is consistent with the principles of design and construction; (v) a prop for delphiniums and Michaelmas daisies, being an iron stick 3 ft out of the ground with a cross on the top, each cross piece ending in a loop. You drive the stick into the middle of the clump when the plants are 3 ft high, later you tie a tarred string on to one of the loops and loop the whole plant into the four quarters of the cross. The stick will never be visible again and my asters stand up all winter like a brown avenue till the young growth is high enough to cut them down. I asked Timms, the blacksmith, how much he would charge to make them, and he said 1s. 3d. each, to which I replied, 'If you can afford it, please make me a hundred', and he did; (vi) for tying up lettuces, instead of slow and arduous raffia and the gardener's always getting behindhand with it, cut foot lengths of thin galvanised wire, turn back the two ends and hook them round the required number of lettuces. When about to slaughter the lettuce pull off the ring and hook it round another, and thus keep the original stock automatically tied up.

It's so perfect and obvious that surely others must be doing it? (vii) To prevent dust flying out into the room and over the maid when she rakes out the fire, an apparatus similar to a shallow sunblind with side curtains through which every particle of dust goes up the chimney, rake and shovel how she may. A frame of 5/16ths iron to fit round top and sides of the grate (generally one frame can be made to fit several different grates). Half-way up the legs are attached on pins two struts which fall some inches lower than the legs. When the apparatus is in position these struts come forward onto the hearth and hold it tight against the grate. From the top of the frame hangs another 3-sided frame which, when lifted, projects about 15 in. and is held up by a cord hooked on to the big loop on top of the frame. This frame (which makes the roof of the tent) is covered with sateen and from its sides also hang curtains reaching down to the hearth. The whole thing when held up by the iron loop at top collapses flat, is taken out and hung against a wall.

A girl friend of Mary Dowdall's luxuriant daughter Buzzy told me today that she had been here once, five years ago, walking with her father and mother from Bognor. They came into the hall and then discovered that they had very little money, so asked if it would be very dear to stay. − 'But how much would bed and breakfast cost?' − 'Three and sixpence each,' and so they stayed. This sounds either eleemosynary or high commercial. It was neither; sometimes one may have one's little joke with delightful people, even in trade, if they are amused enough to take it.

Wit Antisociable

A witty young man is Jock Weir, son of the engineer peer. He has a spontaneous joy in talking rot that makes it jolly to follow and join in, not that of Reggie Turner, Robbie Ross and Oscar Wilde, which forbade active collaboration. Oscar Wilde told me that old Sir Somebody was the only man he allowed to talk at his own table. Reggie Turner's wit is so outlandish that one feels desolate after it, much as one does after a pun. When I was 19 and straight from our Lake District fastness, finding myself, shy and tender, in the thick of that witty society at a big dinner-party, Ross's sister, Miss Ethel Jones, took pity on me and talked to me about my home. 'We live at Grasmere,' I told her, and seeing a chance to get in a literary touch, added, 'quite near Wordsworth's grave,' but unhappily a silence had just dropped upon the party and Reggie Turner called out from the other end, 'And don't you find it very unhealthy?' Robbie Ross, with a natural sensitiveness to the often devastating effect of wit upon the hearer, mitigated it by laughing loudest at his own jokes, and now, fifty years after, comes Harold Acton, carrying on their business, and who knows but what these exaggerated types of exquisite talk and manners do not affect the standard of conversation and behaviour down even to the lowest orders, just as without the fanciful Show Ring terrier we should not have everywhere such a tolerable ordinary dog.

A curious, sweet-mannered old hand here, Newman, mental pathologist, brought Peter, Prince of Denmark, Prince of Greece, (sounds like the Prophesy) to dinner, and in my garden Peter the Prince said,

'I like these English gardens because they grow wild flowers in them as well.' I suppose it is that abroad they use flowers more as a gaudy decorative medium — hence begonias and geraniums — than as plants of interest or individual beauty, so that anything that looks to the foreigner at all ragged or small-flowered or thin, looks like a weed. I told sister Eva Bicknell the other day that her round bed of prize begonias looked like a heap of butcher's meat in various stages of decomposition.

Prepare to Meet...

I offered some Turkish Delight to a pretty girl. I'd put it on a Sunderland lustre plate with the words 'Prepare to meet Thy God.' At first sight she looked a little frightened, then she suddenly lighted up and said, 'And a very nice way of *being* prepared!' And once an estimable young parson called Mortimer irritated me by arguing with me, for the edification of his party, that blanquette of veal was a dull dish. I tried to defend it, at least my own blanquette, but he argued me out of the room. So after dinner, I put down before him Turkish Delight on this 'Prepare to meet Thy God' plate, neatly arranged round the inscription, as my answer to him, a suggestion that he would be better occupied thus than in arguing about blanquette.

Founders

There are limits to forcing a trade. I don't think this place could ever succeed financially. We have made a profit this year and it all went as usual on keeping the fabric together. Our overdraft is funnier than ever before at this period of the year, and the turnover is less. What can be expected with a 100-miles drive for dinner and back? Very little more than we get now and there is Reigate and Dorking with not a decent meal to be had anywhere with thousands, almost, complaining. Lucas Scudamore told me tonight that he simply couldn't attempt a meal at Reigate the other day, so he went to London instead. I took this place for what its local trade was worth, and I never dreamt of Oxford which has made a losing job at least a living and a great privilege. SEYMOUR LESLIE, *Founder* in that he brought the first person from Oxford, Arundel del Re, who were quickly followed by the right kind of undergrad and better class don. Piers Synott, Benoit Tyzkiewicz, Basil Murray, Lord Elmley, Patrick Balfour, Lord Donegall, MARY SOMERVILLE, John Pilley, John Tailleur, Robert van der Berg, Lord Longford and Christine Trew, Vere Pilkington, Romney Summers, brothers Colefax, Lord Clydesdale, John and Roger Spence, Patrick Waddington, David Greene, Michael Russell, Peter Knox, Richard Norbury, Diccon Hughes, Thomas Alston, Frank Filleul, D. Goodbody, Nigel Sligh, A. B. Rodger, Kenneth Bell, George Gordon, C. S. Orwin, John Bryson, Maurice Bowrer, A. Akers-Douglas, Girouard, Edgar Lobel, E. M. and Mrs Ridley, T. Best-Dallison, Lord Pelham, Harold Acton, Lord Weymouth, Greville Worthington, Brian Guinness, Elizabeth Harman, Billie Price, Beverley Nichols, Roger Campagnac, R. de Candolle, Guy and John Vaughan-Morgan, John Bell, Malcolm Macdonald, Patsy Richardson, Archie Chisholm, Peters Scarlett and Coleridge, brothers Lennox-Boyd, Lord Stavordale, Alfred Beit, Billie Coster, Dudley Williams, Dunstan Skilbeck, Malcolm Messer. *I put up a tablet in my heart to these early founders, and to these from the outer world*: CATHLEEN MANN (Lady Queensberry), Francis Meynell, Musgrave and Aminta Dyne, Mr H. H. Asquith, Sir Arnold and Lady Lawson, Mrs Dowdall, Augustus and Dorelia John, Charles and Clare Neilson, A. E. Kingham, Agnes Hannay, Joan Fothergill, Gerald Gould, Langdon Davies, Reggie Higgins, Leslie Hartley, C. E. Bates, A. E. Housman, Tonks and Steer, the Plimsolls, O. J. Llewellyn, David Garnet, John Nash, Euan Cox, John and Mrs Mavrogordato, R. St C. Talboys, Arthur Fox-Strangways, Winifred Phillips, E. S. P. Haynes and Mrs Oriana, P. Sainsbury, Rebecca West, Albert Rutherston, Peter Gregory, Harrington Mann and lovely daughters, Grant Richards, H. G. Wells, Sir Montagu and Lady Pollock, Evan Morgan, Mrs Sydney Ball, the Bergel brothers, Michel and Chattie Salaman, Knox E. V., R. A., and A. D., Ernest Gye, Jim Baird, E. V. Lucas, Mina Kirstein and Henrietta Bingham, James and Gwen Gibbon, Geoffrey and Mrs Whitworth, A. P. Herbert, J. C. Squire, the Selfridges, Bertram and Mrs Long, Willie Makins, Gerald and Dorothy Gurney, Chris and Marcia Arnold-Forster, Lady Ottoline Morrell, Mrs Ellen Shipman, Hugo and Mrs Pitman, the Bourne End Jacksons, Captain and Mrs Parker, Curtis Bennett, Aubrey and Mrs Dowson, Mary Grey and J. B. Fagan, George Lansbury, Nellie Legh, Gwen Otter, Spencer and Hope Hoffman, Eldred Curwen, the Mayos of Pinner, Ethel Bullmore, Mrs Rhys (Oxford), Cecil Aldin, David and Mrs Way, Lady Slade, John and Mrs Buchan, Daisy Blunt, Arnold and Mrs Angus, Albert and Mrs Vandervelde, Sir William and Lady Beach-Thomas, Eric Gillett,

W. D. and Mrs Scott *and many that don't come to my forgetful mind for the moment, and oh, my God, what a stream of life's consolations since*!

A bright talkative little Dutchman, Dr Renier, writing a book on England, *The English, Are they Human?*, whiskers it is true, but otherwise with only a foreign look, came from our Agricultural Show and told me he was standing close behind two 'county ladies', he called them, near the Dog Ring, when one, looking back and seeing him, said across him to the other in a clear voice, 'Good Heavens, how dreadful!' And he was bright enough to recognise that this sort of thing is peculiar to England alone.

Phyllis Lomas and Lyons

Affectionate little Moser and his beautiful attachée brought Oliver Bernard to lunch two months ago. O. B. is artistic adviser and decorator to Messrs J. Lyons. He saw Phyllis Lomas's vase of flat floating concentric rings of little flowers, a Victorian throw-back invention of her own, and asked me if she would do that for Lyons's smart affairs. I suggested a 'demonstration' to the Board of Directors and their floral decorators for £5 5s., and they took it on, and up she went and gave great pleasure and admiration. When she had finished, she didn't think to leave her work for study and research but being very conscientious she poured out the flowers and brought back our bowl! ... Yesterday, Lyons telephoned for 'wild flowers' (i.e. little flowers, I suppose, or anything not poinsettias or carnations) for twenty-four centre vases for today at Olympia. I accepted, but at once found myself confronted with four problems and their solutions: (1) How many 'little flowers'? Two thousand five hundred. (2) How long will it take to pick fresh and pack in time for the nine-o'clock train? Two hours for three of us at 6.30 a.m. (3) How to pack in their thirty separate colours and sizes? In thirty Bibby's soap cartons. (4) How much to charge? —s. —d. per dish, and out of the dewey garden we rushed them into the milk-train just in time. At two o'clock, I rang up Olympia to see if I could help. A man told me that they would not begin till 5.30. How will they get the twenty-four done in time? . . . And today we see in the paper the picture of the dinner-tables. The bowls are there all right, but they were outdone in this 'stunt' dinner to Builders' Foremen by model cranes for lifting the salt and concrete mixing-machines for making the cocktails.

The Collingwoods

I asked R. G. Collingwood and Stevens, a young scholar and birdwatcher, who is writing on the Ro-mans in Gaul as the safest of unexplored subjects for a thesis and is one of the few younger scholars to carry on the thin mandarin voice, e.g. Schiller's and A. D. Knox's, to dinner as a return for Collingwood's father's giving me tea at Coniston thirty-six years ago. Colling-wood is one of those two or three selected super-beings, each of whom is called the cleverest man in Oxford. The last time I saw him was at this tea when Mr Ruskin sent me over to see his father and his magnificent and enormous watercolours. Prof. C. must have been a pioneer in the Bohemian or Chelsea style, for he had a pink-checked tablecloth and they ate in the hall! Never having seen the like of it, I was rather shocked, but what put the lid on it was when a little

maid to mind the children sat down along with us and
worst of all the little Collingwood's jam-covered face.
When I talk to this brilliant man, I can see on his clean
and incisive face jam even now. And now almost all
this little Coniston set is dead. Ruskin had a very little
bedroom in his beautiful house at Coniston, a little
bed, a few sticks of furniture but about a dozen sumptuous Turner watercolours. Arthur Severn showed
me a Turner watercolour of his own. 'It used to be
Ruskin's', he said. 'Once I made a copy of it so exact
that when I showed it to Ruskin he flew into a rage
because he couldn't tell the difference between the
original and my copy and I wouldn't tell him. Finally
he said if I would tell him he would give me the original and we could tear up the copy. So well I remember
doing, for instance, that little bit of earth in the fore-
ground which looks like a rabbit.'

Old Mr —— has come back and told me of his exciting process in pursuit of a quarter million pounds for
breach of contract, in which most of the well-known
barristers were being retained, and then pulled out of
his pocket the bill he'd had here last weekend, and told
me how, on looking it through, he'd found we had
charged him a shilling for coffee for himself and
friend, when he alone had had it. One always encour-
ages saving people, it helps them, they take help so
gratefully. I didn't say, 'What about ——' (the good
turn I'd done him) or about keeping his kit here week
after week, or of the old socks he apparently gives to
our staff to darn? But when he told me he'd been to
Monte Carlo, and taken a doctor with him, I told him
that one didn't generally take a doctor to Monte, but a

mistress. Perhaps it was a lady doctor, as someone in the room suggested.

John Freeman

John Freeman came for the weekend. He has given John Michael four injections and cured his malady for nothing. I suppose the only thing to do with this really saintly person is to accept the service and feel lucky, and give him a bill for his staying here. Easy! Dr Gayner, a quaker saint, is another who asks for his bill as greedily as if it had been his sole purpose in coming here.

We went to Lewes to the sale of E. P. Warren's furniture. I saw sold for £2,100 the refectory table which I bought for E. P. W. thirty years ago for £25 from George Justice, who still deals there, older and perhaps wiser now. On the way home we stayed at a 'new-style' Inn that is walked about in by a fat fellow in plus-fours. The ten or twelve people we saw about were all second-raters. In the smoking-room bar I thought it proper to talk to this gentleman, who apparently has no room of his own, but wanders wherever his victims are, and he snubbed me so badly that I gave up. On getting back here, I found that he hadn't charged 5s. for cigarettes. I sent it him with a polite word – no answer. How gladly we ourselves would have acknowledged that sort of thing! Why, it's very, very rarely that people send money to reimburse me for sending on parcels of things they've left behind them here, it's quite an industry, though often they have troubled to write their grateful thanks.

So ——, who stayed here last week and gave us a stumer cheque for £10, has shot himself and fell dead

in the arms of the detective arresting him for fraudu-
lent conversion. When I look back on his behaviour
here, especially as he has been here before, I can't be
sorry about him because everything he did and said
here – he said a good deal and we couldn't avoid him –
once I ran up into our bedroom to avoid him and found
Kate already there for the same reason – everything
shows him to have been a cold-blooded, good-looking,
calculating scamp.

Atmosphere

Philip Gosse said that Irene and he went to a smart
Inn on the river last week and sat down to tea on the
lawn, a most beautiful site. They smiled pleasantly at
one another, looking round at the press of people, and
smiled again. But soon the atmosphere and the foul
people took hold of them, Philip all the time thinking
that Irene liked it, and Irene that he, till the truth
came out between them just in time for them to share
one another's shame for the place and people before
two very distinguished-looking Oriental ladies step-
ping down from a launch. They paid quickly an awful
bill and fled the place. What is atmosphere created by
then? One would think by the people alone and to pro-
cure these was my main preoccupation here at the
outset, long before the food was anything worth talking about, even if it is now.

The lad, Harry Oppenheimer (Ch. Ch.), had a twenty-
firster here, with his father, Sir Ernest, a delightful
good-looking youngish man, General Smuts, and
eighteen others. It was a fine show on 18 ft of Empire
mahogany pedestal tables. General Smuts told me he

had wondered why they were being brought from Oxford into the Bush to dine and that now it was all clear. Half of them were South Africans, half undergrads, including Grant Lawson and Akers-Douglas, both of great manners, Lysaght and Fraser 6 ft 7 in. Katie came into the office in a semi-levitated state and told me that Sir Ernest had given her, deliberately counted out, a six pounds tip, 25 per cent of the bill, which, she said, almost knocked her down. It's good when the princely and deserving meet. And today Dr Rouse, with whom and Tonks, I have a sentimental correspondence, each time I get an order for malt whiskey or sherry and Cheddar cheese, writes to me and asks me why I don't write a book about keeping this place. Well, I live it instead, and you can't properly do both. When actually on the cross or in bed you can't write about it or be conveniently interviewed.

The Mitchisons continue to dine here with their ribald parties of six or eight, always with Mrs Spring Rice, a handsome Scottish sculptor, red-haired Rumanian Mitrani and his pretty wife (Ena Limebeer, 'Market' Town) all looking absurdly young. Mitrani has assimilated all that is good in an English country gentleman's nature and habits and interests. This party is typical of the best that I want here, though it does look, as Tim Brooke's mother observed, like the cast of 'Sanger's Circus', with the addition of Sanger himself in the person of Mitrani.

The Silence of Lord Beauchamp

Lord Beauchamp lunched. I told him I would give him a different kind of hock from last time, rather lighter but more exquisite. After lunch I was talking out of

the Office window to Algernon Ashton about the
attractions of his daughter, Mrs Basil Murray, as Lord
Beauchamp went back into his car. He waved and
smiled pleasantly. Then Bessie came in and, in order to
reassure herself, asked if it was the 45*s*. Rüdesheimer
that I had given him. 'No, it was 11*s*., another kind of
Rüdesheimer, not on the list, and I forgot to explain to
you – did you charge 45*s*.?' – 'Yes.' – 'What on earth
did his Lordship say?' – 'Oh, he only said, "Well, I
didn't want such an expensive wine, but it was indeed
very good"'; and on top of this my apparent breach of
hospitality and highwayman-like exploitation he had
smiled and waved to me! That wants doing. Anyhow I
caused him to have the explanation as soon as he
arrived in London, till then I and perhaps he had a
bad time.

Talking with two undergrads today, it was said that it
seemed strange and indeed impossible that we alone of
life on earth should admire our surroundings. 'But
dogs enjoy getting out of London into the country',
they said. 'Yes,' I agreed, 'but that is only because they
can run after rabbits and on soft turf, a physiological
pleasure, not like our aesthetic pleasure in the sight of
trees or hills . . . and yet, isn't this also physiological,
i.e. excitement to the eyes, a running after colours and
forms and soft clouds? So why call it aesthetic? With
this then, out goes the word "aesthetics" and all the
books upon it. But perhaps there's a distinction at least
in our appreciation of nature and of art, of which at
least the dog has none of any sort, viz. the abstract? . . .
Yet here too, unless we are bothering about the
subject-matter which is non-aesthetic, we are again

running about after forms and colours and composi-
tion, an optical exercise, so there is really no difference
after all – a proof that body and soul are one, and only
body at that.'

Nephew Alan Bicknell, who has too big a personality not to find himself one day on his still bigger feet,
asks me if I would lend my name and advice to a new
venture in London. But the fact is, having had here a
kitchen staff for seven years composed mainly of half-
wits, degenerates, dishonests, drunkards and hysteri-
cals, and having done it daily ourselves, I can't
conceive lending my name to any establishment
where I don't also do it all myself. It's this kitchen
business that has knocked the initiative and courage
out of me. I suppose everyone who drives his own fur-
row, especially a romantic one like this, suffers from
self-pity at times to compensate for the praise he gets
at other times, and for an awful loneliness due to
people's not knowing what he had done to do what he
has. When, looking at the fellow in a circus today in a
ring packed with loose horses walking stupidly on end,
I could feel for him what he must often feel himself,
viz. the staring multitude's ignorance of all that he
must have done to achieve this monster and de-
plorable result. But now, 1931, Ronald Walker who was
a kitchen boy when the last cook 'put on her hat' has
done more for me in a year than all those 'cooks'
together did in seven years and Ted Surman and Jack
Johnson, boys, have done in two years between them
more than seven years of other kitchen staff.

Feeling that we must have an aeroplane landing
ground (*a*) for our clients and (*b*) for Thame, for
plainly every town will or ought to have one in a year's

time, I wrote to the Brooklands Flying School for an
expert opinion. Two directors, Captains Jones and Old-
meadow, flew down and pronounced in favour of a
field, provided only we could get a square 100 yards
out of the county gentleman's attiguous one. So I
wrote to him . . . Will he be willing to lend this bit or
will he be like the people of Thame who, some years
ago, when the Great Central offered to bring the main
line through here declined the offer and so stayed off
the map, this time, for ever? So the railway went
through 'silly' Haddenham instead, the home of the
Aylesbury Duck, where they 'thatched the pond to
keep the ducks dry' . . . He too has declined . . . And
surely there must be something curious about this
Haddenham where they say, and it is true, that once
you get into it you can never find your way out – something more than a Boeotia ridiculed by cultivated
Thame. Once a man staying here wandered into Haddenham and, getting lost in it, got into conversation
with an inhabitant and said he was staying at Thame.
'What! That *dull* place!' exclaimed the native. H. R.
Barbor told me of a Haddenham man who had a row
of three houses, one he inhabited himself, the others
he rented. As their common drinking well became
unfit for use he got a fellow to dredge it and then
applied to his two tenants for their share of this labour,
viz. 2s. apiece. But they said they'd be damned if they
would, so next morning he shovelled back the dredg-
ings. Charming Mrs Barbor's stories are even better
tho' not true.

A young schoolmaster, whose schoolmaster father I
used to know and who was apt enough in the nice conduct of a cane, preached a new doctrine to me, viz. that

a homosexual tendency is necessary if you are to be a success with boys. I agreed that it probably might make them kinder to the boys, usually, but it might sometimes be that the master, under the strain, might become cruel. If parental love is also sexual, this sort of master would come into the difficult position of half-way between the parent who is not inspired to practice and the irresponsible homosexualist. But all this is to me remarkable, showing that, for once, times must have really changed – I can't imagine that masters talked like this in my days, whatever they did in secret, and now homosexuality is being worked in as a salutary factor towards efficiency in schoolmastering! But wouldn't even that be better than the cane?

Delahaye, with his pretty, always prettier wife, said that some people told him of this place where a fellow called John Fothergill is rolling in money whilst others ask why he chooses to lose money on keeping an Inn like that. The former come on Sundays, I suppose, the latter on Mondays. I neither lose nor roll in it, but I often think that unless the decent and discriminating for whom I keep this place don't come more of them I'll turn the place into a vast charabankerei to spite them.

Distraction for Evelyn Waugh

It was good to give Evelyn Waugh an afternoon with tomboy Rebecca West, her Stowe boy Anthony, and Mrs Frankau and pretty daughter, then an evening with John Fernald and Mollie who, having had a thirty-six-hour honeymoon a year ago, are now having their next holiday here for forty hours . . . and break-fast this morning with Diccon Hughes like an overgrown pink-cheeked false-bearded boy. Three years ago D. H. had a strange laconic manner from which one was always expecting bitterness, but nothing but wit and kindness ever came out of it, as now.

In a German archaeological book with reference to the Boston 'Venus throne' pendant, I see written, 'As Fothergill has clearly laid down!' Consolation to an obscure publican in Oxfordshire. Here we are doing nothing, almost as bad as two years ago when at the end of a day of doing absolutely nothing we sold a piece of cake for fourpence to go with a man's sherry and I got to hear of it just in time to run out to him and ask him to take it back, with the pretext that 'the sherry had been over-charged for', just in order to reach real rock bottom. But I am undisturbed owing to Kate's optimism. She has taken on so much of my work, remembers everything I forget, whilst I sweat away at a gravy and grease extracting invention, a new theory and practice of learning French idioms, and other odd jobs, almost in peace and comfort. Arnold Gomme, A. D. Knox and R. G. Collingwood all think the idiom theory good. I once told John Marshall that some theory of mine seemed to hold water, and he replied that it seemed to hold little else . . . Professor Campagnac has also approved the theory and is going to see what can be done with it. Besides being so comic a book that an ordinary publisher would blush to print it, it would be up against the vested interests, pride and prejudices of teachers.

Tonight Commem. finished. I had had already sentimental good-byes with one or two undergrads who had finished their time and at 11 o'clock I asked two

more lads whom I really didn't know, just by way of
something to say, being beastly tired, not to forget me.
– 'I don't think *I* shall return', said one of them. – 'But
why?' I asked, though not very interested to know the
reason. – 'Because your man's lavatory isn't what it
ought to be!' Instead of telling him that I hoped he
would return even if it involved his bringing his own
lavatory with him, I told him how when I came here I
hadn't more money to make a better one and that now
after nine years I had still less. Curious how large the
lavatory looms in this Diary.

Eric Gill came. I was so glad to meet him so as now
to dispel my ungenerous feelings towards him derived
from what has always seemed to me in his art a
pseudo-religious attitude towards copulation, and a

pseudo-copulatory attitude
towards religion and to find
that, instead of someone
like Great Agrippa, he's
after all a charming, very
human being – rather like
Clutton-Brock with his
witty contempt for gener-
ally accepted people and
things.

1930

Quite a pretty woman came in with her husband to lunch and as I pushed her down the room to her table she expressed much delight in it, 'What a beautiful tapestry,' etc. – 'Yes,' I said, 'very jolly, but when I came here I had to take over all the disgusting furniture . . .' – 'Yes, I agree,' she broke in, looking down at my very passable collection of old furniture with which I had replaced it. So to help her out I pretended not to notice her remark and proceeded 'and *these* things . . .' but she broke in again, 'No, not the sort of things one would buy oneself,' and so I gave her up . . . I thought at first that this was an awful peep into the vacuous mind of one who shammed knowledge and appreciation, but a young man, Bassett, friend of Cobden Sanderson, lunching at the next table sympathetically suggested, that in order to be polite this lady would agree to anything, even though it might not be her own feelings.

The Lost Art of Giggling

Dunstan Skilbeck and Roger Campagnac brought three pretty women to dinner, after which I was telling them of my idea for stopping skidding by shooting sand under the wheels as they do in engines. 'Yes,' said one of the pretty ladies, 'so when I go round a sharp corner I simply break sand?' – 'Do you, really?' I asked, and we all found it very funny and I said it was like another pretty lady, Marjory Marshall, who when describing how to get to Hampstead from here, said, 'And after Hendon, you must pass water three times on the left, and then turn, etc.,' and how when Winnie

Phillips told me of a rude and very red-nosed man giving out passports, I told her she should have said, 'What a lot of port you must have passed in your time!' And then the party degenerated into a salubrious giggling affair, too volatile to describe but which will ever be remembered by each of us.

To the secretary of a very reputable distillers who wrote rather harshly and, as I thought, tyrannously about my delayed payment, I wrote that I, as their distributor and not the consumer of their goods, was their agent or servant, or indeed part of their own business, and that in these exceptionally bad times, I had to spend their money as well as my own with which to keep up my, and to a certain extent their, establishment and pay the taxes, etc., till what time trade got better when I could sell more of their stuff. The argument may be fallacious, but to my surprise the secretary replied most charmingly that at the moment they were 'so under the influence of my letter that they couldn't press me further', and asked me to pay them when I could. I'm ashamed to say that I then tried this argument on my German Hock merchant, who declined to have it at any price, saying that if all his clients so argued he would not be able to carry on himself. Fortunately he's an amiable person.

What is one to do? There was no one to lunch this cold Monday when a black-coated elderly commercial with plenty of false teeth and conceit came in and asked, 'What have you got?' – 'Soup, lamb, beef pie, two sweets and cheese.' – 'I don't want soup, what joint have you?' – 'I have already told you, lamb.' – 'Is the lamb hot?' – 'Yes.' – 'What joint is it?' – 'You are

rather particular.' – 'Well, it makes all the difference
whether it's a shoulder or a leg. Have you anything
cold?' – 'Yes, pork.' – 'Well, I'd like a nice cold pork
chop.' I sent one in, and he complained to Bessie that it
wasn't a chop. 'But it comes off the loin,' she protested.
'It will do, but I like the bone with it.' Then two ele-
gant lads of some 24 years old came in to lunch and
when the old commercial had gone, in order to get
sympathy, I went to regale them with this story, but
first I said, 'How did you like it,' referring to the
mince-pie that I had told them to have. 'Oh, all right.'
– 'Wasn't it good?' – 'Well, the meal's not worth coming 100 miles for.' – 'What did you expect? Fireworks?'
– 'No, but it isn't like the Berkeley exactly.' – 'But it
isn't the Berkeley. I don't know what you mean?' –
'Well, you have such a tremendous reputation, so
we've come specially to lunch here.' – 'How far have
you come?' – 'From Beaconsfield.' (20 miles away.) I
can't help disappointing weekday people who know
of the place from Sunday people, so I merely said we
didn't spring good food and expensive on workaday
people in the week unless asked to, and I didn't make
things worse by telling them of the cold pork chop
who had just gone out. This is not the only of the
many anomalies, problems and impossibilities of this
out-of-the-way, out-of-the-ordinary, and, I think,
wasted effort. Wasted, not quite perhaps, because yesterday four very loud-voiced, ordinary people blew
in on account of a breakdown, had tea at half-past
four, and sat round the fire till cleared out for laying
up dinner, when they migrated into the Common
Room and sat tight round the fire there, heaping it up
constantly, and were haughty and offended when at

10.15 I got the maid to tell them we were shutting up the place. They had had 1*s*. 3*d*. worth of drinks there between them, so our efforts for 6½ hours were not wasted on *these* people at least.

Butlers' Shortcomings

Mrs ———, County, ordered some cyder and lager, so as I hadn't seen the inside of what looked like a beautiful house, new and old, I took it up myself, determined with some excuse to see inside. I drove handsomely my yellow four-wheeled dog-cart round to the back door whose narrow approach and turning was dangerous for a horse that could be turned sharply round in only one way, viz. on its hind legs. The butler took my stuff, and then I asked if I could see Mrs ———. He came back and said I could, and led me down a passage when suddenly he stopped and said 'the second door on the left'. Abandoned thus, I proceeded, and going through the half-open door found myself standing in a big room alone and unexplained, whilst Mrs ——— and her mother were squatting in the middle of the floor having to do with some tapestries. I then realised how comforting even though unappreciated is the servant's introduction of you as you enter a stranger's room. He is your devil's advocate or visitor's friend, and very properly is paid by his employer for this important job. I felt utterly lost, and the 'County's' unimaginative reception didn't relieve my feelings. I spoke of this later to a nice old butler who said that the fellow must have been a very inferior servant to have treated anyone at all in that manner. Once I got a wire from some 'County' to go over immediately and discuss the doing of a tea party. I arrived at the house,

several miles away, cold at 4.45, and was conducted by
the butler with a good deal of 'Mr Fothergill', as if I
were a respected villager, into the drawing-room. On
the left of the fireplace sat the very handsome lady of
the house in hunting kit before a tea-table covered
with the biggest silver pots I'd ever seen, another table
had eight plates of various food. On a huge sofa across
the fire sat the gentleman. The butler didn't give me a
chair but I found one and drew it up between the sofa
and the silver. The gentleman was drinking tea from
an outsize cup. We discussed and I watched them have
their tea, which when they had both finished, I asked
if they would mind my smoking. 'Not at all,' and I
believe the gentleman set up a sofa effort to get me a
cigarette, but I produced my own, and then, I couldn't
help it, for out of the emptiness of the belly the mouth
speaketh, I volunteered apropos of no invitation, 'I've
had tea already, thank you.' And I wondered afterwards whether I was more childish than they were
more gauche. To be addressed by butlers without a 'sir'
is distressing; there is only one now in the district who
gives it me, and I feel like thanking him for it. One
footman always gives me a rain of 'Mr Fotherjills', so
last time I delivered the goods I told him that if he
must call me affectionately by my surname it was
Fothergill but that 'sir' would be shorter. Being social-
istic temperamentally, I shouldn't want it if I thought
they were merely wanting to show their equality with
me, but I know that it is because they want to show
their superiority and independence, or even to put into
practice their contempt for the people and the class
they serve. Only a period of declining aristocratic
forms and a struggling socialism would give this

opportunity to certain people to tread upon another. They know they call you 'sir' in the front of the house – but at the back door they've got you and let you know it.

Good Clean Irish Fun

During a busy lunch an old lady with spinster daughter, shabby county style, caught me in the hall and asked for sandwiches and coffee: 'Egg sandwiches or ham sandwiches,' she said. – 'I haven't got any ham.' – 'Well, egg or anything, will do.' So taking them at their word, I sent them lamb sandwiches. After a bit, I went into the Common Room and saw them at a very good fire. 'Are you quite comfortable?' – 'Yes, very, delightful room, but you didn't give us our egg sandwiches.' – 'But you said anything would do.' – 'Well, you see we are vegetarians.' – 'Then why did you ask for ham?' – 'Well, anyway, we had to put up with beef.' – 'It wasn't beef, it was lamb.' – 'No, it was beef, wasn't it, dear?' – 'Yes, mother, it was beef.' – 'I tell you it wasn't beef; I haven't had beef in the place for a month.' – 'Though we *are* vegetarians, we know one meat from another; it was beef.' – 'Good God, do you want me to bring you in the cook and the butcher's slips.' – 'You should know that I am obstinate.' – 'Then they ought to have been donkey sandwiches. But, look here, is this a joke, or do you want simply to make me angry.' – 'Well, it's no good being Irish for nothing.' The silly old thing – with no feelings apparently other than good ones towards me, merely putting up a mild row for the fun of it! I smiled sickly and thought that if Irish want to be Irish, let them be Irish at home. Next day I told this story to Shaw Desmond, who was angry about it. He

said the Irish were cold-blooded, but it very seldom
happened that a woman could be as cold-blooded as
that. He said I treated her too well. Desmond is as
unlike old St John Ervine as you could wish, yet they
both have kindness. From Ervine you always expect an
outburst of dogma or attempted advice with violence.
Desmond is very alive to beautiful things and the
charm of this place (I feel it myself, just having
returned from a holiday in hotels). He is more like
George Kennedy with his softness of heart, so apparent, and, I would think, genuine.

An Innkeeper has won his appeal from a County
Court judge against an infamous demand from a guest
or Insurance Company for a new radiator to replace
the one that burst with the frost in the poor three-
sided 'garage' of his Inn. The appeal was allowed
mainly on the ground that a traveller had to take the
accommodation as he found it or leave it. I was a vic-
tim once to the hard and humiliating Innkeeper's Act.
A man took away after lunch, presumably for his own,
the coat of a very tall man and left behind his own, an
absurdly short one. 'It's all right,' the tall man assured
me, 'I'm fully insured.' The short man, thinking perhaps that he wouldn't get his own coat back even if he
wrote for it, preferred that if he lost his own through
carelessness the other man should lose his also, so he
kept it and I couldn't make an accommodation. Some
months afterwards the tall man wrote that the Insurance Company had declined to pay and he demanded
£8. As advised I paid up. The implication is that if I
have thirty men's coats in the hall during luncheon, a
useful fellow with a lorry could land me with a claim

for £250, for no one will insure me, an Innkeeper, and I couldn't afford an attendant nor have I room for a cloakroom. But what hurt most in the paying for the man's coat was that if he had left it on a chair in a shop, or on a gate, or in the house of a friend, he couldn't reasonably or indeed legally claim, yet he claims from me with no more moral justification but simply because I am subject to the law, which in this case is one for the publican and another for the public. I wonder what the law would have said had Donald Lennox-Boyd sued me for the loss of his hat which he saw disappear from the peg amongst a charabanc crowd that had descended upon us for a drink. Liability by law makes one feel morally liable also, though this thing might have happened anywhere, so I compromised with my conscience by forcing upon him a pot of Greek honey, whilst his father gave him a new hat. To the Lennox-Boyd family of four giant sons, with a father who looks like a stage peer, I would like to give Greek honey every day.

There are two kinds of people who lose things: those who leave things in the place, go away and never know it — instead of being sorry for these and ultimately assimilating or throwing away their leavings, I suppose I ought to report the loss to the police. And for those who say they have left things and haven't, I can't be sorry. But the other day I mixed the two kinds myself. Coming in from a walk I met on the steps a nice woman who had called for a hat that a friend said he had left behind. Not seeing any on the hooks, and Bessie denying that any hat had been left in a bedroom, I was rather irritated by her certainty, evident even through her politeness, of its being here, I sent her off. When she was out of sight I found the hat on my head. I could think of only one clue towards tracing her or him. The man had had a friend staying the weekend at Brill in a house where he had told me there was no bathroom, so I telephoned to the postmistress there, who, after laughing merrily at this anguish-making incident, told me that in Brill *all* the houses had no baths!

Gwen Otter

Gwen Otter came here today to stay indefinitely because her boiler had burst, only to find ours had burst also. She is another of the 'nineties, but you never know who she will bring here out of the 'thirties, Alec Waugh, Layton the coloured pianist, and so on. When she likes, Gwen Otter is rather deaf – a witty lad called Till met her here. He said to me, 'Gwen is deaf today and we've been talking in tangents. I said to her, "I saw Tallullah yesterday; she is so pretty still." "Yes," drawled Gwen, "she's the worst . . . cook . . . I ever . . . knew . . ., and I really . . . must . . . get . . . rid of her." ' Gwen Otter knows everyone; she is not a lion hunter; she collects from the whole human Zoo and loves everyone and everything. What she doesn't love isn't worth loving. Her more usual parties here are with Aubrey and original generous Mrs Dowson, and Dr and Mrs childlike Elliott of Stokenchurch. How many people have been grateful to her for her existence!

Frank Vosper told me he was getting very afraid about his not thinking any longer of the words he's speaking when he acts. 'It's all right,' he said, 'sometimes in the middle of the thing to wonder whether you should go down to Brighton for the weekend or not, but now I find myself, whilst acting one part, repeating whole chunks of the part I'm rehearsing for the next show!'

Mrs Shanks

Today's joke: I asked the very attractive Mrs Shanks if she was Irish. 'No,' broke in Edward Shanks, 'she's half-American, half-witted.'

Some months ago we gave up all idea of going else-where and dug ourselves in again as if for life. But rumour got about that we had gone or were going, which was working detrimentally, so I published a 'démenti' in *The Times*. It's uncommon remarkable that this notice, though half-way down amongst adver-tisements (which some thought it to be) of all dull sorts in the 'personal' column was seen by so many. The *Weekly Despatch* made a funny half-column upon it, saying that the landlord of this sleepy village Inn got so worried by Jim and Tom, and the others in the bar ask-ing him if he was leaving that he denied the rumour to Jarge, Giles and to one and all of the local gossips by a notice in *The Times*. Geoffrey N. Foster, kind, curious man, our greatest athletic event here, wrote that he was pleased – a grateful word when here we are with lovely food every night and almost no one to eat it. Mr Keen came again with Mrs Ellis Roberts, and pro-pounded his proposition for us to transfer to Pasadena taking 'our whole joint with us' where he would build a place the spit of this to take the 'joint' as it stands. He is only waiting till he can say the proposition is a sound one . . . He has now decided against it.

Loftus Tottenham to a crowded lunch. I haven't seen him for thirty-five years, and now I saw him for only thirty-five seconds, having just time to remind him of his Divinity Schools when he ended up the enumeration of the events of the Last Day with 'the Last Supper and the subsequent Agony in the Garden'. And H. V. Routh and wife to stay here — he writes books and lectures at London University. His and his fine wife's peculiar forms of self-indulgence are 20-mile walking, good wine drinking and building a lovely house in Sussex with the plan of the whole estate and every detail of it suited to the whims and habits of Quintus the dog.

A grey little elderly man in the hall told me the Greek honey reminded him of Crete. 'So you've been to Crete, have you?' I replied encouragingly and said good-bye. I don't know why I patronised him unless it was that he looked lonely. But as soon as he was outside I thought that it must have been Sir Arthur Evans whom I'd never met so I went out to his car to find that I'd guessed rightly and being a good deal the younger it was fun to tell him that I knew his father well — patronising again. I seem destined to patronise this Baronetcy. I didn't tell him how I first met his father. Coming back one evening from the Museum at Olympia, very tired and aged 22, I saw in the distance an old man with a huge beard, poking in the dusty road with his stick and pick up something. 'Poor old lad,' I said to myself, 'I suppose he thinks he's excavating.' Coming up to him I said I would show him and the lady (his young wife) over the Museum next day. 'Thank you very much', he replied, 'but we have to go tomorrow and I've been here every year for over

'Poor old lad ... I suppose he thinks he's excavating.'

twenty years.' Nor did he let my humiliation stay
there. After dinner he said, 'Just before you came up I
found on the road this beautiful gold stater,' producing
it from a pocket, then from another pocket another
and another from another till the table was covered
with Greek coins and my head with shame. At breakfast he quoted Horace all the time and so sweated into
me a lasting respect for this old scholar with a naughty
wink in his eye.

Katie Lomas Landed us

Katie Lomas has just told us that she is going to be
married some time this year, which after 7½ years of
her is depressing enough. When I came to look over
this place in 1922 for the second time – it was Tuesday,
Market Day, for the vendor worked it that both my

visits of inspection were on a busy Market Day – tired and confused by such a dirty ramshackle-looking show, I was passing down the yard trying to make up my mind, when I saw Katie standing at the kitchen door, and I decided then and there to take it, and sure enough she has been a considerable part of the making of it. She has the strength and constitution of a horse in her neat person. For all these years, five and six nights a week, she has read out of her counterfoil books every item received – would it be fifty thousand or sixty thousand pounds or more? – mainly in shillings, with Kate transcribing and analysing them. Many people perhaps, even thousands, will remember her in this god-forgotten spot, and how many will miss her, and miss her more were it not that we have still three of her sisters! . . . And now Phyllis has left us on the same errand whom Steer used to say had the face of a Madonna, a look which she deserves. And Bessie remains, equally wonderful, to perform heroics in this lunatic asylum.

Four rather expensive-looking people, two men, two women, City type of men, came for the night. At dinner they ordered my cheapest Burgundy. When I went to them with it, uncorked and in a cooler of tepid water (which sometimes offends the dogmatic), one of them said, 'Mr Fothergill, I've heard such great things of your wonderful cellar; you weren't in the room at the time so we had to order without you, but do let us now have your advice – which is the *best* wine that you have?' As I couldn't suggest re-corking the cheap Burgundy, or mention the Hock at 45*s*. a bottle, I tried to be polite in this embarrassing situation, but they began to talk of Latours and Lafites and finally I left them with their Burgundy, which, when tasted, the spokesman called 'pedestrian', as if it was good only for tired feet. Very soon after, Phyllis asked for another bottle for them. Being rather doubtful, I asked them if the bottle was for *them*. 'Yes, and I believe you are right; it *is* rather pedestrian – yes, rather pedestrian.' – 'Then why did you order it?' – 'Well, we thought quantity would make up for quality – but it is not a really fine wine, rather pedestrian.' I couldn't stand this buffoonery any more, so I said, 'But it's a very cheap wine, and you can't discuss a cheap wine for a week'; he agreed politely and I cleared off. Later he told me they had just come from Great Fosters; again, I suppose, to impress me. Instead of being bewildered or irritated by people like this, I suppose I ought to feel flattered that with only a little learning in Greek archaeology I have in so few years made such a reputation as an Innkeeper that certain people should put up such a fight to impress me; or do they think I'm a beer-house proprietor to swallow their nonsense?

To Charles Prentice, of Chatto and Windus, I sent these Diary books for him to see what, if anything, could be done with such industry . . . he writes suggesting that I publish excerpts just as they are . . . I hate the thought of it now. I'm better than this Diary, the product of the fag ends of my daily supply of energy. I act and don't write; I can't see any interest to others in it . . . anyhow if you don't write about yourself nowadays someone else will . . . I asked Prentice down to talk about it. He, or rather, his affectionate silence, like David Garnett's, Kate and Maisie

Somerville finally persuaded me. I can't help it, so here goes. Let people reading it think, perhaps, less of me than I really am. And yet, if those who have been here, the lovely and the unlovely too, will think of me as an Innkeeper at best and as the best Innkeeper, I am content.

The Garden

Extract from Prep School Annual Report
c. 1889. 'Gardens – Fothergill ma. and mi.
a wilderness of mignonette. Poor show,
garden taken away.'

Let me remember twenty years hence our garden here.
Through the coach-house into the pig-yard where you
pass along a high wall of Babylonian willows which I
planted in weeping memory of a barmaid for giving
notice. But the barmaid stayed on and was for years the
only one who didn't know the sentimental joke till I
told it to what turned out to be a dishonourable journalist, who published it next day in a Bristol newspaper. Behind the willows a little squash racquets court
with sun and air in it and an odd-shaped mound for
flowers ('The family tomb, I suppose,' I once overheard
said), and then the pigs of Colonel Ashton's breeding,
and into the garden which, when I came here, was a
parallelogram of parsnips and cabbages, fodder for the
weekly farmers' dinner. The gardener I took over with
it had done one thing, at least, in making two standard
gooseberries, the shape for preference to be born under.
This fellow's thirst kept him more out of the garden
than in it – 'popping out', as he called it – and I got so
inured to this popping-out disaster (after all, it wasn't
worse than many others of the abuses we had taken
over), that when he popped out for good and William
Stevenson came, I was disturbed whenever I went into
the garden to see him always there: I felt he was an
interloper abusing his position or perhaps plotting

against those standard gooseberries. Stevenson is so kind and efficient that I am quite certain that if I asked him to bring the bottom of the garden up to the top and vice versa he would do it in a few days without question. Before breakfast this morning I saw him going round with a sort of hoop-stick, agitating the rain out of the soaked flowers!

In this patch of 300 × 70 ft, there are at least 550 species (not including hybrids and varieties) and 120 species of aromatic plants. Having no idea as to how to design the patch, I decided at once that any architectonic design was to be avoided. They are not suitable for little gardens. At the back of a Golder's Green bungalow you are taken into the carefully planned little bit; you say at once 'Oh, that's it, is it,' and there is no more to be seen. Just as a ten-acre garden has to be cut up and divided into rosary, rockery, maze, water and formal garden, so a tiny garden must be cut into as many units and surprises besides having a great number of species. So I ran a path diagonally through half the length of it, tapering it to give distance. Then to increase the illusion I did a thing for the first time, I would think, in planting it in atmospherical prospective, i.e. from hot to cold, red and yellow, purple, dark, light blue and pink. If it doesn't look ten miles long as it ought to it's at least a good natural scheme for varying a long border. Moreover, the path when looked at from the other end looks totally different in length and colour and thus you get two gardens in the same space of ground, surely an economy. I demonstrated the idea one day to a man and it all came out next week in *Country Life* with no acknowledgment which made it difficult for me to speak of it ever after as my

invention. The working out of this scheme necessi-
tated the compiling of my *Gardener's Colour Book*, a
tabulation of flowering plants arranged according to
colour, height and periods of blooming, which will
always be in print since no other idiot would be like to
make another and better. In the thirty-five yards of
this path there are 150 species flowering at one period
or another. Well, into October, today, it seems, but
isn't, as bright as ever it was, and the three most beautiful things in it are *Salvia Uliginosa* and a new
magenta Michaelmas Daisy which Denis Wood of
Taplow has produced and gave to me (I asked him
why he named it 'Red Rover', and he said that the
public couldn't yet stand up to the word magenta), and
a long mauve campanula with scalloped ends which
Eunice Edwards, liquid-voiced, a beauty from the Isle
of Man, said 'looked like girls falling off rocks'. 'What
on earth do you mean?' – 'Oh, don't you know the story
of Mrs G—— who, when a girl, was climbing rocks
with a young man and she slipped and was hung up by
the seat of the voluminous drawers of the period and
there she stuck, looking like these campanulas, till the
young man came and picked her off, and her mother
below said to her father, "That young man must
marry Jane," and he did.'

One day I asked A. E. Housman how he pronounced *Oenothera*. His reply was, 'Evening primrose',
so by way of punishment for priggishness in a garden I
proceeded to point out all the plants with vile names.
'There's *Herniaria*; there's *Fothergilla major*, good for
piles; that's *Monarda fistulosa*; that's *Lobelia Syphilit-
ica*, I got it to give it a good home; and over there I
have a *Phallus amorphus*, but it hasn't come up yet.' –

'Perhaps modesty forbids?' he conjectured in his attractive thin mandarin voice.

To take the place of a handsome double row of asparagus, 'the oldest in Oxfordshire', as my predecessor told me when selling me the place, and the worst, I made a crescent of green lawn raised on the outer edge and sloping down with a pear-shaped pond towards the bottom. 'I wish I could get that water to take the same slope as the lawn,' I said to a man who answered quietly, 'That will *all* come in time, Mr Fothergill.' Unhappily I missed taking his name for his consoling wit. But soon after, Maurice Chesterton, architect, returning from the new Stratford Memorial Theatre, said, 'Of course it could be done. Put a jack at the bottom and freeze the pond!' So, with that asparagus gone and a row of seventy beans from which, owing to a disease, I had only seven beans and sixty-three might-have-beens, ended our vegetable growing.

Mrs Harding of Chepstow, now Hitchin, told me that if I brought a car she would fill it with plants, and so she did. One day two middle-aged ladies in hard county hats and suits drove their big Daimler into the yard for the night. I asked them to tell me what there was in my garden that they would like. At dinner they handed me a long list, saying, 'These are the plants you have of which we should like bits.' In the morning they handed me another list three times longer than the last, 'These are plants which you haven't got and which we should like to give you.' Later, we stayed a sumptuous night with these affectionate and competent Misses Bulwer and their Cotman watercolours. When I mentioned *Epimedium*, Miss Bulwer said, 'We call it 'appy medium here.' To G. M. Marshall of

Farnham I pointed out some *Commelina*. 'Common Lena!' he exclaimed, and then we traced the rise of this poor slut to the *Abutilon* nearby with her fine orange bodice, yellow silk petticoat and dark red drawers and back somewhere to her ultimate fall. Mrs Mayo of Pinner brought me some plants in perfect condition all the way from Chile. Gifts also from Mrs Ellen Shipman, NY, Mrs Pigott, Durrington, J. Parsons, Peradeniya, Ceylon, generous enthusiast, Major Dorrien-Smith out of his staggering garden in Scilly, Theo Ingwersen, with whom I started 'rock' things. He has more feeling for plants as children or weaker brothers than anyone I know, not that he calls them 'little chaps'. Clarence Elliott gives me things that haven't grown in England before; *he* makes the plants laugh when he goes into a garden. John Nash, who is one of the few amateurs to know almost every species, and F. A. Hampton, whose books on aromatic plants are written by a scholar who has grown them, and General Prichard who, when a subaltern, built his house and planted his trees and let it to his several superior officers till he retired to take it and the now old trees and himself for life. He had a garden during the siege of Mafeking, a garden everywhere. And gifts from other kind people with the same gardening infirmity: that last infirmity of noble minds.

Wilfrid and Mrs de Glehn brought Ruth Draper, the genial mocking bird who has queered the pitch of every sensitive soul who would show off his temporarily dull garden to permanently dull people. I, not so to be inhibited, rubbed her nose in species after species – I thought Mrs de Glehn at first resisted a bit this onslaught – but Ruth Draper will make no crowded house out of me at least. But before I had finished, the rain came and drove us before it out of the garden, that old flying picture of the garden of Eden and how well we know it here too.

At the bottom of the garden there is an old and worthless apple-tree for which I paid nearly twelve thousand pounds. Eight years ago when my predecessor was showing my broker James Motion and me over the place, boasting and making a great to-do about everything, he declaimed so cleverly, this Thame-born man, upon the earliness and juiciness of the apples of the tree that we, the men from London, were wholly seduced and walked away in silence. Then my broker, perhaps the biggest in England, touched me on the shoulder and whispered, 'Mr Fothergill, you've a pretty little shop here.' Suppressing my emotion I replied proudly, 'You are right,' and we made our way back through the waving rows of asparagus and savoys to the house, blind to the insecurity of the roof, walls and foundations and the great beastliness of every detail in the place, which I bought and was told afterwards that it had been on the market for years for £4,000!

Roses have no snobbish place in this garden, but they do fairly well in their struggle with the rest. There are two roses which I give to wedding couples – 'You have on your table two roses,' I tell them, 'the one, Red Letter Day,' and they think how banal, 'and the other Independence Day,' and Mrs Jermyn Moorsom, for one, got appendicitis on the way to her new home.

Right in one corner, 5 ft × 10 ft, is Kate's garden village, miscarpentered by herself and brought indoors for the winter. There's the 'Stately English home', the cottages, church, graveyard and vicarage, shops, doctors' and stockbrokers' and alms-houses and a zoo, and just outside, a tiny hill with a farm and windmill on the top, the view as seen from the village. Gradually dream people are coming to live here, Kate says. 'The man in the big house is not really a nice man, and the parson is pedantic who dug up those Roman remains.' 'Observe the working of the child's mind,' Kate once overheard. When people are so careless as to ask me if that's the children's garden I say 'Yes,' for much the same reason as John Michael told the boys at his school that I, with the buckles and long hair, was his uncle. Denial does not always imply shame but sometimes a nice sense of unfitness. Charles Wade showed us his stupendous 'model village', but this is too good for any dream person to walk its streets or light a fire in a cottage, look over the quay at the yachts and steamers, steer a barge down the canal, or drive the train through the tunnel. If this inhumanity pervades it you are dumbfounded instead by the marvellous conception and craftsmanship of everything down to the tiniest door-knocker. This and Clovelly, quite inhuman now, are surely two of the world's wonders.

Last July a beautiful girl, Jane Herriman, and a friend came to dinner two or three times running, but always too late to see the garden, their primary object, they said, in coming, so this time I took them round in the dark to smell only. To start with I gave them coffee and *crème de menthe* in *Codonopsis* and *Pelargonium tomentosum*, then *Salvia Turkestanica*, smelling of armpits, *Sududuru* of the devil's coachman, *Xanthoxylon piperitum* which Elliott said smelt like a courtesan that had been embracing a tom-cat; *Chrysanth-*

cinerarifolium that smells of and makes Keating's
powder, *lemon-mint* that elevates, *Hyssop* like cedar
pencils, scented *Edelweiss*, not the Edelweiss that
Victorians broke their necks to get and which Clutton-
Brock told me he had found in the valleys below but
smelling of dried orange skins, *Camphor plant* (Hampton), turps and verbena *Pelargoniums*, *Melaleuca
leucadendron*, *Diosma gracilis* (Mr Boscawen), *Micro-
meria corsica* that smells strong of ether in which the
cats roll deliriously in spite of the sharp iron spikes
I planted amongst it. Then two *Basils*, cloves and
aniseed (Basil Murray told me that the first time he
was here he overheard me say to some people as he
came near, 'That's Basil, stinks like anything') and
pineapple *Salvia rutilans*, *Agathosma imbricata*,
Patchouli, *Barosma foetidissima* and *Incense plant*, and
then to clean up these heavy aromas *Cedronella tri-
phylla*, like a douche of seaweed fresh from the rocks
till the thing became emotional, so back in the hot
evening into the quiet pig-yard – 'Dear God,' I said,
'the very Berkshires seem asleep.' J. H. afterwards sent
me a postcard from Villa d'Este with 'This garden
doesn't look as well by day as your garden smells by
night.'

And right through the winter these smellers are
your friends in the greenhouse, and no wonder you
keep faithful to them during the summer and perhaps
bore people with them. Moreover, as they have generally poor or no flowers they are a silent population in
the garden, private and unnoticed by others save very
few or those to whom you act as olfactory guide.

Index of Significant People